# AN INSIDIOUS INHERITANCE

A CLARA DAWSON MYSTERY

AMELIE WEST

This is a work of fiction. All names, characters, and incidents portrayed in this production are a product of the author's imagination and are used fictitiously. Any resemblance to actual persons (living or deceased), places, or events is entirely coincidental.



Cover design by Miblart
Developmental editing by Friel at Grey Moth Editing
Copyediting by Mallori at Fiction & Fable Editorial
Proofreading by Maria at The Intuitive Desk

First Edition: January 2025

ISBN: 978-1-7387711-7-2 (ebook)
ISBN: 978-1-7387711-6-5 (paperback)

For those who were forced to find their strength in the absence of the love they deserved.

# Content Note

This book contains themes that may not be suitable for all readers. For more information, please see the detailed content warnings at the back of the book.

". . . may you not rest as long as I am living; you said I killed you—haunt me, then! The murdered *do* haunt their murderers, I believe. I know that ghosts *have* wandered on earth. Be with me always—take any form—drive me mad!"

—Emily Brontë, Wuthering Heights

# Chapter 1

## *September 1933*

It was an unseasonably warm day in September when Clara was notified of her father's suicide. She was nearly finished typing up the last page of a report when she was pulled aside by her boss who told her there was an officer waiting to speak with her in the front lobby. She was given no further details, left to let her imagination wander and her stomach churn as she pushed through the door of their small unit on the second floor and walked toward the staircase.

In truth, Clara had always felt unsettled by the police, unable to sink into the sense of relief that those in her social circle seemed to feel while in their presence. When she'd pass an officer on the street, she couldn't help the way her heart quickened in her chest, the way her mouth suddenly went dry as cotton. Being near them always seemed to take her back to childhood, back to those moments when strangers in uniform had pushed their way into her home, demanding answers to their questions as if they were entitled to such information. As if her honesty did not hold the power to break her family apart.

It wasn't that she often engaged in criminal activity—she didn't, aside from the occasional indulgence in libations despite Prohibition, but that made her no different from anyone else in Rochester. In fact, she had gone out of her way to follow the rules wherever possible, not wanting any reason for an encounter with the law. But surely an officer waiting for her in the lobby could never mean anything good, and she felt the weight of it as she began down the steps to the first floor.

Clara's chest tightened as she reached the bottom step and saw the man waiting there for her. He wore a black double-breasted jacket and matching trousers and had his cap tucked under an arm. She wondered if he'd simply removed it to be polite in the presence of a lady or if it was an attempt to seem less intimidating. As Clara neared, she saw that he was younger than she'd initially thought, perhaps recently out of training.

"Miss Dawson?" the officer asked.

"That's her, officer."

Clara glanced toward the owner of the voice—the receptionist, Peggy, who she'd passed with a polite smile every day of the last six months she'd worked here as a typist. There was an energy of anticipation in the woman's eyes as if she had gotten the best seat in the house for what was about to unfold.

"Yes," Clara said, forcing a smile on her face as she greeted the officer. She knew better than to show her concern. He would only take it as a sign of guilt, an indication to press deeper, dig further. Although she had no indication of why he was here, one thing was certain—she would offer him nothing.

The officer introduced himself, though her heartbeat was so loud in her ears—her thoughts of what would come next such a distraction—that his name seemed to slip past her completely. He led her out onto the sidewalk, likely seeking privacy from the curious ears of Peggy at the front desk.

The street was quiet around them, the office built on a side road that turned off from a busy street in downtown Rochester. Clara had always felt a sense of relief as she diverged from the crowd of commuters, turning down this little slice of road, the sounds of vehicles and people growing more muffled the closer she got to the office. But as she stood there alone with the officer, her stomach roiling with uncertainty, she almost wished for a crowd.

"Your father was Al Dawson, is that correct, miss?" the officer asked. Hearing the name sent a cold shiver across her skin, as if uttering those words could make Al appear suddenly like a wraith. Clara nodded stiffly, confusion whirling through her. The officer continued, "I'm afraid he passed two weeks ago."

She blinked, waiting to understand. Al had . . . died?

Clara looked at the officer, a mix of concern and pity in his eyes, and waited to feel the impact of his words. She waited for some depth of emotion to find her, to take her to her knees right there on the pavement like the death of a parent should. But all she felt was a slow unraveling of something else . . . relief. There was a loosening in her chest, a tightness she hadn't known was there finally easing, as if she'd been living in the constraints of a too-tight corset and was only just now plucking the laces free.

The chatter and noise of the city streets echoed in the distance, and Clara found the officer watching her. "Miss Dawson?" It took a moment for her to realize that he'd spoken again.

"Yes." She exhaled. "Sorry, can you repeat that?"

"I asked if you've been to Briar Hollow. The town where your father was living before he passed."

She frowned, trying—and failing—to picture it in her mind. She wasn't certain she'd ever even heard of the place, let alone visited. A warm breeze tousled the dark strands of hair that had escaped her chignon, and she tucked them behind her ear. "No, I don't believe I have."

"It's a few hours south of here," he offered. "Never been there myself, but I'm told it's a small community."

Clara nodded, discomfort settling into her as she dared to ask the only question on her mind. "How did he die?"

The officer stared at her, silence falling between them. It hardly seemed like an unfair question given the circumstances, yet she felt the sudden warmth in her cheeks as shame trickled into her gut.

"From what I was told, it seemed to have been done at the hand of the deceased." He cleared his throat. "Anyway, the coroner can tell you more, miss." He pulled something from his jacket pocket, a small rectangle of paper, and handed it to her. She took it, reading a name and phone number that meant nothing to her. "Said he couldn't find a working telephone number for you—the one on file was out of order, so he asked our department to notify you on his behalf." Concern arose in her at the thought that somewhere out there was a file with her information in it, tying her to Al Dawson. "He'd like you to call him to discuss further arrangements."

She stared down at the card again, pressing the pads of her fingertips into its sharp corners. "Arrangements?"

"For the funeral, I assume."

Her chest tightened. She'd decided long ago that, one day, when Al died, she wouldn't be attending his funeral, and now here she was, the one left to arrange it on his behalf.

"Are you sure I'm the best person for this?" She looked up at the officer, his expression unreadable. "It's just that I haven't seen him in over ten years. Surely he must have some . . ." Some what? Friends? Loved ones? She knew the kind of man Al was—had known it her entire life. He was not one to build genuine connections, to become part of a 'small community' like Briar Hollow. He saw people simply for what they could do for him, for what he could acquire by being in their proximity.

"I understand how difficult this must be," the officer said, his tone indicating that he did not, in fact, understand how difficult this must be. "Please, just give the coroner a call."

With that, the conversation was over.

Clara felt like she was floating as she walked back into the building. A haze had fallen over her mind and nothing seemed quite real anymore. She ignored an upbeat "How'd it go?" from Peggy and found herself gliding up the steps to the second floor, then turning down the hall. She'd almost expected everyone to look up at her as she slipped through the door, to feel the shift that had happened within her at the news she'd been given. But she went unnoticed, and, in some way, that was more of a comfort to her.

Clara sat down at her desk and looked at the page fed through her typewriter, the letters appearing jumbled for a moment before she placed her hands above the keys and focused her eyes. After a moment, she began to type, thinking of nothing but the letters on the page and the sound of each key clicking beneath her fingertips.

She didn't move from her desk for the rest of the afternoon, occasionally feeling her boss' curious eyes on her but knowing he would not ask any further questions. She tried to lose herself in her work, in each word on the page, but with each moment that passed, she felt the weight of that card tucked inside her pocket.

It wasn't until her walk home that evening that she pulled the card free, tore it into tiny pieces, and let it float away into the wind.

# Chapter 2

## *October 1933*

The last of September's warmth had burned away and Clara pulled her jacket tightly around her as she weaved through the other pedestrians of downtown Rochester. She and Mabel had finished their biweekly shopping spree feeling sore-heeled and famished, and now they were headed toward Clara's apartment to drop off Mabel's bags before they went to lunch.

Clara, of course, didn't have any bags to drop off—she never did—but neither of them minded. Mabel was happy to have someone help her pick out a new outfit for whichever event was upcoming and to have an audience while she twirled in and out of dressing rooms like a paper doll modeling her extensive wardrobe. Clara was happy to be the audience, to have something to consume her Saturday, to distract her and stop her mind from wandering to the places it tended to linger when she was alone.

After the day's events, they would drop the bags off at Clara's apartment nearby and go to the Crystal Dining Room at Hotel Seneca for lunch. Despite Clara's objections, and the fact that Mabel was technically the younger of the two, she would insist on paying for the meal—both of them knowing that Clara couldn't afford a lunch for two at Hotel Seneca—labeling it as a thank you for Clara's assistance in helping her choose the perfect outfit for this gala or that event. Clara would leave the afternoon feeling a mix of gratitude and shame, but, unable to decline a free meal, the cycle would repeat in a fortnight or so. It was a pattern of theirs, a ritual.

This afternoon had gone no differently, and a cool breeze brushed alongside them as they stepped into the small entrance of Clara's apartment building.

"Who's there?" called Mrs. Gibbs, her landlady, from the room just off the front entryway. The door was always, to Clara's annoyance, ajar.

"It's Mabel and Clara," Mabel replied, fixing a pin that had loosened in her honey-brown hair. Clara walked past the nosy woman's door and made her way up the narrow wooden staircase that led to her apartment upstairs.

"Oh, Clara, you've got a letter there," Mrs. Gibbs replied, still hidden within her unit, likely in the middle of crocheting another blanket for the upcoming winter.

Clara reached the landing and turned, her hand scrounging around her purse for her keys, as Mabel approached the small table next to the staircase and sorted through the letters there.

"Got it," Mabel said, taking an envelope from the tray before following upstairs.

Clara carried on up the steps, reaching her door and unlocking it, the hinges groaning as she made her way into the apartment. Her eyes scanned across the space to ensure nothing of embarrassment lay in sight. The apartment was small, the circular dining table nearly too large for the kitchen on the right, and the old couch filling the living room on the left.

It was then she noticed that the hole in the couch—the one that had appeared one day and prompted her to worry that mice had gotten into the unit again—was left uncovered. The sound of Mabel coming up the steps urged Clara forward, and she crossed the room quickly, grabbing a nearby pillow and throwing it over the gap. Heat rushed to her cheeks as she turned, expecting Mabel to comment on her odd behavior. Instead, Mabel was consumed by the letter in her hand, now opened and unfolded between her fingertips.

"What is that?" Clara asked, alarmed. Mabel paid her no mind, continuing to read the piece of mail. Her mind swirled with all the possibilities of who the letter could be from, and she reached out, snatching the paper from Mabel's grasp.

"A little sharp there, aren't we?" Mabel said with a look of distaste.

"Serves you right for being nosy." Clara forced a laugh despite the concern that pooled in her stomach. "Poor Walter must never get a thing past you." She turned away from her friend and walked over to the kitchen. She wanted to look at the letter, to see who it was from and what it said, but instead, she opened a cupboard and pulled out a drinking glass, eager to find something else to fix her attention on.

"Who's Al Dawson?" Mabel asked, standing in the doorway. "Is that your father?"

Clara stilled, the envelope feeling hot within her grasp. Was this a letter from the man himself? Something from before his death? Or from the police officer she'd spoken to weeks earlier? Her curiosity nagged at her to open it, but she didn't want to encourage Mabel to approach and read it over her shoulder.

"Yes," was all she said before turning around again to lean her back against the countertop. "Didn't you have to use the bathroom?"

"You didn't tell me he died."

Clara tried to appear unaffected despite the way her heart pounded furiously in her chest. This was not a topic she discussed. In fact, she couldn't recall the last time she'd even said the man's name out loud. In the years that she and Mabel had been friends, Clara had avoided the topic as much as possible. "It didn't seem important," she said with an air of feigned indifference.

Mabel stepped into the room, her voice soft and her brown eyes wide with pity. "But he's your father."

Clara's stomach twisted at the words. Words that had been spoken to her before by those who would never understand how she could have so much apathy toward her father. But how could they?

How could someone like Mabel possibly understand what it was like to grow up in a house like hers?

"I haven't seen him in over a decade," Clara said, forcing a lightness to her tone. "And anyways, we're going to be late for our reservation. Hurry up and use the bathroom so we can go. Tick tock."

"Are you sure—"

"Certain. Please, I'm famished."

With an uncertain expression and a final glance back, Mabel obliged, leaving her bags on the floor next to the table and returning to the hall that led to the shared bathroom.

The moment she was out of sight, Clara opened the letter, scanning the words on the page. Her hands shook slightly, making it even more difficult for her to absorb the words before her. As she reached the end of the letter, something coiled tight in her chest, and a handful of words echoed through her mind: inn . . . sole heir . . . inheritance.

Footsteps sounded down the hall a few moments later and she tossed the letter into the cupboard behind her. Clara scooped up Mabel's purse and sped across the room, meeting her at the door.

"Shall we?"

As the girls made their way out into the afternoon sun, relief washed through Clara with each step they put between them and the apartment. Throughout the afternoon, her mind occasionally wandered back to the letter, but she pushed the thought away, distracting herself with Mabel's latest gossip, indulging in details about people she didn't much care for.

When Clara returned to her apartment later that evening, she avoided the cupboard and the letter calling to her from behind the cabinet door. She walked into her bedroom and changed into more comfortable clothing, then flicked on a lamp in the living room, the small space filling with a warm glow. But she felt the letter's pull with every step, its presence calling out to her until she eventually gave in. She fetched the letter from the cupboard and sat down on the couch, crossing her legs beneath her as she read.

The letter had been sent by a lawyer from Briar Hollow, supposedly hired by the county. Apparently, Al Dawson had not written a will before his untimely death, and as his only child, that meant she was entitled to his estate. His funeral had already been dealt with—a fact that left her with a mix of guilt and curiosity as she wondered which of the unopened envelopes stuffed in her kitchen drawer had included details on the event—and all that was left was for her to come to town so they could begin the process of transferring the ownership of Hollowfield House.

Clara didn't know much about property or inheritance. There hadn't been much to inherit when her mother died, seeing as they'd already shared an automobile and the one-bedroom apartment she sat in now. It had started when her mother had gotten her diagnosis and was left to put most of her income toward treatments and medications. It had only made sense for Clara to move in, to help split the expenses, since she had already been coming here most days of the week to help her mother get to and from her appointments.

Over time, Clara had taken on a larger share of the bills, having just enough from her meager salary as a typist. But then her mother had gotten the news that her treatments had failed, that she only had a few weeks, perhaps a few months, left to live. Her mother then quit her job, choosing to accept her fate and spend the last of her days in the comfort of that small, cramped apartment. In the weeks that followed, Clara had said nothing as the financial responsibilities fell entirely on her. She'd started to fall short a few dollars with each bill, but that was nothing. A few dollars could be covered on the next bill, the next paycheck. Then her mother died, leaving Clara to pick up the pieces.

Now, after the death of another parent, Clara suddenly had an opportunity to get out from under her compounding debts. She wouldn't keep Al's property—the last thing she wanted was to be shackled to some small town by the responsibility of a mortgage—but she could own the place just long enough to put it up for sale. Granted, the economy wasn't in a great place at the moment. She'd heard the stories of people down on their luck, needing to travel across the country in search of employment as they struggled to make ends meet. But New York had seemed to do better as a state than those in the South. Surely there was someone, a local perhaps, who'd been wanting a business opportunity such as the inn to support their family. And even if she sold the place for less than its value, that would still leave her better off than she was now.

Hope was something she didn't often allow herself to feel, but with the letter in her hands, she couldn't help but feel it spark within her chest. After all the ways Al Dawson had broken her, permanently damaging something vital within her, maybe there could be a silver lining. Perhaps, despite Al's carelessness in not drawing up a will, he had inadvertently given her a gift greater than just his absence.

Clara barely slept that night, her mind racing with possibility even as some part of her tried to remain tethered to the ground. This could all end badly. She could end up disappointed, maybe even worse off than where she'd started, given that she hadn't a clue what the place looked like or what condition it was in. But by morning light, she knew this wasn't something she could turn away from. They likely wouldn't hold the property forever—if she didn't accept the inheritance, surely the county would step in and claim the inn. It was now or never.

And so she got up from her bed, her body tired but her mind alert, and began to pen a response to the lawyer, Mr. Baker.

She was going to Hollowfield House.

# Chapter 3

"Are you sure you don't want me to join you?"

Clara closed the lid of her suitcase and buckled the straps in place. "Positive." With a swift tug, her luggage cleared the edge of the bed, and Clara nearly toppled over with it. She glanced up at Mabel, the perfection of her honey-brown curls in stark contrast with the frown on her face. "I'll only be gone a few days."

"But what if I need you while you're gone? My party is only three weeks away. You know I can't make all those decisions alone."

Clara fought back a sigh. This year would be the fourth year that Mabel hosted a festive dinner party with her husband on Halloween, and she was hardly in dire need of assistance with the task.

"I'll be back well before then," Clara promised, maneuvering her case through her bedroom doorframe. She puffed a breath upward, trying to push away the baby hairs that had escaped the braid twisted into a low bun at the nape of her neck.

"How far did you say it was?" Mabel called from behind her as they moved through the apartment. Clara scanned over each surface as she walked, making sure she wasn't leaving behind anything she'd need for the next few days.

"Five or six hours." She likely should've left earlier in the day, but she'd foolishly put off packing until just that morning.

"Are you sure it's safe to be traveling that far on your own?" Mabel asked, concern weaving through every word.

"Quite." They pooled into the apartment's small hallway. "I live alone—I think I can handle a drive through the countryside." Clara dropped her case on the wooden floor with a thud and pulled the keys from her purse. There wasn't much to steal if she was honest, but the allusion of security gave her some small semblance of control nonetheless.

"But what if you pop a tire? What if your vehicle gets stuck at the side of the road?" Mabel's voice grew in concern as Clara shimmied the key into the old lock. "There's a reason our mothers' generation didn't drive, you know. It's dangerous out there for a lady on her own."

Clara refrained from pointing out that while Mabel's mother had never driven, Clara's mother actually had learned to drive out of necessity, not having the luxury of a chauffeur or even a husband to take on the task.

"I suppose it's a good thing I'm not a lady, then," Clara said as she tested the door to ensure the sticky bolt had slid into place. She felt a nudge at her side and glanced down to see an envelope of money in Mabel's hands. "Oh, Mabel. Put that away before you get jumped."

"It's in case of emergency," Mabel insisted, following Clara down the creaky steps to the first floor. "Come on now, don't be so stubborn. What happens when you're stuck in a ditch on the side of the road with no money to pay a tow truck?"

For a moment, Clara indulged the possibility, her mind playing out the scenario before she pushed the thought away. That wouldn't happen. Her Ford Model A, despite being a few years old and secondhand, was in great condition. And even if the worst did happen, surely she would figure it out. She always figured it out.

"I have money for a tow truck." The lie slid easily through her lips.

It was no use trying to convince Mabel she'd be fine. They were two different types of people who'd led very different lives. Mabel had grown up as the baby of her family, close to her parents and older brothers, before she started dating her husband, Walter, when she was just fifteen. She had never known a life untethered from another person, never known what it was like to need to survive on her own, to find her way in the world no matter how uncomfortable it was, and she likely never would.

"Somehow I don't believe you," Mabel said.

A wash of city noise swept over them as Clara pushed the front door open, stepping out onto the sidewalk. It was nearly noon on a Tuesday and the sidewalk was sparse of people for a brief time, soon to be filled by those on their lunch break.

Clara shoved her case into the back seat of the Ford Model A and slammed the door shut before returning to the sidewalk to say her goodbyes. After a hug that lasted several moments too long, Clara climbed into the vehicle, smoothing the flaps of her long coat beneath her as she sat down on the leather seat and turned the key in the ignition.

Mabel appeared at the passenger side window and Clara leaned over the seat to roll down the glass. "Maybe you should have Peter go with you," Mabel said.

Clara paused, agitation sparking in her chest. "Thanks for the suggestion," she said flatly before she began to roll the window back up.

Mabel placed her fingers on the edge of the glass, a guilty look on her face. "Don't be angry with me. It's just . . . don't you think he'd want to know?"

The last person Clara wanted to call to join her on this trip was her ex-fiancé, the man whose family was the epitome of good stock, with not a singular skeleton in their closet. While he'd always tried to sympathize, she had seen it in his eyes the few times she'd spoken of her family—he simply didn't understand. No matter what she told him, snippets of her father's poor behavior, Peter would always follow with something vaguely like, *But that's in the past, why don't you give him a call? I'm sure he'd be happy to hear from you. He is your father, after all.*

Clara supposed that some people were so well-adjusted, their lives so steady, that it simply wasn't possible for them to understand a family like hers. That all they knew was a set of parents who were good folk, and that beneath each mother and father must be a well-meaning person who had done their best. But Clara knew better.

"We split up months ago. I don't particularly care what he'd want to know," Clara said, leaning away from the window. She wondered if Mabel had already told Peter about the trip and felt a sudden eagerness to be on the road, far from the city. "I need to get going."

Mabel sighed, leaning back into the window to say, "You'll call me when you get there?"

"From what the lawyer said, there's no electricity at the house, so I highly doubt they'll have a telephone." The look of horror on Mabel's face prompted a laugh from Clara, despite herself. "I'll give you a call once I find a phone in town."

"Don't forget," Mabel said, that same look of concern still on her soft features. "If I don't hear from you by Thursday, I'll be sending the police."

Clara sighed. "I'll be fine, mother dearest."

"Well, if you're not, call me. I mean it. Walter and I can be there in a blink."

Mild discomfort spread through Clara. She should be grateful for Mabel's concern—that someone cared enough for her to worry about her—but the worry of others always felt more like suffocation than comfort.

"I'll be fine," she insisted.

They said their final goodbyes, and as Clara pulled the motorcar out into the street, any anxiety about Hollowfield House was quickly replaced by the stress of navigating amongst the other cars. Buildings crowded in on both sides of the street and pedestrians spilled over the sidewalk, dodging cars as they crossed this way and that. Clara hated driving in the city, but once she left downtown behind, and the shops and buildings became more spaced out, she began to enjoy the feeling of freedom it afforded her.

As offices and retail stores gave way to open roads and rolling fields, her shoulders relaxed and her tight grip loosened on the steering wheel. The sound of the city was replaced by the rustling of autumn leaves and the swaying of stock in cornfields. A couple of hours into her trip, she stopped to fill up her gas tank and couldn't help but marvel at the peace of the open land around her.

But as she reached the halfway point between Rochester and Briar Hollow, the reality of where she was going settled in like a weight placed on her chest. This wasn't a vacation in a quaint cottage in the country. She was going to meet with a lawyer about her estranged father's estate. She'd spoken to the lawyer—Mr. Baker—over the phone, and he told her she was welcome to stay at Hollowfield House while she was in town, even giving her the address, which she'd used to mark the paper map sitting on the seat next to her. While the thought of staying in her estranged father's home unsettled her, she didn't have the funds to stay elsewhere for several nights. She could barely afford to fill her gas tank, let alone shell out some coins for a room.

It would all be fine. After all, it was just a house—just four walls where Al had happened to spend his last few years. But with every mile of dirt road Clara covered, her mind began to wander . . . What if all of this was a ploy to get her there? The thought was ridiculous, of course. Al hadn't shown an interest in her even when they lived under the same roof. Why would he go to such lengths to set up an elaborate ruse? What would he even gain from such a thing? But the absurdity of the idea did nothing to quell her nerves.

The terror from those first twelve years was so deeply embedded into her skin. He'd rarely laid a hand upon her—compared to her mother, Clara was lucky, really—yet even to this day, the thought of seeing him, of being near him, sent her heart racing. It wasn't physical breaks and bruises that he'd left behind but something deeper, a mental terror of sorts. It was the way he could walk into a room and change the atmosphere, putting both her and her mother on edge, waiting for what he might do. Even now, a wave of nausea swirled through her at the memory.

Clara took a deep breath, trying to calm herself. Al would not be there waiting for her at Hollowfield House. He was dead. The officer had said so, the lawyer had said so—it wouldn't make sense for them to lie. And besides, she wasn't a child anymore. She could leave. She could get in her car and go at any time, the moment she felt uncomfortable.

Outside her windshield, the sky turned from soft blue to light grey, slowly darkening as the sun was blotted out by clouds. By the time she reached the final few miles of the drive, night had fallen and a light drizzle had begun. She'd already pulled over once to look at her map, certain she should have been there by now, yet she had not seen any sign of an inn.

Raindrops tapped against her windshield as the realization settled in—she was lost. Frustration and fear built within her as she looked out into the darkness ahead. Perhaps it was a sign to turn around and go back home. Even from beyond the grave, Al Dawson was rejecting her. Rejecting the notion that she could truly inherit something that so clearly belonged to him. He was territorial of what was his in life, why not in death as well?

Eventually, she pulled over to the side of the road and pulled out her flashlight, unfolding the map onto her lap once again. How did her father make money from an inn that was this difficult to find?

It didn't make sense. She might be a bit directionally challenged at times, but this seemed excessive even for her.

With her finger, Clara traced the path she'd taken here, trying to estimate her current location. It was difficult to find her place with each dirt road, each field, looking like the last. She felt a sense of dread quickly approaching as the night's cold air seeped into her skin, even from inside the cabin of the vehicle. Maybe she'd be better off sleeping in her car until morning when she'd have a better chance of finding the inn in daylight. Or at least a better chance of encountering another human being who might point her to the inn. But she shouldn't need help—that was the entire reason for the map.

She leaned forward, squinting past the rain and out into the darkness, looking for any distinctive landmarks. There was nothing but fields and forest, and for the first time, she felt the impact of her isolation. As she looked into the dark trees off in the distance, she couldn't help but imagine someone out there, watching her from some hidden place in the shadows. She thought of a legend she'd known since childhood: a man on a horse riding free through the countryside late at night, appearing to lone riders and swiftly removing their heads.

Clara chastised herself for entertaining the story, nothing more than a childish fable. Yet she couldn't help but glance behind her, out the back window, and look for movement, for a shadow to cross her path. Sleeping in her vehicle no longer felt like a viable option, so she turned the key in the ignition and pulled back onto the road, willing to drive aimlessly until she found Hollowfield House.

A few minutes down the road, by some miracle, she came upon a faint glow through the dark of the night. Hope sparked within her, though she was unsure whether the light came from a house or another vehicle. As she got closer, Clara realized that the light was coming from a one-story brick building with white block letters atop the awning that read *DINER*. Only a single light shone above the front entrance, but it was enough. Two vehicles were parked out front, not giving her much hope for assistance, but she turned into the gravel parking lot anyway, her car rattling as it drove over a pothole.

Hesitation fluttered in her stomach as she stared at the building. She couldn't see past the blinds that covered the windows, but there was a faint perimeter of light around the glass from where something inside must be switched on. Someone had to be in there; surely, they wouldn't be wasting electricity like this without purpose. With a deep breath, she cut the engine. She would go try the door. Either someone was inside, in which case they could hopefully point her toward the inn, or they were not.

Her heart quickened as she stepped out of her car and ran the short distance to the front door, wet drops landing on her hair and skin. She reached out and tugged on the door handle, which mercifully swung open, and a bell chimed above her head as a layer of warmth enveloped her. She stepped onto a thin red rug, so relieved to be out of the downpour that it took a few moments for her to realize the room had gone completely still upon her entrance.

Her skin prickled as she met each pair of eyes that stared back at her without a word.

# Chapter 4

The lights were dimmed inside the small diner, chairs had been placed atop tables, and the only sound in the room was a radio playing softly in the background. It was empty save for three men sitting at the bar top and a woman serving them from behind the counter. Each of them stared at Clara, their expressions unreadable, but she found no hint of warmth in their watchful eyes. So much for small-town hospitality.

"Hello," Clara said with a warmth she didn't feel. The two men nearest her looked to be in their forties or fifties, and while the man at the end looked closer to her age, all of them wore similar attire—high-waisted dark trousers and button-front shirts in need of a good wash, the sleeves pushed up to their elbows.

Clara turned her attention toward the only other woman. She was older, her hair a blend of soft brown and grey, and she wore a uniform with a name tag that Clara couldn't read at this distance.

"Can I help you, miss?" The woman's tone was clipped, one of obligation rather than a sincere desire to assist.

Clara considered how much she should disclose to a room full of strangers, out in the middle of nowhere on a quiet autumn evening. The thought of telling them she was lost seemed far too vulnerable a confession for this time of night, so she opted to stay as vague as possible with her response.

"Yes. Could you point me toward Hollowfield House?"

There was a shift in their silent demeanor—a change she could feel in the room, though no one had spoken. Clara kept her smile in place as she met the gaze of the first man, who promptly looked away, as did the second. The third man at the end, the one who appeared to be in his late twenties, held her gaze. He had a handsome face with full lips and a dusting of scruff that shadowed his jaw, yet when she looked at him, all she felt was annoyance at his boldness in staring at her, despite his utter lack of urgency to help.

Just as she was certain none of them would answer, he spoke.

"What's taking you there?" His voice was low, his gaze unmoving from where she stood.

Her smile faltered.

"I hardly think that's any of your business." The words slipped out before she could think better of them, and the other two men suddenly turned, their interest piqued once again. She refused to look away from the third man, pride sparking within her despite a small voice in her mind that urged her to back down. But why should she tell this stranger her reason for going where she needed to go? Either he knew where the inn was or he didn't.

"The inn is closed for the time being," the woman said, drawing Clara's eyes away from the agitating man.

"That's quite alright," Clara said with another attempt at politeness. "I'm not looking to stay as a guest. I just need to be pointed in the right direction."

"What's your name?" the man at the end of the counter asked.

The urge to glare at him nearly overpowered her, and all at once, Clara regretted ever bothering to step inside this diner. She didn't need their help. She was perfectly capable of finding the damn place on her own.

She made a show of glancing back at the window behind her. "You know what, it looks like the rain is lightening up after all," she said, her tone pleasant. "I'll be on my way." She turned and pushed open the door, an unpleasant warmth rising in her gut as she ran toward her vehicle.

The rain—not actually lightening up—sprayed down upon her as she reached the driver's side and climbed in, slamming the door shut behind her. So much for getting help. She grabbed her map and snapped it open in frustration. At what point should she just give up and admit defeat?

She hadn't even wanted to stay at the property to begin with. She was only here to sign the papers and sell the damn place so she could go back to her life and get out from under the pile of outstanding bills in her name. But she should've known it was too good to be true. For all she knew, the inn was no more than a local legend used to mess with tourists—a place that didn't actually exist at all. It would certainly explain how useless the group inside had been in her attempt to locate it.

Through the steady rap of rainfall against her windshield, a sudden movement in the dark outside her vehicle made her pause. Just as she looked up, her passenger door opened and a man jumped inside, bringing a gust of cold wind with him before he shut the door. It took a moment for her to recognize him as the man who had been staring at her—the one at the end of the bar.

Perhaps she should be afraid, but all she could feel was anger at his ongoing audacity. "Get out," Clara demanded.

He lifted his hands in mock defense. "Hold on now—"

"Get out of my car," she repeated, feeling the dampened fabric of his cotton shirt beneath her fingers as she tried to shove him toward the passenger side door. Even as she pushed with all her might, he barely budged, which only agitated her further.

"Do you want to know how to get to the inn or not?" In the shadows of the vehicle, she couldn't quite see the emotion in his eyes, but she could hear the frustration in his tone. Good.

"The time to be helpful was five minutes ago," she informed him, pushing the map off her lap and into the shadows by her feet, hoping he wouldn't pay any mind to the sound of paper crinkling as she subtly tried to refold it. Clara glanced through the front window of the automobile, squinting through the rain to be sure the rest of his posse hadn't decided to funnel out after him.

"Just take it easy. I'm not trying anything here. I just—"

"Take it easy? Need I remind you that you just followed an unknown woman out to her car in the dead of night like some kind of criminal? You're lucky I haven't started screaming yet."

He tilted his head, seeming to consider her words. "I suppose you've got a point there. I apologize. I didn't mean to frighten you—"

"You didn't," she cut in. "I'm not frightened. I'm annoyed and a bit puzzled as to why you're still sitting here, getting the seat of my motorcar wet."

He glanced down at himself, and she took the opportunity to toss the folded map into the shadows of her back seat, its presence not likely to convince him that she didn't need his assistance.

"It seems I'm not the best with first impressions," he said, his voice now softened. "But you said in there that you were looking for the inn. Do you happen to be Clara Dawson?"

She stilled, fear crawling over her skin as she heard her name in this stranger's mouth. "How do you know that?"

"I'm the groundskeeper at the inn. I heard you might be coming into town, but I suppose I imagined Al's daughter to look rather . . . different."

She stared at him, unsure of whether his comment was an attempt at insulting her, but more concerned with whether or not he was lying about his identity. He didn't have the weathered appearance of the groundskeepers she'd previously encountered, but she supposed the older men she'd often associated with the job had likely held their position for many years by that point. "And how do I know you're telling the truth?"

Initially, she was met with silence, but a moment later he leaned over and pulled his wallet from his pocket. He dug a card out from it and handed it to her. It was his driver's license. She hesitated for a moment before grabbing hold of it, her fingers on the farthest end from where he gripped it. His name was Jonathan Tucker, he'd turned thirty last April, and his address was a match to the one Mr. Baker had given to her for Hollowfield House.

"You live there?" she asked hesitantly, handing back the card. She'd known there was a groundskeeper nearby, but she certainly hadn't been expecting a roommate during her stay.

"I live in the cottage on the property," he said, slipping the card back into his wallet.

"And you couldn't have said as much when I asked for directions?"

His gaze landed on her through the dim light of the parking lot. "Considering the inn is closed to guests, it didn't seem necessary to disclose. Besides, I didn't see you offering up your identity."

"To a room full of strange men?"

He shifted in his seat before he said, "I'd hardly say strange. And Sylvia was there too." She gave him a flat look, though it didn't seem to impact him as he carried on. "So, what'll it be? You can keep driving around looking for an inn that has no sign—"

"The inn has no sign?" she questioned.

"Well, it did. But I took it down after . . ." His voice trailed off as she filled in the rest. After the owner took his own life. Annoyance and relief simultaneously spread through her at the realization that it wasn't her lack of direction that had caused her struggle in finding the place—he'd just taken down the damn sign. "As I was saying, you can try to find it on your own or you can save Will the drive, and I'll show you the way myself."

"Am I to assume Will was one of the charming fellows I just met?" She stared out into the night, her mind playing through her options. Either she could trust this stranger and pursue the possibility of finding the inn, or she could sleep in her car, out alone on a dark country road, a choice she wasn't convinced was a safer option. With a deep sigh, she said, "Fine."

The engine came to life beneath them as she put the key in the ignition. Her heart pounded quickly as she backed out of the lot, driving into the darkness of country roads with a stranger in her passenger seat. As they turned onto the main road, leaving the light of the diner behind them, she only hoped that she hadn't made a grave mistake.

An uncomfortable silence sat between them as they drove. Although Mr. Tucker's presence didn't feel particularly threatening, Clara couldn't help but glance at him out of the corner of her eye, memorizing details in case she needed to identify him later. He was taller than she'd initially thought when he was seated in the diner, but here in the proximity of her car, he filled the space with his presence, the top of his head almost grazing the roof of the vehicle. His dark hair was pushed back off his face haphazardly, different from the polished type of good-looking she was used to seeing in Rochester.

"We're not too far," he said, meeting her gaze for a moment before she looked away.

She fixed her eyes on the path ahead of them—a long gravel road with no streetlamp in sight. There was only the stifled light of the moon and her headlights to lead the way. Clara followed his direction as he told her to make another left turn onto yet another road that looked the same as the first.

"Slow down. It's just up here on your left."

She looked to where he was pointing but saw only trees, a sinking feeling settling into her stomach. If she needed to get away on foot, she had no idea where to go—it all looked the same out here in the dark of the night, the rain doing her no favors either.

She slowed the vehicle and saw a small clearing between the trees. It was hardly the size of a driveway, more like the opening of a walking trail.

"Just turn down here." His voice was confident, but she hesitated for a moment, looking between him and the opening of the shadowed pathway.

"This doesn't look like a driveway," she said, her voice steady despite her heart racing in her chest.

"I assure you, it is."

Slowly, she turned the wheel, her car pushing through the entrance. The branches overhead clawed at the top of the vehicle as her headlights illuminated the vacant windows of a house at the end of the short driveway. As they pulled into the empty space before the building, her eyes wandered over the structure.

The inn was a square, two-story house with white clapboard siding, the paint peeling away in some places. As Clara looked up at it through her windshield, she couldn't help but imagine Al staring down at her from the shadows of one of the windows. She swallowed a wave of nausea, chastising herself silently for her fear. It was just a house—nothing more.

Before she could think better of it, she cut the engine and opened her door, stepping out onto the gravel lot. They were surrounded by forest, nothing but darkness around them and night above them. Across from the house, there was a path that appeared to lead to a small cottage shrouded in shadows. Clara lifted the navy cotton scarf around her neck over her dark hair and squinted against the rain. Movement caught her attention at the tree line that bridged the gap between the inn and the cottage at the edge of the property.

Her eyes strained as she struggled to focus on a silhouette in the darkness before her, shifting in the forest. The shape almost looked like a woman with her long skirt billowing around her legs in the breeze, the figure seeming to stare directly at Clara. A tingle crawled up her spine at the sight, even though the idea of a woman out here in the cold and dark, standing in the forest and watching her from the trees, was ridiculous. Clara blinked, hoping to make sense of the shadowed figure, waiting for the shape to suddenly reveal itself as a tree or plant of some sort.

She startled at the sound of the car door slamming behind her and turned to find that Mr. Tucker was now carrying her trunk toward the house. Clara looked back to the forest, scanning the shadows for the woman, and found nothing but the silhouette of trees and leaves swaying in the wind. She exhaled, relief mixing with annoyance. She'd been here for all of sixty seconds, and her imagination was already running away with her.

"Do you plan on standing out here all night?" Mr. Tucker called across the lot.

His words brought her back, and she became aware of the moisture against her skin as the rain soaked through her jacket, down to the clothing beneath, her toes numb within her shoes. She turned to follow Mr. Tucker up the front steps, finding solace under the covered porch as she pulled her scarf down around her neck.

The hinges groaned as he pushed open the front door and crossed the threshold, carrying Clara's case in one hand as if it weighed nothing at all. Just before she stepped inside, she took one final look out into the dark shadows of the trees, unable to shake the feeling that she was being watched, even now.

# Chapter 5

The scent of old tobacco overwhelmed Clara as she stepped across the threshold into the small entryway of the inn. It was dark and cold inside the house, dampness clung to the air, and she could see little more than the vapor of her breath as she exhaled. Mr. Tucker had left her suitcase by the stairs and disappeared into the room to her right, leaving her to hover by the open door, debating whether she should shut it and seal them inside this dark box of an entryway.

"Just a minute," he called between thumps. By the sounds of it, he was either very clumsy or was not as familiar with the layout of the room as she would've expected. She tried not to let the thought concern her as she shut the door closed with a firm click. Perhaps it was a sign he wasn't close with Al, that he'd had no reason to come into the main house as the groundskeeper. After all, he'd had a key to the inn and had shown proof that this was his residence.

With the flick of a match, a soft glow emanated from the room that Mr. Tucker had slipped into, a room she could now see was a small kitchen. A countertop lined the wall across from her, only broken up by the presence of a wood-fired stove. There was an icebox along the wall to her left and a window taking up most of the wall to her right, though little moonlight broke through the cloud cover. A rectangular wooden table in the middle dominated most of the room, leaving no more than a foot or two of space to pull out a chair and sit.

"Sorry it's so cold in here," Mr. Tucker said as he moved past Clara, holding an oil lamp in one hand as he walked through the hall toward the living room. He paused suddenly, looking down at the floor beneath him then back toward the path he'd taken. She followed his gaze to find mucky boot prints trailing behind him. "I'll clean that," he grumbled before stepping out of his shoes.

Clara followed suit, taking her shoes off and following him into the living room while keeping a few feet of space between them. In the dim lighting, she saw that there was a couch in the center of the room and two chairs on either side of a mantle where Mr. Tucker placed the small lamp. He knelt before the hearth, pulling pieces of chopped wood from a nearby basket. She turned away, burying her frigid fingers into her pockets, and looked toward the far side of the room that was still cloaked in shadow.

The room extended beyond her view, appearing as a darkness with no end, but as the fire flickered to life, she saw that the room extended quite far, nearly twice as long as it was wide. The far end of the room was likely meant to be a dining space, but it sat empty, nothing but an expanse of wood flooring. A single window sat farther down the wall from the fireplace, a curtain framing the pane that overlooked the forest surrounding the house.

In contrast, the left half of the room was fully furnished. There was the couch and chairs she'd noticed earlier, and to the right was a gramophone with a rich mahogany base and a faded bronze horn, a stack of discs tucked neatly beneath its stand. A thick patterned rug lay beneath it, adding a bit of warmth to the cold room. The furniture in this half of the room had clearly been left behind by the previous owners, and the thought gave Clara a strange sense of satisfaction. Further evidence that what she had always known had remained true long after Al had left them. Even though he'd always been desperate for control over everything around him, he had never been bothered to care for anything once it was in his possession.

Mr. Tucker stood from his crouched position, brushing remnants of bark from his hands. "Did you want something to warm you? Tea or . . ." His voice faded off and she wondered if, after weeks of this house standing empty, he had anything left to offer.

Clara looked over her shoulder toward the kitchen, confirming her own suspicion. There was no kitchen sink. "Do you have water for tea?"

"Not presently," Mr. Tucker said as he walked past her, toward the kitchen. "But there's a pump out front. I can just—"

"That's alright," Clara said, the thought of this stranger walking out into the rain to pump water for her tea leaving her with an odd feeling of discomfort. "I'm perfectly fine. The fire is more than enough." She walked over to the hearth, took a seat in one of the chairs there, and stretched her numb fingers toward the heat of the flame. Part of her wished that he would leave now, his eagerness to help making her feel unsettled, but another part of her wasn't quite ready to be alone in this house.

"It's really no trouble," he insisted.

She heard him open a cupboard in the kitchen and turned in her chair to assure him it was truly not necessary when she saw him with a cloth in hand, disappearing behind the couch to wipe the prints from the floor. When he came back into view a moment later, the question was still in his eyes. She gave him a polite smile, knowing that for each kind gesture, she would only owe him further—a tab that would be left unpaid if she couldn't sell the property quickly. And she didn't like owing people.

"Mr. Tucker, I assure you, I'm quite content," she said, sweeping a strand of dampened hair out of her face. "I just need to warm up by the fire for a bit before I go to bed."

He nodded slowly, though he remained seemingly unconvinced. "Alright. Then I'll bring your case up."

"You don't—"

"Miss Dawson," he said, cutting her off and lifting her suitcase into his grasp, "my mother would roll over in her grave if I allowed a woman to struggle with her luggage. On this, I must insist."

Guilt bloomed uncomfortably at his subtle admission. If Mr. Tucker was only thirty, how old could his mother have been when she died? Had he been a young boy, or had it perhaps been a more recent loss? It made Clara think of the death of her own mother and she found herself unable to protest, suddenly eager for the interaction to end. She cleared her throat before saying, "If you must."

Clara turned away from him, toward the fire that crackled in the hearth. At the sound of him going up the stairs, the wood groaning beneath his feet, her shoulders relaxed. The heat of the flames began to melt the ice from her veins as she sat there, lost in the memory of her mother's final days, before she caught sight of movement in her periphery. She looked to her right, toward the dark end of the long room, and noticed the curtain shift ever so slightly. She stilled, the fine hairs along her arms standing on end as she watched the curtain sway before falling back into place.

But then, the curtain moved again, and Clara huffed a sigh of relief with the realization that the window must have simply been left ajar. She stood, walking away from the light of the fire and toward the window—toward the shadows—and found it had been left open barely an inch. A sudden gust of wind blew through the crack and caressed her skin, leaving gooseflesh in its wake. Clara looked out into the forest, to the same place where she'd imagined the shape of a woman watching her when she'd first arrived. She blinked, waiting for her eyes to adjust to the blackness of the unbridled night before her.

The trees swayed restlessly against the wind, the scent of wet earth slipping in through the window. She'd always loved the rain. The scene before her, the sounds and smells, should have comforted her. Yet as she looked out into the darkness, suddenly she was all too aware of the glow of the fire inside, the way it lit the room, leaving her exposed to anyone who may be outside looking in.

Clara scanned the tree line, unease seeping deep within her bones, akin to the sensation of walking down an empty street at night and noticing a stranger walking several paces behind her. It wasn't the fear of being alone, but rather, the realization that someone had been near for some time, lingering just out of sight.

The floorboards groaned behind her and she jumped, turning toward the noise only to realize it was Mr. Tucker returning down the staircase. Her hand went to her chest, her heart pounding furiously before she felt a flush of foolishness at how jumpy she'd been. It was an old house. It wouldn't do for her to be startled at every creak and groan. She shut the window and flipped the latch, trying to feign a casual air as Mr. Tucker appeared in the doorframe, his eyes searching the furniture before landing on where she stood across the room.

"I gave you the first bedroom at the top of the stairs," he said, a look of confusion on his face as if he were trying to determine why she was standing off in the shadows.

"Oh, thank you." She walked toward the lit side of the room, gesturing back to the window. "Don't mind me. The window was open, so I was just closing it."

He furrowed his brow and looked between her and the window before crossing the room to inspect it. "I can't imagine how that happened. No one's been in here for weeks. I was sure the place was locked up." He knelt down to examine the lock, and Clara couldn't help but feel a bit defensive, as if he thought she'd imagined the whole thing.

"Oh. Well, it was hardly open," she said. "I only noticed because I saw the curtains blowing from the breeze." His expression remained unconvinced. She fought the urge to explain further, to prove to him that the window had, indeed, been open, but instead, she put a polite smile on her face. "Anyways, thank you for . . . your assistance with everything."

He dipped his head in acknowledgment before he spoke. "Is there anything else you need? I'm afraid there's not much in the way of food." He walked toward her, leaving a few feet of space between them. "I'll have to go into town tomorrow and get some things."

"Don't trouble yourself with that," she insisted, all too aware of the ever-growing list of things he'd already done on her behalf. "I have to go into town anyways to meet with the lawyer. I'll just pick up a few things for myself while I'm there."

He was silent for a moment, seeming to analyze her as if trying to read into her words for some hidden meaning. And then he said, "Alright then. I suppose I'll leave you to rest." He walked toward the front door. "If you need anything, I'll be in the cottage just there."

"Thank you," she said, relieved that he hadn't pushed the matter. "Despite our strained introduction, you've been very helpful, Mr. Tucker."

He stopped at the doorway, hesitating for a moment before he said, "No one around here calls me Mr. Tucker. Just Tuck is fine." His voice was softer now, and she felt the weight of his gaze from across the room.

"Tuck," she said, trying out the name on her lips. "Well, then, you can call me Clara."

He pulled the door open and the sound of rain intensified. "Goodnight, Clara." With that, he shut the door behind him, disappearing into the shadows beyond.

Clara waited a moment before she crossed the room and locked the door behind him, letting out a deep exhale as she took in the sight of the room around her. She felt a pang of homesickness move through her, a desire to climb into her small, rickety bed and get under the covers, to be back in her little apartment in Rochester. But she wasn't home in Rochester. She was hours away, officially alone in Hollowfield House.

# Chapter 6

Clara returned to her seat before the fire, but a few minutes later, she found herself falling asleep, the crackling of the wood and the heat of the flame making her eyelids grow heavy. The thought of letting sleep take her away from this house, from this strange situation, was suddenly very alluring, and she stood, walking over to the oil lamp Tuck had left behind. She picked it up and began up the staircase, the wood protesting beneath her feet, filling the air with a symphony of groans and creaks that cut through the quiet house.

A yawn escaped her as she reached the final step. She was just thinking about the book she'd brought with her, the way she didn't have the energy to read before bed as she'd intended, when a creak—clear and loud as the chime of a bell—sounded from the end of the hall. Clara stilled, staring past the glow of her lamp and down the dark hallway, her heart pounding furiously. She knew it was common for houses like this one to make noise, sighing and groaning in their old age. Yet, this didn't sound like an old house shifting in the wind. This sounded like the creak of shifting weight, a foot stepping on a loose floorboard.

A shiver ran down Clara's spine as she waited for another creak, but the only sounds she heard were the wind and the rain outside picking up into a gentle howl. Inside the house, all was still. She stared into the darkness of the short hallway, two open doors on the right side and two on the left, each shrouded in shadow.

After a moment, her logic returned to her, and she exhaled the breath she'd been holding. No one was here waiting for her in the shadows. She was simply tired, her exhausted imagination setting her on edge in this isolated house. It would do her no good to let her mind wander. She stepped into the room closest to her, the one where Tuck had placed her suitcase, and closed the door behind her before setting the lamp down on the small nightstand.

Clara turned back to lock the door but found there was none. Unease washed through her, but she pushed the concern away, returning her attention to the room that would be hers for the next few days. The bedroom was small, the only furniture in the room a poster bed with white bedding, a night table, an armoire on the wall at the foot of the bed, and a wash basin by the small window across from where she stood now. Her case had been placed on the bed, and she unbuckled it, laying it open and sifting through her clothing for something dry and warm.

She peeled off her layers before slipping into an old nightdress, the material a light cotton, but its sleeves long enough to cover her exposed skin from the chill. Clara lifted her dampened clothes from the floor and laid them over the mirror of the wash basin, hoping they'd be dry by morning. She walked over to her case and flipped it shut before dropping it onto the floor with a thud, then slid it across the wooden floor, pushing it up against the closed door to act as a make-shift doorstop.

The sheets felt soft against her skin as she climbed beneath the covers, and she was grateful to whoever had taken care of the laundry in this inn, as it certainly hadn't been Al Dawson. She lay on her side and watched the flickering of the oil lamp, knowing she should turn it off but not wanting to extinguish the only source of light in the room. She lay there, watching the flame, as she drifted off to sleep.

Clara woke some time later, unsure of whether it had been minutes or hours since she shut her eyes, to the sensation of having just missed something. The aftermath of a word spoken or a sound ceased. The feeling still lingered in the air as she opened her eyes to complete darkness, the flame in the lamp having somehow extinguished. For a moment, the impenetrable blackness was suffocating, as if she were buried beneath the earth where no glint of light could reach her. Panic swept through her as she waited for her vision to return, lying completely still.

*Creak.*

Her breath caught at the noise.

The sound had come from down the hall.

She thought of the creak she'd heard earlier as she came to bed. Surely, she was imagining things again, nothing more than her own fear conspiring against her. The thought brought her no comfort, and despite the part of her that felt foolish, she didn't dare move.

Her eyes slowly adjusted to the darkness, making out the vague shadows of the furniture in the room around her.

The wind howled outside her window, leaves rustling as they clung to their branches.

But inside, all was still.

*Creak.*

Clara's heart hammered in her chest, but she didn't dare move, fear seizing her limbs.

She waited for another sound, for something distinctly human that could confirm that these were not the echoes of the house itself but of someone moving within it.

The world outside seemed so far away as she listened, every nerve in her body on edge.

It could be Tuck. He could've forgotten something. He could've needed something but, not wanting to wake her, decided to tiptoe—

*Creak.*

Slow and long—the evidence of a patient step, of someone creeping down the darkened hallway. Bile climbed up her throat at the image her mind evoked.

This wasn't Tuck.

She had no proof, no evidence to believe it, but she could feel it somehow. Feel that something was not right.

Sweat dampened her brow and slicked her palms. Her muscles ached with tension, but still she couldn't move, too afraid to make a sound, no matter how quiet.

Her mind went to the one place it should never go—to the fear buried deep down inside her. What if it was Al? What if he had sensed her presence in his house? What if, wherever his wicked soul lay, he'd awakened and come to—

*Creak.*

The sound was closer now, louder than it had been.

But dead men didn't walk.

Dead men didn't creep down the hall late at night, floorboards groaning beneath them as they shifted their weight.

This was not an apparition of her father. This was someone very real.

Clara recalled the figure she'd seen in the tree line—the shape of a woman, her skirt billowing in the wind.

But that couldn't have been real. The sight had seemed no more than a product of her own imagination. Why would a woman be there in the shadows, in the rain, watching the house?

*Creak.*

Closer. The sound—the person—was coming closer.

She should run.

She could see it in her mind, could imagine herself slipping out of bed, opening the door, running down the steps—the painfully loud steps—then out the front door and into the night.

But then what?

Where would she go?

The house sat miles away from any neighbors.

What if the trespasser caught her? What if she didn't even make it down the stairs before they were upon her?

What if there was more than one intruder? What if there was another one downstairs and she'd run right into their arms?

*Creak.*

This one was just outside her door.

So close she could've sworn the person had stepped through the closed door and into the room with her. But the door remained shut.

Even the wind outside seemed to hold its breath and wait.

Whoever it was, they would hear her.

They would hear the pounding of her heart and know she was awake, know she was listening. Her pulse roared in her ears, and she wished she could reach into her chest and grasp her heart, holding it still, silencing it.

She waited.

Waited for a sound.

For the click of a doorknob turning.

For her suitcase to slide across the floor as they pushed their way in.

She waited, seconds stretching into minutes, feeling like hours.

Her body was alight with electricity, every nerve on edge in anticipation.

But nothing came.

She swallowed, fear consuming her. Her nightgown was damp with sweat.

What if they were there, just outside that door, listening? What if they, too, were waiting? Waiting for her to let her guard down, to feel momentarily safe again.

So, even as no further sound came, she continued to wait.

She waited until the silence that had swallowed her whole cracked, the howl of the wind outside returning.

She waited until the ravenous pounding of her heart eased.

She waited until the crackle in her veins weakened to fatigue.

And somehow, as she lay waiting in that dark room, she fell into a deep slumber.

# Chapter 7

The chirps and flutters of birds outside Clara's window pulled her from sleep the next morning. She tried to open her eyes but quickly shut them against the bright sunlight spilling onto her pillow. She flipped onto her back, rubbing her eyes before staring up at the ceiling. Some part of her hoped her journey last night had been a dream, hoped she'd wake up to her drafty apartment with its leaky pipes—a place that was unglamorous but had been the closest to a home she'd ever had.

Clara pulled the blankets further up over her shoulders, fighting against the chill in the air. She closed her eyes and turned away from the light, relishing her final moments of warmth beneath the covers. She was meeting with Mr. Baker today—a meeting she'd been dreading for the past week. She couldn't help but feel like the inheritance wouldn't be as simple as it seemed, like they would discover some secret clause that snatched away the possibility of her owning the property and, therefore, ruin her only chance of gaining some semblance of financial security.

It was in rare moments like this that she almost wished she had stayed with Peter. How much easier he made her life, the way he was always willing to take the lead in situations like this. But instead, it was just her left to deal with all of this, stepping into territory way over her head.

She squeezed her eyes shut tighter, hoping sleep would reemerge, but her stomach twisted with anxiety. With a sigh, she opened her eyes, accepting that she was awake now and would need to face the day.

As she stared through the open door, her eyes landing on the wooden floor out in the hall, something nagged at her. It didn't hit her right away, the realization of what was wrong. It took several moments before the events of the night came back to her—the footsteps in the hall, and the moment before that, when she'd slid her case in front of the door. The suitcase that was now placed neatly at the end of her bed.

Clara sat up abruptly, a wave of dread coursing through her. She pushed her way out of bed and into the hall, the wood flooring cold beneath her bare feet. The doors in the hallway were all left ajar, just as she'd remembered. To the left was the staircase leading down to the front door. She scanned the floor, looking for footprints—some sign of the presence she had so clearly heard last night—but there was nothing.

She walked down the hall, peering into each bedroom as she went, but only found replications of her room. As she moved, she felt the floorboards shift gently beneath her, at moments hearing the same creak she'd heard last night, the memory of it sending a chill up her spine. But as she glanced into the final bedroom at the end of the hall, the furniture looking innocuous in the morning light, she couldn't help but wonder how the intruder had managed to make such noise—had managed to find each creaky board down the hall.

Clara looked at the floor beneath her, at the cracks where the boards lined up with one another. She wondered now, what path did one need to take to land on each and every creak? She stepped on the slat of wood farthest to the left, right up against the floor. Then she moved to the next board, testing each until she heard that unsettling creak, felt the give of the old wood beneath her feet.

By the time she reached the other side of the hall, Clara came to an alarming realization: whoever had been here last night had walked down the hall slowly, strangely, nearly zig-zagging at times, as if they'd done so intentionally.

Clara swallowed, nausea climbing up her throat as she turned and looked into the room she'd slept in last night—at her suitcase that had been moved to the foot of the bed. Whoever was here last night had wanted to be heard, had wanted her to know of their presence. And it seemed they wanted her afraid.

Clara readied for the day as best she could without running water, settling for a dry toothbrush and toothpaste in the wash basin in her room. She exchanged her cotton nightdress for a cream sweater and long navy skirt, grateful to have brought her thickest pair of stockings with her considering the briskness that lingered in the air even here inside the inn. Then she ran a brush through her dark brown shoulder-length hair, sweeping it off her face and pinning it in place. All the while, there was a building sense of anticipation in her chest, an eagerness to hurry up and put space between herself and the house.

Clara tossed her grey wool overcoat over her arm and grabbed her purse before heading down the noisy staircase. As she reached the bottom of the stairs, she shrugged into her coat and found her shoes where she'd left them the night before, slipping them on and reaching for the door handle until she saw the lock still firmly in place. Her hand paused just before it, hanging in the air as she stared at the lock.

Did that mean whoever had been here last night was not an intruder but someone with a key? Her heartbeat quickened as she thought of Tuck and the way he'd been so eager to help. Could he have snuck back inside after she'd gone upstairs? She glanced at the floor where he'd cleaned his shoeprints, then to the staircase, recalling the way the wood had groaned as he climbed the stairs with her suitcase.

It seemed unlikely that she wouldn't have heard him if he'd snuck back into the house and made his way to the second floor. And then she remembered that moment at the top step, the sound at the end of the hall when she'd been here alone. She shivered at the realization that perhaps someone had not needed to break in, but perhaps they'd already been inside, waiting.

She thought of the open window, the swaying of the curtains. Suddenly she was desperate to be free of this house, away from its walls that smelled of smoke and mildew. She flipped the latch on the door, the hinges creaking as it swung inward, and a wash of crisp morning air pushed past her, making its way into the hall. Without another look back, Clara stepped out onto the covered porch, not bothering to lock it behind her. She told herself it was in case Tuck needed quick access to the house for his work, though some part of her knew that anyone who wanted into this house already had a way inside.

Birdsong sounded from the trees nearby, but otherwise, the morning was quiet, especially compared to what she was used to in the city. Fog clung to the grass and the base of the trees that lined the gravel lot. Clara stood beneath the morning sunlight, letting the rays warm her skin as she waited for her tension to melt away. But even now she could feel the remnants of last night, a fear so tangible it had stilled her, frozen her in place. If she had just gathered the courage to open her bedroom door, to confront the intruder, then she wouldn't be dealing with these questions now. But instead, she'd cowered in fear like a child. Her inaction strikingly reminiscent of the one person she'd worked so hard not to become—her mother.

Clara had known from a young age that no one would save her, especially when it came to her father's tyranny. She'd seen the way her mother was willing to cower in her own home, time and time again, willing to let her child experience the same fate rather than face the unknown fear of what life might be like if they left. But instead, Al beat them to it, leaving one day when Clara was twelve. While Clara no longer had to protect herself from Al's temper, that also meant that she had become the protector of their household, knowing her mother certainly wouldn't fill the role.

Yet that tenacity she'd had as a young girl seemed to vanish last night. She was a grown woman now, but all she'd done was lie in her bed, too terrified to move, too terrified to face whoever was in the hall. Emotion thickened Clara's throat as shame spread through her. She could see now how her relationship with Peter had softened her, weakened her, made her feel as though she no longer needed to come to her own defense. She'd become so comfortable within the protection of a man—a good man, at that—but where had that left her now that she was on her own?

A sound cut through the morning air. She looked across the lot, toward the crunch of leaves, and saw a shadow move through the trees, away from her and around the cottage.

Tuck.

What if, somehow, it had been him? What if he was so familiar with the house, with its creaks and groans, that he knew just where to step so as not to draw a sound from the stairs?

The memory of last night returned to her, the way he'd fumbled around the kitchen in the dark, and suddenly that seemed unlikely. She supposed it could have all been part of his plan, a ruse to trick her, but the possibility of him having thought ahead and crafted a plan to unsettle her seemed strange when he hadn't even seemed to be expecting her arrival last night.

Clara looked over at her car, where it sat in the shade waiting for her, waiting to take her away from this dreadful place. She should get in her vehicle and head to town, yet her feet moved in the opposite direction, following Tuck's path through the trees and around the side of the cottage. What if it had been him inside the house, sneaking in only because he thought she was asleep, not wanting to wake her? But no, that couldn't be. She'd seen the path he must've taken, woken to her suitcase moved across the room. She felt a sudden urgency to confront him, to watch his expression as she caught him off guard and see if there was something there in his eyes, in his movements, that might give him away.

As she walked across the gravel, the leaves crunching beneath her feet, doubt crept in. Even if he'd had a key, how had he made his way up those stairs without her hearing a thing? How had he returned down those same steps and not given away his exit? For just a moment, she couldn't help but wonder if the reason she hadn't heard the groan of the stairs was because there hadn't been anyone at all—it had been a product of her own fear. What if the door to her room had not been opened by an intruder, pressing their way in slowly to prevent her from waking, but if she'd done so herself in sleep, her body acting in response to the fear and anxiety running through her?

Clara paused at the edge of the cottage. What if there was something even more insidious going on? She thought of those moments in the dark shadows of her childhood bedroom, the memories she'd tried so desperately to forget. What if she was losing her mind? Losing her grasp on reality? It wouldn't be the first time.

She shut her eyes tightly, trying to push the thoughts away. Many children had overactive imaginations, saw monsters beneath the bed or in the corners of their room at night. It hadn't been real and it hadn't been madness, she knew that.

The sound of gravel underfoot caught her attention, coming from the direction of the house. She looked over her shoulder, her attempt at sanity suddenly slipping away as she imagined the unknown figure from last night, here again to face her in the daylight.

Clara's pulse thrummed as she listened, waiting, some distant part of her knowing she was being foolish. She heard another sound then, coming from the opposite direction. Just as she turned back toward her original path, toward the back of the cottage, a dark figure came into view and she screamed, lurching back.

The figure yelped in response, and it took a mere moment before she recognized the man as Tuck. "Christ Almighty, why are you screaming?"

"Well it wasn't intentional," she replied, trying to catch her breath as embarrassment heated her cheeks. If she wasn't so busy trying to think of an excuse for her being here, lingering around his cottage, she might've laughed at his expression. There was a mix of shock and horror in his eyes, which, she realized in the daylight, were somewhere between green and grey, a soft sage, the irises lined with a ring of black, making the color all the more breathtaking. She pushed the observation aside.

"What exactly were you trying to do?" he asked, visibly exasperated. "Did you get lost on your way to the car? The house is *that* way."

Clara felt a flare of agitation in response to his tone. Perhaps she was being nosy, poking around where she shouldn't be, but he certainly didn't have evidence of that. For all he knew, she had wandered outside in desperate need of assistance, and here he was greeting her with a rather brash disposition.

"I . . . I was looking for you. I wanted to ask for your assistance with something," she lied. "However, it seems you're in no mood to play the part of a gentleman, so forget I mentioned it." She spun on her heel and walked quickly around the cottage, hoping he would let it drop there.

"Well, you might as well come out with it. I'm certainly awake now," he said, keeping pace just behind her.

"Don't bother. It's of no importance to you." She carried on quickly, digging into her purse for her keys.

"Wait a minute. You went through the effort of scaring the daylights out of me—"

"We already agreed that was an accident," she said without a look back.

Tuck scoffed. "We certainly did not."

Clara slipped inside her vehicle, eager to shut the door between them, but he moved quickly into the gap, stopping her from closing it. She reared back at his show of audacity and said, "Your lack of etiquette where cars are concerned is truly appalling."

There was a twinkle of amusement in his eyes that disarmed her for a moment before she huffed and put the key in the ignition. As she turned back to glare at him, a cold draft of air brought in the scent of shaving soap, and she noticed the scruff along his jaw from the night prior was gone. She had the brief thought that perhaps he'd cleaned himself up because of her unexpected arrival, but quickly reminded herself that she didn't care either way.

"Are you truly not going to tell me whatever had you creeping around my cottage?" he asked, his tone revealing that he found the whole thing quite humorous.

"I was not creeping around," Clara protested. She found him looking a bit too smug for her liking so she added, "And if I were to creep on anyone, I assure you, Mr. Tucker, it would not be you."

"Tuck." He smirked, and it took a moment of confusion before she realized that he was not regarding her remark but rather correcting her formality.

With a scowl, she grabbed onto the handle of the door and said firmly, "Please move, *Tuck*." This time he shifted out of the way, and she yanked the door shut, giving him a pointed look as she clicked the lock between them.

As Clara pulled out of the lot and drove down the short driveway, she refused to glance back at him, but, to her great annoyance, found herself tempted. Her heart only returned to a normal pace once she pulled onto the road and Hollowfield House was completely out of view.

She let out a sigh, replaying the whole scene in her mind and feeling rather foolish as she muttered, "That went well."

# Chapter 8

The diner was only a few minutes away and involved just two roads, an embarrassing truth when Clara thought about being so hopelessly lost the evening prior. The sky overhead was blue, and she rolled her windows down on the way, the crisp air energizing her. She checked her watch and found that she had nearly half an hour before her meeting in town, just a minute or two up the road.

In the light of day, the diner appeared much more docile than it had initially, if not a bit rundown. Gravel crunched beneath her tires as she pulled into the small parking lot, and just three cars were parked out front, but as she walked in through the front door, the bell above her head announcing her arrival, she was surprised to find that the room was nearly half-full of patrons. A group of men sat at a booth each nursing a mug of coffee. At another booth, an elderly couple sat quietly, neither looking at the other, each with a bowl of some sort of porridge in front of them. The scent of bacon made Clara's stomach grumble as she made her way to the counter where two young men sat, talking to a pretty young waitress.

"Excuse me," Clara said to the girl in the uniform. "Do you have a telephone I could use?"

She felt the weight of their eyes on her, and there was a slight pause before the young woman responded. "Just behind you." Her tone was polite, but the warmth Clara had overheard in the conversation moments ago had vanished.

Clara looked over her shoulder and saw a pay phone on the wall farthest from the tables.

"Thank you," she said, turning and walking across the room.

As she pulled her coin purse from her handbag and inserted the nickel into the slot, Clara's movements suddenly seemed loud, the other patrons having lowered their voices to a mum. She glanced self-consciously at the room behind her as she lifted the handset off the cradle, wondering if it had been a mere coincidence that the crowd had quieted just moments after her arrival.

"Number, please?" asked the operator through the receiver.

Clara turned away from the room, lowering her voice. "I need to place a long-distance call to Rochester, please."

After giving the operator Mabel's information, Clara heard a familiar voice come through the line. "Livingston residence."

"Hi Beatrice, it's Clara. Is Mabel in?"

"Yes, miss. Let me fetch her. Just a moment."

Clara moved the receiver from one ear to the other, looking out through the large windows and into the fields beyond. Behind her, she only heard the hushed tones of the waitress and the two men at the counter, and when she looked in their direction, she found one of the men was watching her. A strange feeling settled into her stomach, though she couldn't say why.

"Well look who's alive," Mabel said from the other end of the line. "It's nearly been twenty-four hours. I thought you were dead."

Clara couldn't help but smile at the familiarity of her voice. "Glad to hear that your plan under such circumstances would be to do nothing at all."

"How was the drive?" Mabel asked, her tone light—all agitation forgotten. "Did you end up getting lost?"

"Of course not," Clara lied. Part of the reason Mabel had expressed concern over Clara's trip was her past tendency to lose direction in her own city, but it wouldn't do to tell Mabel the truth now. That would only give Mabel a reason to stress.

"Well, aren't you something?" There was a note of distraction in Mabel's voice, and Clara could just imagine her sitting in her beautiful home with the phone cradled between her head and her shoulder, painting her nails with a fresh coat of polish. "And how's the inn?"

"It's . . . there alright." Clara twirled the phone cord between her fingers, her mind returning to the footsteps she'd heard last night.

"Well, I didn't know that was ever disputed," Mabel replied. "How's the town? Any eligible bachelors?"

Clara flicked another glance at the room behind her, accidentally making eye contact with an older woman who looked away quickly. "Hardly. Anyway, I have my meeting with the lawyer soon. I just wanted to check in and let you know I'm alive." For now, at least.

"Oh, alright. When will you be back? You know my Halloween party is coming up—"

"In a few weeks, yes, I remember. And I'm not sure yet. No more than a few days."

"Well, if you change your mind about needing me to come down—"

"I won't," Clara interjected. "Thank you though."

After saying a quick goodbye, she hung up the phone and turned in the direction of the exit. A hush still blanketed the room, and she found that men and women alike were watching her with varied levels of interest. She swallowed her discomfort. Perhaps they did not have outsiders very often, but all the same, she was eager to return to her car and get out of there. Clara's shoes clacked loudly in the quiet of the room, the only competing sound the distant sizzling of frypans in the kitchen.

As she reached the last few steps before the door, she caught the stare of one of the men sitting at the counter. He was smaller in stature, his dark beard close-cut, and he had turned completely in his seat, leaning back against the counter to watch her unabashedly. Even at a distance, she could see the contempt in his dark gaze, and she felt fear coil in her gut. The air in the room seemed tense, and she looked away from the man, ignoring the thrumming of her pulse as she pushed through the door and walked to her vehicle.

She started her engine and drove out of the parking lot, glancing in her rearview mirror continuously, until she was certain she wouldn't be followed.

# Chapter 9

A few minutes up the road, the open fields gave way to Main Street—a short slice of road with single-story businesses placed along either side of the lane. As Clara slowed her vehicle, she noticed that for each store that was open, there was another that was closed. Between a hardware store and a pharmacy was an abandoned café, boards covering its windows and door. She passed a small theatre, it too boarded up, the sign out front reading *WE'LL BE BACK*. She thought of the many theatres in Rochester with their glowing lights and advertisements and wondered if they were headed in the same direction.

Clara was well aware of the hardships of the Depression. After the stock market crashed at the end of the twenties, unemployment across the country had risen to the highest it had ever been. Then a drought had spread through the Great Plains, killing crops and livestock, forcing farmers to walk away from their land in search of some other way to support their families. Clara had seen the newspaper headlines, had heard the grim stories of a friend-of-a-friend who'd lost everything in the dust storms that ravaged their homes. In those moments, when she let herself truly feel the gravity of it, it almost felt like the apocalypse was upon them.

But the truth was that she rarely allowed herself to acknowledge the depth of the tragedy splashed across the newspapers. It was easy to spend the day with Mabel—her husband a well-paid executive, their finances padded with the promise of a future inheritance—and feel as if most people weren't struggling to make ends meet, that Clara's own financial struggles would eventually be overcome with just a little more time. But how many of these people in Briar Hollow, the owners of these businesses, had once thought the same?

The town itself had a strange air about it, a somber weight clinging to each building like morning dew. From one end to the next, she saw no more than a handful of pedestrians, each walking at a pace that indicated they were in no rush to reach their end destination, if they had a destination at all. She couldn't imagine living here. There was something about it that felt suffocating, like a heat wave in the height of summer when each breath felt strained. As she pulled into one of the empty parking spots along the sidewalk, doubt cropped up. What were the chances that someone local would even have the money to purchase the property from her?

Her stomach flipped as she stepped out of her vehicle, nerves overtaking her now that it all began to feel real. A bell chimed above her head as Clara opened the front door to the office, and she was immediately greeted by a reception desk filling the small space. A young woman sat before a typewriter, the clack of her keys filling the air. Her blonde hair was smoothed into a neat updo, and she looked to be just a couple of years out of high school.

"Good morning," the young woman said, her eyes bright and enthusiastic, a stark contrast to the ghost of a town that stood just beyond the door. "Are you here to meet with Mr. Baker?" She had a glow to her, an energy that Clara could only envy.

"Yes," Clara replied, pushing her hair off her shoulder nervously. She suddenly felt unprepared with so much riding on this meeting. "Miss Clara Dawson."

"Wonderful," the woman said as she pulled a clipboard from the side of her desk, scanning down the page before seeming to find her name. "Wait here for just a moment." She smiled and stood from her desk, then disappeared down a short hallway that took a sharp left. From around the corner, the woman's hushed tone was met by a deeper voice.

"Mr. Baker will see you now," the woman said, reappearing a moment later.

Clara followed, taking a deep breath to ease her nerves. This was it—the moment she'd been thinking about for the past week. This meeting was all that stood between her and owning Hollowfield House. After this, she would go back to the inn and clean it up, go through her father's things, and prepare it to be sold. And then she would have the funds to start a new life without the burden of debt hanging over her head like an axe, ready to fall at any time. Al's death would be the beginning of her new life. Or so she hoped.

"This is Miss Dawson," the woman said politely.

As Clara turned the corner, she was momentarily startled by the sight of Mr. Baker. In her head, a lawyer was a much older man—perhaps in his fifties or sixties—but this man couldn't yet be forty. Compared to the lawyers she'd seen in the city, this man more closely resembled someone she might find in an issue of *Photoplay*, with high cheekbones, dark hair slicked back, a tailored black suit, and perhaps the most vivid blue eyes she'd ever seen. As she stepped forward to shake the hand extended to her, she smelled the warm, woodsy scent of his cologne.

"Lovely to meet you, Miss Dawson." His hand was solid and warm around hers, and she felt her cheeks flush before a flame of annoyance rose up in response to her own foolishness. He was her lawyer; this was not the time to be taken with a handsome face.

"You as well," she replied, breaking his gaze and taking a seat in the chair across from his desk.

"My condolences to you on the loss of your father," he said. "I wish we could meet under different circumstances, but I appreciate you coming all the way from Rochester."

Clara nodded, ignoring the way her stomach flipped. "Well, I appreciate your assistance in the matter."

After the initial letter, she'd sent a response expressing her desire to move forward with the property, and he had shared more details in a brief telephone call, stating the address and even mailing her a key should she wish to stay on the property during her visit.

"Certainly. We're a small town, albeit spread out by land, but we're a community, all of us. And your father was part of that community." He gave a dazzling smile, and she found herself returning one of her own before wondering what it must be like to be so good-looking. She felt fairly confident in her own appearance, her large dark eyes and full lips features she'd received compliments on throughout her life, but she certainly didn't consider herself beautiful. What must it be like to be the kind of attractive that a mere smile could affect a stranger's demeanor so effortlessly?

Clara looked away from the intensity of his gaze, fiddling with her handbag as she reminded herself of the topic at hand. She sincerely doubted Al Dawson had been part of the community, but it didn't seem the time to state such an opinion. "I'm happy to hear that."

"Will you be visiting the property today?" Mr. Baker asked, sifting through the papers on his desk.

"Oh, I already have. I stayed there last night."

He paused, his eyes alight with surprise before he asked, "And how did you find the condition?"

She thought of the creaks in the hall, the shifting of weight outside her door. "It's . . . nice."

He laughed lightly and she softened with relief.

"It's quite secluded," he said. "And the lack of electricity—I imagine it's quite the contrast from what you're used to in the city."

"Yes," she agreed, folding her hands on her lap. "It's definitely an adjustment."

Clara was relieved when he moved on, asking for the documentation they'd spoken of in their call. Mr. Baker beckoned the receptionist, Isabelle, and had her make a copy for their files before she disappeared again, leaving just the two of them in his office.

"Before I have you sign anything," Mr. Baker said, "it's important we discuss what comes along with taking ownership of the property."

Clara sat up taller. "Please do."

"I've been appointed administrator of your father's estate by the county, so we've handled most of the preliminary work." He leaned back in his seat and crossed his hands on the desk between them. "And by taking ownership of Hollowfield House, you will become responsible for all property taxes and outstanding debts related to the inn."

Her mouth went dry. "Are there outstanding debts?"

"Most of the debts have already been paid against the estate, but I can't speak to any debts of a personal nature that may still be owed. But there's still the matter of taxes. And of course, my fees are also paid out of the estate, which means that if you sign for the property—"

"I'll be responsible for paying your fees," she finished for him, her chest tightening.

He nodded. "Unless you sell the property quickly, in which case my fees would simply come from the sale of the inn."

Her stomach twisted into knots at his words. This wouldn't be a problem if she could sell the house quickly—but what if she couldn't? What if she was stuck with this inn that wouldn't sell and even more debt on her shoulders?

"And what if I'm unable to make the payment?"

He gave her a compassionate smile, pity in his gaze. "Miss Dawson, may I ask, what is your intention for the property? Is Briar Hollow a place you see yourself living?"

"No." The word came out quickly, and his brow furrowed in concern. She shifted in her seat. "You see, my job is back in the city, so I intend to sell the inn. Preferably, as soon as possible."

He took a deep breath before leaning forward onto his forearms, lowering his voice. "To be frank with you, Miss Dawson, the economy is in a bad spot at present. Many folks don't have the funds to pay their own mortgage, let alone pay for a new property entirely."

She felt the weight of the words crash down around her, the hope she'd dared to kindle tamped out beneath them. "I understand."

Suddenly, Isabelle appeared in the doorway, giving Clara a smile as she placed her documentation on the desk between them. Then she left, shutting the door behind her, leaving them to simmer in the discomfort of the conversation.

"You also have the option of refusing the inheritance," Mr. Baker continued. "You can simply walk away, nothing lost, nothing gained."

Clara considered it. The money she was losing from not working these next few days. The gas she'd used—and still would use—on the hours she'd driven here. The wear on her vehicle. And the thought of returning to Rochester with nothing to show for it. She could picture it—the quiet drive back, the sight of her apartment, the letters from debt collectors piling up. It almost felt difficult to breathe, the weight of it all.

Seeming to sense Clara's apprehension, Mr. Baker spoke again. "I'll tell you what—why don't you take a few days and think it over? You're already here, you've got the keys. Spend a few nights and decide what you'd like to do. We can meet back here on Monday morning, ten o'clock, and you can let me know how you'd like to proceed."

A part of her wanted to turn down his offer, to get in her car and leave—never look back, never return to this dreadful place. But another part of her, the part that had started to hope, wasn't ready to give up just yet. Clara pushed aside the disappointment within her and put on her best attempt at a smile. "That's a great idea, thank you. Let's do that."

Her eyes fell to the desk before her, catching sight of her documentation still there, and she reached for the paper. Before she could pull away, she found the warmth of Mr. Baker's large hand over hers, his bright eyes swimming with sympathy as she met his gaze.

"It will be okay, Miss Dawson. It'll all work out for the best. I promise."

She nodded, pulling her hand away and folding the document back into a small square to slip into her purse. "Yes. I hope so," she said as they both stood.

Mr. Baker reached for the door, opening it for her as he spoke. "I really am sorry you're dealing with all of this. No woman should be put in this situation—made to make these kinds of decisions. I know Al wouldn't have wanted this for you."

She didn't know what to say to that, so she simply nodded and stepped into the hall, her mind clouded with thoughts of the inn. She paused when he called her name, and she turned to look at him over her shoulder.

"If you need anything else, you know where to find me." He gave her a warm smile, one that she knew had dazzled many women, had dazzled her mere minutes ago. But she couldn't feel moved by it now. She was too distraught by the situation, by the decision she would have to make.

With a "thank you," she walked through the small office, past the reception desk, and out into the chill of the morning, uncertainty swirling in her stomach.

# Chapter 10

As she walked down Main Street, the cold nipped at Clara's skin, helping to keep her emotions contained. It would do no good to fret about the situation now. Whether she signed the papers or not, she'd be in Briar Hollow for at least another few days, so she might as well push aside her gloom and make use of the time here should she choose to take ownership on Monday.

She made her way toward the general store she'd glimpsed on her way to the lawyer's office. The place was small and square, with a large window offering a view inside. A bell chimed above her head as she pushed the door open, making her wonder if such a feature was a business requirement in Briar Hollow.

"Hello, miss." A plump woman with a kind face stood in one of the aisles, organizing some items on a shelf. "Can I help you with something?"

"No, thank you. I'm just here to browse." Clara returned a small smile and disappeared into a vacant aisle. If there was one thing she appreciated about the city, it was the feeling of anonymity. The way she could disappear into a crowd of strangers, make her way through a grocery checkout exchanging little more than a "hello" and "thank you" with the cashier. It took the pressure off, knowing that everyone was in their own world, not bothering to take note of those around them, and even if they did briefly take notice, their attention was fleeting before they moved on with their day.

She looked at either side of the aisle, noting that most items were lined up only one product deep and spread out, giving the appearance of more stock than there actually was. Clara recalled the empty icebox in the house, realizing there likely wasn't any ice inside and that her best bet would be sticking to items that wouldn't require refrigeration. She went through the aisles, pulling jarred and canned items, then looked at the price and wondered how much canned peaches were really worth to her.

A few minutes later, after skimming through the aisles empty of any other customers, she stood at the checkout counter and placed a handful of items at the till. The woman from earlier came around and greeted her, her name tag reading *NELLIE*.

"Well, you're a quick one, aren't you?" Nellie smiled at her as she punched the first item into the register.

"Yes, I suppose I am," Clara said, returning the smile.

"Are you visiting someone?" Nellie asked between items. "I don't believe I've seen you in town before."

"I'm just here for a few days," Clara responded vaguely. In the city, that would have been enough to curb the questions, but she had a feeling Nellie's curiosity wouldn't be quelled so easily.

"Oh," Nellie said as if the news was a pleasant surprise. "Where are you staying?"

"Hollowfield House."

Nellie stilled, something flickering behind her eyes that Clara couldn't quite place. After a moment, the woman seemed to return to her senses, her attention back on the items she punched into the register. "Well then," she said with a tight smile.

The door chimed at the front of the store and Clara looked over her shoulder as a tall man stepped inside.

"Morning, Nellie," the man said. He was slender with a full mustache, one not in the current fashion, and he looked to be near her father's age, perhaps in his early fifties.

"Morning, Randy," Nellie replied pleasantly.

Clara turned back toward the counter, finding Nellie bagging up her things as if the tense reaction moments earlier had never occurred.

"I don't believe I've seen you here before," the man said, turning his attention to Clara. She wondered if this was how every conversation with an out-of-towner began for the people of Briar Hollow.

Clara turned toward the man and gave a polite smile, the muscles in her cheeks nearly cramping from the overuse. "Just passing through," was all she managed to say.

"What did you say your name was, dear?" Nellie asked.

"Clara."

"Oh, how lovely. I had a friend named Clara once," Nellie said.

"Hm. Doesn't ring a bell," Randy said from behind her. "Are you visiting someone?"

Clara stifled the urge to sigh at the blatant nosiness of the man. How had she finished her shopping in less than five minutes and then found herself caught up in conversation against her will?

"She's staying at Hollowfield House," Nellie offered, placing the last item into the paper bag.

"I thought Hollowfield was closed," Randy said.

Nellie glanced at Clara for a moment before responding, "I suppose not."

"How much do I owe you?" Clara asked, hoping that if she didn't stoke the conversation, she could pay and be on her way.

Thankfully, Nellie turned, then read out the total so Clara could count out her coins. Just as Clara paid and scooped the bag into her arms, Randy spoke again.

"Say, you didn't happen to know Al Dawson, did you?"

Clara looked up at the man, her heart quickening suddenly, though it seemed an unreasonable reaction to such an innocent question. But prior to a few weeks ago, Al Dawson was not a topic she discussed with anyone. At most, he was 'her father who she hadn't spoken to in years,' the conversation always dying out after that.

"We weren't close," she said, side-stepping the question. "Did you know him?" She didn't particularly care about the response, but Clara had learned long ago that the best way to avoid sharing one's truths was to distract the other person with questions about their own.

"Well, of course," Randy replied. He smiled then, wrinkles forming around his eyes, a soft blue against the tan of his complexion. "I worked with him for a decade."

Clara paused, confusion and surprise running through her, her mind snagging on the word *with*. Worked *with* Al, not for him. "Did you own the inn as well?"

Both Nellie and Randy laughed, and Clara felt heat rush to her cheeks.

"No, no," Randy said, clearly amused by the notion. "I'm a carpenter by trade. I helped with some projects around the inn when he first bought the place."

Clara pictured the inn and couldn't quite imagine what projects he might've been referring to. The place wasn't exactly a luxury resort, but she supposed she hadn't seen its condition before Al bought it.

"We were thick as thieves." Clara fought the urge to cringe at the expression, wondering if Randy knew how accurate an assessment that was when it came to Al. "Say, how did you say you knew him?"

Clara tensed. It wasn't necessarily a secret that Al was her father, yet the thought of making the admission to this stranger discomforted her. She didn't know the kinds of activities her father had gotten involved in during his time here, and she wasn't sure she wanted these strangers to make that association with her.

Just as Clara accepted that this man might not be satisfied until she clarified her connection to Al, Nellie cut in, "Don't badger her with questions, Randy. I'm sure she's got places to be."

Clara gave Nellie a grateful smile and said, "Actually, I do need to get back. But it was nice to meet you both." She walked toward the door, but Randy was faster, cutting ahead to hold the door open for her.

"Have a good morning, Clara," Nellie called after her.

"You too," Clara answered before walking through the opened door and out onto the sidewalk. She gave Randy a polite smile, though she couldn't shake the unease that had settled in her. "Thank you."

Randy gave her a nod of acknowledgment, and she turned her back to him as she walked toward her car. She hoped the interaction was over, but a moment later he called out to her.

"Hey, you're not having any trouble at the house, are you?"

She turned, blinking in confusion. "Uh, no."

Randy was still by the open door, the street empty aside from the buildings, a few parked cars, and the two of them.

"If anything comes up, you let me know and I'll take a look. I'm very familiar with the house, so I wouldn't have you going to anyone else for the job."

Clara nodded, pushing down her discomfort. "I will," she said, turning toward her vehicle. Before she could cross those final few feet, Randy spoke again, calling out across the street.

"I'm always around town."

"Alright," she called back, not bothering to turn around this time. Her heart quickened, and in the reflection of her vehicle, she could see him there by the store, still watching. She tried to reason with herself that perhaps he wasn't good with social conventions, or perhaps he was just feeling the effects of the Depression and was desperate for work. Or perhaps, everyone in this blasted town was bizarre.

As Clara climbed into her vehicle and subtly locked the door, she felt a wash of relief to see that he had finally gone back inside. Without another glance at the store, she put the key in the ignition and drove away from Main Street, toward Hollowfield House.

The entrance of the inn was far easier to see during the day. There was a slight break in the trees at the side of the road, and as Clara pulled in, she saw the outline of a sign lying in the grass beneath a dusting of fallen leaves. The air was crisp, carrying the scent of wet earth and pine as it slid through the gap of the open window, and for the briefest of moments, she forgot about the stress of the morning.

As she reached the clearing, the house coming into view, there was movement to her left. She glanced over to find Tuck standing there before the footpath that led to the cottage, but he wasn't alone. Before him stood a petite blonde, her hair tied into a neat bun at the nape of her neck. The woman was turned away from Clara, but there was tension in Tuck's expression that instantly made her feel as though she was interrupting something.

It was oddly silent as Clara stepped out of her vehicle, the pair's conversation having ceased completely, reminding her of the hush that had fallen over the diner that morning. As she came around the back of her car, she glanced at Tuck. There was a stiffness to his posture, a tightness in his shoulders beneath the faded buttoned shirt that had seen better days, and her eyes fell to the sleeves pushed up to his elbows, exposing the muscle of his tanned forearms. Then his gaze met hers and she looked away quickly, turning her attention to the woman next to him.

"Miss Dawson," he said, his voice suspiciously jovial. "How was your meeting?"

The woman looked over now, her glance seeming to be one of cold assessment rather than innocent curiosity, and it was then that Clara noticed she'd been holding something in her left hand.

"It was good, thank you," Clara responded, disguising her unease.

"I'm Evelyn," the woman offered, seeming to sense that Tuck would not properly introduce them. "I just wanted to bring you something to give my condolences." She extended her hands, offering Clara the item she'd been holding—a baking dish covered with cloth, the scent of cinnamon and baked apples hinting at the pie beneath. It was a luxury of living in upstate New York, that even during these times when costs were cut and fresh fruit was scarcely available, there was still an abundance of local apple orchards.

"Oh, thank you," Clara replied, taking the baked good from her. "That's so kind. Did you want to come inside?"

"No," Evelyn replied, her tone light, "I don't want to impose. Just wanted to drop it off for you."

Clara nodded, holding a half smile in place while trying to decode the strange air between Tuck and this woman. In the distance, leaves swayed on their branches, a hushed moment landing upon the group.

"Evelyn worked here," Tuck said. Clara glanced at Evelyn to find the woman's attention was on Tuck, and she did not seem impressed with his admission.

"That's wonderful." Clara waited for some further explanation from Evelyn, but none came. Her eyes had moved from Tuck down to the ground at their feet, something about her mannerisms seeming as uncomfortable as Clara felt. "Well, I should be getting inside. It was lovely meeting you," Clara offered. "Thank you so much for this." She gestured to the pie in her hands.

Evelyn nodded. "Of course. Nice to meet you too."

Clara turned toward the house, gravel crunching beneath her feet as she walked. She couldn't help but notice the quiet that followed her departure, neither Tuck nor Evelyn speaking as she opened the door, the groan of the hinges cutting through the tense silence. It wasn't until she shut the door firmly behind her that she heard them return to their conversation, their tones low.

She walked into the kitchen, placing the pie on the kitchen table and lifting the cloth. It looked a bit roughed up, likely from the travel over, but the scent of it made her stomach grumble. As she moved through the kitchen, looking for a plate and utensils, she couldn't help but glance back through the window at where Tuck and Evelyn stood, still conversing. There was an air between them that felt intimate somehow, and Clara felt a strange pang in her stomach.

It wasn't jealousy, certainly. She supposed Tuck was attractive in a gruff, unkempt kind of way, but certainly not her type of man. Perhaps she was longing for the intimacy she'd once had with Peter. Though, it would do her no good to let her mind wander down that path.

As Clara sliced into the pie, her thoughts suddenly returned to what she'd seen last night, to the figure who'd seemed to appear in the trees, watching silently from the shadows. In the light of day, she felt foolish at the conjecture that a woman might somehow have been waiting there in the cold, dark, wet forest. But when she thought of those creaks in the hall, suddenly she couldn't help but wonder if Tuck was the only worker with a key to Hollowfield House.

# Chapter 11

The afternoon sun spilled into her father's office as Clara stood in the doorway looking over the cluttered room. A desk sat before the room's only window, and behind it was a tattered chair that was turned inward toward the hall, rather than facing the view of the forest outside.

The wooden desk, though of average size, was nearly too wide for the room—one side of it was pushed flush against the wall, and the other side left only a small gap of space between the wall and the edge of the desk to squeeze through. The surface was piled with dust and an assortment of clutter—papers stained with dried coffee rings, cigarette butts and ash littered over the flat top, envelopes torn open then abandoned in a pile, mugs with dried remnants in the bottom.

On the left side of the room, along the wall just before the desk, sat a narrow bookcase filled with all sorts of books, though a thick layer of dust revealed their neglect. Stress flooded through Clara at the sight of it all—at the realization that she would need to go through each of these items or risk the possibility of throwing out something that could end up being important. It would be just like Al Dawson to treat an important document with no more care than a used napkin.

Clara walked across the floor and squeezed through the tight space, nearly knocking over a small frame hung on the wall. She turned and saw that it was a drawing of a flower, clearly done by a true artist, and no doubt purchased by someone other than her father. As she righted the frame, she couldn't help but imagine the original owner of the inn, likely a woman, who had decorated each room with such care, even down to the finest detail. All for the place to end up in the neglectful hands of Al.

She walked over to the window and opened it up, welcoming the fresh air from outside. A litany of trees lay along the side of the house, their leaves varied in shades of gold and rust. What a shame such beauty had been wasted as her father's view for nearly a decade. She couldn't imagine turning her back on the scenery in favor of the dusty interior of the inn.

Looking at the desk before her, Clara decided it would be best to pick a place and begin. She grabbed the bin from the kitchen and began to go through each of the items one by one, most of them ending up in the bottom of the container. As she peeled back layer after layer of grime, she became more disgusted with the knowledge that her father had lived this way among the sticky surfaces and the cigarette ash.

Most of the paper had been bills—whether paid or unpaid, she had no clue. Mr. Baker had mentioned these things would come out of the estate—perhaps they'd already been paid off. If not, and she chose to take over ownership, she supposed they would fall to her. She separated the bills from the envelopes and placed them on the chair tucked under the desk to get a closer look at later.

It took longer than she'd expected, going back and forth between the kitchen and the office, clearing out the dirty mugs and miscellaneous cutlery, then placing them into an empty wash basin that sat in the corner of the kitchen. She'd expected to feel relief when she got to the bottom of the pile, but instead, a new wave of disgust rose up as she saw the full extent of the ash littered across the desk, the burned wood from cigarette tips, the sticky spills tearing at the papers as she tried to peel them away.

Clara thought of her mother, the way their house was growing up—always bare, lacking the warmth of a true home. It made sense now looking at the way her father treated his belongings—why bother to have nice things if they would just be destroyed by neglect? She went back into the kitchen, realizing she would need water and rags to clean off the desk. With a sigh she picked up an empty pail she assumed was used to fetch drinking water and drudged her way out onto the porch and down the steps.

The wind was brisk but the sun was shining down upon her, countering the chill with the warmth of its rays. She found the water pump at the side of the house, between the tree line and the clapboard siding. She bent over, placing the bucket beneath the spout, and lifted the handle, the metal cold against her skin. She pulled up on the stiff handle and pressed down, feeling resistance in both directions, but after a few moments, water began to splash into the bucket. Pride ran through Clara at her success, and she carried on, her cheeks flushing at the exertion.

The bucket was filled nearly a third of the way before the skin on the back of her neck prickled, and the strangest sensation settled into her like she was being watched. She glanced over her shoulder, scanning the tree line, but saw nothing aside from the swaying of leaves in the breeze and rustling across the forest floor. Clara turned back to her task, trying to ignore her unease, likely no more than the product of her own paranoia, but the feeling only intensified.

The bright sun dimmed overhead as passing clouds cast her in shadow. A twig snapped behind her and she stood, facing the forest. She scanned the woods again, her heart beating hard in her chest. She looked from tree to tree, hoping to spot an animal who'd just happened to wander through, but some part of her could feel the change, could feel the way the energy around her had shifted.

All at once, Clara realized that the forest itself had stilled. The soft chattering of squirrels and birds moving through the trees had ceased. Even the leaves had seemed to stop their dance. And then she saw it—movement in the distance. A darkened figure edged behind the trunk of a tree, someone stepping just out of sight.

"Hello?" Clara called, taking a step closer. She watched the trunk the figure had disappeared behind, waiting to see them emerge. After a moment, a sound cut through the quiet of the forest—a crunch of leaves underfoot.

Without thinking, Clara found herself moving forward. She stepped into the shadows of the forest, her eyes fixed on where she'd first seen the shape, first heard the sound. Her mind spun to the night prior, to the figure in the trees, to the creak in the hall—this had to be them. Whoever was behind that tree had been who she'd encountered last night, she was certain of it.

Fear coursed through her veins, ran across her skin, yet she couldn't stop. She kept walking—stepping over mangled roots, slipping on a mossy rock before catching herself—but she refused to move her gaze from that tree. From where that person was hiding, waiting, just behind the bark.

She came within a few paces of the tree, keeping her distance as she rounded the trunk, leaving a gap between her and whoever was hiding there. Her mind was racing, some part of her waiting for them to jump out at her. But when she reached the other side, to the place where she knew someone stood, she stilled.

No one was there.

She turned, eyes scanning the forest around her, confusion running through her. That couldn't be—she had heard them, seen them, just here.

Clara looked all around her as she walked farther into the forest, trying to understand what had happened. She'd seen someone there—had seen the movement of their clothes as they'd stepped behind the tree. She'd watched that tree the entire time. If they had run, she would have seen it, heard it.

She tried to breathe through the panic climbing up her chest, her mind going to the place she so desperately had tried to bury years ago. Those moments in the dark of her childhood bedroom, the things she'd seen, the way she could feel their presence, watching her from the shadows. Her mother's words, a promise more than a threat: *They'll lock you away.*

It was happening again.

Nausea pooled in her stomach and tears pricked her eyes as she truly considered the possibility that there had been no intruder, that it had been her all along. That she was seeing things, hearing things, that did not exist. The part of her she'd convinced herself long ago had been no more than a child's imagination.

And now she had to face the possibility that Hollowfield House might very well be driving her back to madness.

# Chapter 12

After a few minutes of searching, of looking up at the branches overhead, trying to make sense of the figure's disappearance, Clara was left to accept that she was alone in the forest. Reluctantly, she made her way back to the house, her gut twisting all the while. As she stepped out of the trees and into the clearing, the slam of a car door came from the front of the house. She was hardly in the mood for a visitor, and some part of her was tempted to stand right there in silence, waiting for them to leave. But as she heard the crunch of gravel beneath shoes, she walked forward through the grass and rounded the corner to find Mr. Baker at the bottom of the porch steps.

Concern settled into her stomach at the sight of him, unsure of why he was here unless it was to deliver bad news.

He smiled when he saw her. "Miss Dawson, there you are."

"Here I am," Clara said, exhaustion settling into her after what she'd just experienced in the forest. "Is everything okay?"

The sight of him—his hair perfectly slicked, his suit tailored, his features sharp—hung in strange contrast to the drabness of the house before him. He looked out of place, as if the two things could not exist simultaneously, so close together.

"Oh, yes, of course," he said pleasantly. "I just have some news, and I thought I might as well come tell you myself since the inn doesn't have a telephone."

"I see," she said with a polite smile, some of the anxiety easing within her. She walked past him and up the front steps, though she couldn't help but turn at the sound of a twig snapping in the distance.

"I hope this isn't a bad time," Mr. Baker said, drawing her attention back.

"No, of course not. Come in." Clara pushed through the front door and led him inside, suddenly embarrassed at the state of the place. It was in good condition, all things considered, but a thin layer of dust and grime seemed to cover every surface in a way she hadn't noticed the night prior. "Don't mind the mess."

She opened several cupboards before finding the one that held the mugs and pulled out two from the shelf, stifling a grimace at the brown smudges within them. She kept her face neutral but casually grabbed a rag and buffed the marks away. Suddenly, she remembered the empty bucket she had brought out to the water pump—and never brought back in.

"I'm afraid I don't have water for tea at the moment," she said, placing the mugs down and turning around to face him. Her eyes landed on the pie that sat neatly on the table. "But we do have pie."

"Pie would be wonderful," Mr. Baker replied from where he stood in the kitchen doorway.

Clara turned back to the cupboard, pulling out whatever plates and utensils she could find that didn't look too badly chipped or dirty.

"As for the reason I'm here," Mr. Baker started, pulling a chair out to sit at the table. "I know you were concerned with selling the property, so I made a call to a friend of mine—a real estate agent, the best in the county."

"Oh?" She placed the plates on the table and cut into the pie, her stomach fluttering in anticipation of what he would say next, what it might mean for her future.

“Thank you,” he said as she slid the plate toward him. She’d meant to cut a piece for herself, but she suddenly lost her appetite. “I asked him if he would mind coming out to look at the property. He does real estate assessments, so I thought I’d see if he could take a look, give you his thoughts. Help you make your decision.”

She paused, a wave of discomfort washing through her. “That’s great. And how much will that cost?” she asked, keeping her voice light as she sat across from him.

He waved a hand. “Don’t worry about that. It’s covered.”

She blinked. “Covered by who?”

He gave a small laugh at her response. “Consider it part of my services.” He smiled at her before returning his attention to the pie. “This is great, by the way. Who did you say made it?”

She swallowed, her mind whirling at the thought of accepting this type of favor from him. “Uh, Evelyn. She brought it earlier today.”

“You’ll have to give my compliments to the chef.”

She nodded, giving him a small smile to disguise her discomfort at his earlier words. In her experience, there was no such thing as free, especially when it came to things offered by men. There was always an expectation attached to it, something to be amended after the fact.

“I really appreciate the offer, Mr. Baker, but I can’t accept it. You’ve already done so much for my father, for the estate—”

“Nonsense,” he cut in. “Percy’s an old friend of mine. And between you and me, the real estate market hasn’t been great lately. No one’s buying houses.” The words felt like a punch to her gut. “He’ll be happy to have something to do.”

She nodded, conflict roiling within her. It would be a great help to get his professional opinion—to know whether any of this would even be worth it. But she couldn’t help but feel like the tallies were stacking up with how much she owed Mr. Baker. She looked up at him and found his gaze already on her, and embarrassment flushed through her as she realized she'd gone silent.

"Miss Dawson, let me do this for you." He reached across the table and touched her hand. "It's what your father would have wanted." She couldn't imagine her father caring, couldn't imagine he'd be happy at the idea of something of his belonging to anyone after his death. She was starting to wonder if Mr. Baker had ever even met Al Dawson to be making such declarations. After a brief pause, Mr. Baker pulled his hand away and returned to the last bite of pie on his plate. "Anyways, he'll be here tomorrow."

Surprise rang through her. "Oh, so you already called him?"

He nodded. "Of course. I wanted to be sure he had time this week before I made the offer. I didn't want to get your hopes up if he couldn't come down to Briar Hollow."

Clara supposed she didn't have much of a choice, then. "Well, that's very considerate of you."

"I understand how difficult this must be," he said softly. She couldn't help but be reminded of the officer who'd come to see her weeks ago, the way he'd said the same thing. But while the officer's words had felt hollow, there was a sincerity there in Mr. Baker's eyes as he spoke. "It must feel overwhelming facing all of this on your own, expected to make these kinds of decisions."

A jolt of emotion moved through her at his words, at the consideration of how she might be feeling. So many men didn't bother to understand the experience of women, of what it was like to still have such little agency in these modern times; to feel like there was so much they couldn't do without the presence of a father or brother or husband. Clara felt a sense of affirmation wash through her at his words.

She exhaled slowly. "It does feel a bit . . . overwhelming, I suppose."

"Of course. I imagine it would for any woman in your situation. Please, let me help however I can."

A knock came from the front door, making Clara jump.

"Sorry." She got up from the table, eager to step away from the potential vulnerability of the conversation.

"I should get going anyways," Mr. Baker said, pushing out of his chair and following behind her.

Clara saw Tuck's broad shape through the sheer curtains and opened the door to find him with a bucket full of water. "I thought you'd been abducted the way you left this," he said before looking at Mr. Baker. "Ah, it appears you were."

Clara frowned, confused at his statement. Mr. Baker forced a weak attempt at a laugh from beside her. "Tuck, always good to see you. I actually wanted to drop by your little cottage before I left." He stepped forward, pointing toward the gravel lot. "There's a pile of leaves you missed, just over there." Clara felt heat rush to her cheeks, her eyes going back and forth between the men and their unexpected exchange of thinly veiled animosity. "Miss Dawson, I'll see you next week." He tipped his head politely before returning his gaze to Tuck, who he clapped on the shoulder as he walked past without another word.

Clara and Tuck both watched as Mr. Baker walked down the steps and across the gravel lot. Her attention then slid to Tuck, to the tightness in his features as he watched after the man.

"Care to come inside or would you rather follow him home?" she asked. Tuck *hmphed* before stepping over the threshold and taking the water into the kitchen. "Was the abduction comment really necessary?" she'd asked once she closed the door.

Tuck placed the water basin down. "Not sure what you mean," he said casually before he stood and met her gaze. "What did he want anyway?"

She sighed, feeling a trickle of stress run through her. "I guess someone is coming tomorrow to evaluate the property."

He was silent, seemingly waiting for more. “And that’s a bad thing?”

“No,” she said. “No, it’s not.” She walked over to the table and cleared the plate, carrying it over to the counter. “Thank you, by the way,” she said, gesturing toward the water.

“I should’ve done it sooner but it slipped my mind.” He turned and looked through the front window, at that spot where he and Evelyn had been talking in hushed whispers. Clara’s mind returned to earlier, before she’d gone out to the pump, to when she’d been considering whether Tuck was the only employee with access to the house.

“You said earlier that Evelyn worked here,” she said, a statement more than a question.

He turned and met her gaze. “Yes.”

“What did she do, exactly?”

Tuck met her with silence, seeming to try and piece together a motive for the question. Until he said, “She’s a maid. Why do you ask?”

“I was just wondering if maybe she had a key.” And if she’d used that key to sneak into the house after Clara had gone to bed.

“I assume so,” he said. “Considering she cleaned the place each week.”

“Does she come by often?” she asked, turning back around to lean against the counter as she crossed her arms. “Since Al died, I mean.”

He blinked, and she couldn’t help but feel that there was something calculating behind his gaze, as if he was trying to anticipate her line of questioning. “We haven’t had guests.”

Alarm rang through her at the response. It wasn’t a no. It was a complete side-step of the question, really.

“Was she here last night?” To see him, is what she didn’t add. Perhaps Clara had interrupted something between them, although she had found him at the diner when she first got to town. But maybe

Evelyn had been here, waiting for him, not expecting a woman to be in his company.

"Not to my knowledge," Tuck said slowly, his brow furrowed. "Why?"

She considered telling him about the intruder, but how could she without sounding like she had lost her mind? There was no point in involving Tuck when she didn't even know what was real and what was her imagination. The thought of telling him about all these strange incidents—from the sounds in the house, to the person in the trees, to the strange behavior of the people in the diner—felt too vulnerable. He was, after all, one of them.

The more she thought of it, the more she realized that if anyone had a motive to scare her away, to want her gone, it would be the workers of Hollowfield House. Perhaps they'd expected the place to be left to them after Al's death, thinking he didn't have a family to pass the property down to. For all she knew, Evelyn was in on the whole thing, and so was Tuck.

The thought unsettled her, a chill crossing over her skin as she looked up at him, at where he stood, waiting for her to respond.

For the time being, she needed to keep her suspicions to herself. At least until she could figure out what was going on. So she gave him a soft smile and said, "No reason."

# Chapter 13

Some time later, after Tuck had left and Clara had cleaned up the kitchen, she found herself walking down the hall and pushing open the door to Al's bedroom. The hinges protested, and some morbid part of her was fearful that she might somehow find him still there—what remained of his final act. She hadn't gotten any further information on the suicide, on the method he'd chosen, but as she looked at the room, relief washed through her that all she found was clutter.

The bed was unmade—a tangle of stained sheets and a warped, yellowed pillow. Clothes were strewn across the room on every surface—shirts, trousers, and socks scattered on the floor, draped over chairs, and spilling out of an overstuffed laundry basket in the corner. A sour smell greeted her, and she stepped back involuntarily, taking a breath of the air in the hall before walking back inside.

An ashtray sat on the nightstand, another on the cluttered bookshelf, both overflowing with cigarette butts. A glass jar sat one-quarter full with a clear liquid Clara doubted was water, and a feeling of grim satisfaction emerged at the knowledge that, for all his time away, he hadn't overcome his greatest vice. Her eyes moved to the dresser where she found more unopened mail, crumpled papers, and coins.

She couldn't see through to the floor, yet she desperately needed to get through the room and open that window, to replace the stale and soured air with something that didn't burn on inhale. She stepped over the clutter, reaching the sill and noticing that although it was closed, it hadn't been locked. She opened the window, letting in the fresh air and the sounds of the forest around the house.

Clara turned back to the room, trying her best to ignore an insect that skittered beneath the bed. No part of her wanted to go through this room. At a minimum, it seemed rather unsanitary. Yet, it also felt representative of his nature—not the cool, collected exterior he conveyed when he wanted something, but the real Al Dawson. Chaotic, unstable, vile. And yet, some small part of her felt weighed down with pity at the notion of him being in this room all alone, deciding to end his life.

It seemed so out of character for someone who spent every moment of their existence seeking control and domination over others, but she supposed there might've been a deeper layer, a dark void beneath the anger, that could've been unseen to her.

She stared at the mess, wondering where to begin—how to begin. Should she just throw it all away? If there was something of value—anything at all—it would likely be one of the papers on his dresser. She didn't bother to look where she stepped, more concerned that she'd see something moving within the clothes and lose her nerve altogether.

With pinched fingers, she sifted through the papers. She tilted her head to read them at an angle, unwilling to place more of her skin on the sheets than was absolutely necessary. As was the case in the office, most of the pile contained unpaid bills and notices, though some of them were scraps of paper with a date or time scribbled on them. She didn't bother to pick those up, but she did look at them, taking in the handwriting—her father's handwriting.

She sighed and moved another slip of crumpled paper, finding an ashtray beneath it that had been sitting atop a small black book. She avoided it at first, imagining all kinds of insects living within the seams of its pages, but it looked to be a journal, and curiosity pulled at her. With a single fingertip, she pushed the ashtray off the book and lifted it by its front flap. She gave it a shake, waiting for something to come flying out, but nothing did.

She flipped the first page and found that it, too, was filled with dates and times, almost like a schedule of some sort. As she turned each page, she found several entries with nothing but dates listed. *Aug 10. Aug 11. Aug 13.* After several pages, the entries became sorted by times as well. *Aug 16: 11:03 p.m. 11:47 p.m. 12:16 a.m.* They were written in the same scribbled script as Al's other notes.

Confused by the entries, Clara flipped ahead and found lengthier passages. One was labeled as *Aug 24. Someone watching me in the yard. Hiding in the trees. I felt its wicked eyes on me. Randy don't believe me but I saw it.*

A chill ran up Clara's spine at the words, at how they mirrored what she'd experienced in the forest that very morning. Fear and concern crawled through her in equal measure as she flipped through more pages, finding similar entries.

*Aug 27. I heard it again last night. Walking back and forth. Won't let me get any sleep. Back and forth all damn night.*

Clara dropped the book, the sound of it clattering to the floor cutting through the silence around her. Her heart pounded quickly in her chest. He had heard it, had felt it too. The same things she had—the woman she'd seen, the footsteps she'd heard in the hall. Clara didn't know if that made it better or worse, sharing the same delusions with a man who had clearly still struggled with alcohol, the evidence of it sitting in that mason jar on his dresser. She couldn't say he was a man of sound mind, yet she'd never known Al to suffer delusions. He had been violent, aggressive, manipulative. But mad? Had he been mad?

Clara knelt before the book, suddenly hesitant to hold it in her grasp, as if his delusions might transfer through the ink onto her skin. She flipped through the pages, needing to know how it ended, what his last entry had been.

*Sept 6. It's coming. Getting bolder. Showed itself to me again today. It looks like her, but I know the truth. That's no woman, that's a demon. It can attack my body but it won't take my soul.*

Nausea rolled through Clara as she read the words over and over again. *Demon.* In all of Al's ranting and raving, she couldn't recall him ever speaking of demons. He wasn't a man of faith, wasn't one to pray to a god or to fear a devil. But seeing these words written in his hand, so close to when he must've taken his own life, brought bile up her throat, the taste bitter in her mouth.

She stood, eager to get out of this room, away from this book. She strode into the hall, finding the space darker than she'd left it as grey clouds rolled in outside, threatening a storm. She paced back and forth, up and down the hall, her mind churning as she considered what all of this meant. Were those entries the product of alcohol or something darker? Perhaps the delusions of a man unwell, losing touch with reality.

*It looks like her.* Who was *her*? Who had Al thought he saw in the house? A woman who clearly could not have been there in front of him—that was something he'd seemed sure of. Had it been her mother? Had Al thought his wife had found him, returned to haunt him here? Clara wasn't sure that he had even known of her mother's death—she certainly hadn't told him, hadn't known how to contact him even if she'd wanted to. Or was it the same figure she had encountered? Was something truly haunting this house?

Clara's chest tightened at the possibility that whatever Al had experienced, she was seeing too. And what if it ended the same for her as it did for him? She drew her hands to her face, rubbing at her eyes in frustration. Those kinds of thoughts would only make everything worse. She needed to get out of her head, to find something to distract her from her spiraling mental state.

She walked out into the kitchen and looked at the water basin, now full, and remembered the original reason she'd needed the water. The desk. The sticky, disgusting desk. Clara went through the kitchen, opening and closing drawers, until she found a washcloth and soap. She lifted the cloth and dipped it into the water—the cold biting into her skin, turning it red almost immediately—then she scrubbed the soap into the dampened cloth before carrying the bucket into the office and placing it on the floor with a thud, water sloshing over the edge.

She scrubbed the stick and grime off the wood, going back and forth between the basin and the desk. She funneled all her energy into scrubbing that desk clean until thunder rolled overhead. She jumped, startled to find that the room was dark, the sun having been blotted out as the storm moved in. All at once, the stillness was broken by an army of raindrops pelting the roof.

She suddenly remembered the window she'd left open in Al's room and paused, considering if she really needed to go back in there to close it. It was only his belongings in there, items he himself hadn't cared for, even in life. Did it matter if those things were ruined by rain? But then she thought of that open window, an entry for whoever might have been creeping around the property, and she found herself walking out of the office and back into her father's bedroom.

She nearly tripped over a pile of clothes in the shadows but stumbled over to the window and shut it, sliding the lock in place. On her way out, she could just make out the shape of the book—a shadow still there lying on the floor by the dresser. She wavered, some part of her wanting to pick it up and take it with her, to read through each page, each word, each letter. But fear held her back, kept her frozen in place, as she looked down at the book.

What if Al hadn't ended his life because he was sad or in despair? What if he had lost his sanity? What if that journal was the key to proving the sickness that ran through her veins, the blood of her father coursing through her, taking its toll on her mind?

It was all too much. She'd spent her entire life doing everything she could to ensure she would never end up like her mother—never be the woman that stayed, the woman that relied on a man so completely she was willing to sacrifice her peace to keep him. But what if the person she'd really become was someone much worse . . . her father.

# Chapter 14

Clara felt her way down the shadowed corridor and into the kitchen, pulling open drawers until she found a match. She went out into the hall and lit the wall sconces, grateful for the darkness that disguised what likely would've been dead flies littered within their glass enclosure.

Her body was tired yet her mind continued to spin, pulling her into the past, into memories she'd been sure she'd erased completely. The nights when she was a child and had been awoken by a creak at the foot of her bed, then turning over to find not the eyes of her mother or father but those of a stranger. Even as fear had pumped through her, she'd known there was something different about the figures she saw at night. She could feel it in the air, a coldness in the room, a strange tension that lingered around them.

Sometimes the figures were young, sometimes they were old. The worst had been the men. They had stood at the end of her bed, watching, leering over her as if they could see through the blanket that lay atop her. Of all those who terrorized her with their mere presence on those nights, it brought comfort to her that none had ever touched her. Whether that was because they'd chosen not to or because they simply couldn't, she didn't know.

But being here in this house, seeing the same things Al had, unsettled something within her. It brought back the feeling of shame that had washed through her when she had told her mother of the figures in the shadows of her bedroom at night. It reminded her of the look in her mother's eyes as she'd said, *Don't ever say those words again. Not to anyone. They'll lock you away.* Clara had been young at the time, perhaps no more than five or six, and she didn't know what the words meant, why she'd be locked away or by who, but she could see the fear in her mother's usually vacant eyes as the words were spoken. And so she never spoke of it again.

Clara had done everything she could to ignore the feeling that washed over her when one of them appeared, to ignore the creak of her bedroom door opening and closing, opening and closing, as one tried to get her attention, to get her to look, to see them. She would squeeze her eyes shut and hum—quietly, not loud enough for her parents to hear, just to herself, just enough to fill her mind with something as she tried to grab hold of sleep.

As she got older, the encounters had come less and less, more and more spaced out, until one day they'd stopped altogether. The further she'd gotten from those nights, the more she had convinced herself that it hadn't happened at all. It had been no more than the overworking imagination of a child. And now being here in Hollowfield House was threatening all of that.

The thoughts pressed down on her, making it difficult to breathe. It wasn't enough to clean, to sort, to distract herself with tasks—she needed something stronger. Her mind went back to that jar in Al's bedroom, the one with a clear liquid inside. Either Al had been making his own hooch, or he'd been buying from someone local. Either way, there had to be more somewhere in this house. She looked around the room, her eyes scanning each surface as she moved into the kitchen, opening cupboards and drawers. And then, there at the back of the cupboard, she saw it. A mason jar with the same clear liquid inside. She reached back and pulled it forward, feeling the weight of the liquid as it sloshed within the container.

Clara held it in her hands, knowing exactly what it was—moonshine. She hadn't tried the stuff before, but she'd heard of it. She'd

# Chapter 19

Clara awoke the next morning, a wave of confusion washing through her at the stiffness in her limbs until she opened her eyes and found herself in the back of her car, her memory returning to her. She was going back to Rochester. Back to relative safety, which was as much of a comfort as it was a discomfort, but at least it was familiar.

She lay in silence, sorting through her thoughts. She thought of what it would be like to return to Rochester now, with the inn unfinished and unresolved, leaving her no closer to the money she'd hoped would finally give her some semblance of financial freedom.

A memory came to her from the dream she'd had last night. She didn't remember most of her dreams, but this one had felt so vivid. She could still smell the fire, still feel the rocks digging into her spine. She pushed the thought away and sat up, looking around in the early morning light.

She was parked at the end of a long drive in the middle of wheat fields. The morning was foggy but bright, mist clinging to the ground as far as she could see. She heard the engine of a tractor in the distance, echoing across the flat land.

Clara climbed out of the vehicle and stepped out onto the empty road stretching her arms above her head. She breathed in the morning air, a heavy feeling on her chest. Her mind pulled her in two different directions. One piece of her still wanted to run, to leave it all behind and return to her normal life. No matter how unhappy she was, it was predictable. Staying in Briar Hollow, even for just another few days, felt complicated. That was something she avoided at all costs.

But the other part of her—the part of her she'd tried to stifle all her life, that had experienced things she couldn't quite explain—whispered for her to stay. That part of her realized that no matter how terrifying the woman's presence had been, it had never once hurt her. Time and time again, this woman—whether alive or dead—had been close to Clara in her most vulnerable moments, and yet had never tried to hurt her.

She'd been so confident when she'd told Tuck that she was leaving, been so determined to leave the inn behind and pretend that these last two nights hadn't happened. It was what she always did when she started to question things—she ran. She ran to prove to herself that she could leave. And last night, she'd needed that confirmation. Nothing could shackle her to anywhere she didn't want to be. And she had proved it to herself. Here she was, over an hour away from town, and she had survived.

Yet now, the thought of leaving behind the chance of money, of gaining some semblance of freedom, was not the only thing pulling her back. As much as she thought herself foolish for even considering it, she couldn't help but feel the presence of a question left lingering in the air. Was someone trying to communicate with her beyond the grave? Had Al been the reason the apparition still lingered around the inn? The entries in his journal had been fueled by fear—he'd been so sure that the woman he saw at Hollowfield House couldn't truly exist, couldn't be living, that she must be a demon. *It looked like her.* What if he'd felt so strongly about it because he'd been the one to cause her death?

There was a bitter taste in her mouth as bile climbed up her throat. She swallowed, breathing in the cool morning air. Clara knew Al wasn't a good man, but was he a murderer?

She thought back to the dream, her chest tightening as she considered the possibility that it hadn't been a product of her overactive imagination, but that it was a memory somehow—something that was not her own but had been shown to her. She shivered, crossing her arms over her chest as she considered what to do next. She looked down the road at the long path ahead of her, toward the city, toward her life. Could she return to Rochester with this weight still on her chest? The possibility that Al had killed someone and never been caught?

And there was, of course, the matter of the inheritance, the money. But somehow, that now felt less important than what had started to emerge. She thought of her own life, of how easily it might be taken from her by a stranger, a man who'd ended it all simply because he wanted to, simply because he could. The thought of such a person going uncaught, unpunished, filled her with cold anger. And in that moment, she knew that she couldn't go back without at least trying to find the truth. It was Friday morning, and she wouldn't be returning to work until after the weekend anyway. She might as well hold out for the weekend and see if she could find anything else before her meeting on Monday.

Clara returned to her vehicle and climbed inside, turning the key in the ignition. She would go back to town and see if she could piece together some semblance of what might have happened in that house, what this apparition was trying to show her. And then, she would tie up any loose ends with the property, and after her meeting on Monday, she would return to Rochester.

The morning fog began to clear by the time she reached Briar Hollow, the sun just starting to break through the clouds. She slowed the vehicle as she reached Main Street, finding a spot to park along the road. It was early and the small town was surprisingly empty. She stepped out of her vehicle and walked toward the market, hoping she'd find Nellie inside.

As Clara pushed into the market, the bell jingling overhead, she felt a flush of relief to see Nellie behind the register.

"Hello, miss. Lovely to see you again," the woman said, wiping down the countertop with a rag.

"You as well," Clara replied as she approached the till, trying to exhibit an ease she didn't feel. If there was anyone who knew about the happenings of Briar Hollow, it had to be someone like Nellie.

"Can I help you find something?" Nellie asked.

"I was actually hoping you could help me find some*one*," Clara said, reaching into her pocket and pulling out the locket. She opened it, revealing the picture inside. "Do you know who this is?" She remembered what Tuck had said, that he was the Reynolds boy, but she wanted that confirmation from someone else.

Nellie glanced at the locket before her eyes flicked up to Clara. Something flickered behind the woman's brown eyes before she averted her gaze, suddenly eager to return to wiping down the counter. "I'm afraid I'm not sure, dear. Where'd you find it?"

"Inside the inn. In my father's office."

Nellie paused, her eyes moving up from the rag to where Clara stood. "Your father? Al Dawson was your father?"

In that moment, Clara got the sense that she'd need to tread gently here or risk scaring Nellie off. It was clear that Nellie was one to gossip, but perhaps Clara would need to earn her trust a bit more before the woman would be willing to share information. Perhaps the way to do that would be to appeal to Nellie's sympathies—to make her think she was being confided in.

Clara glanced over her shoulder before leaning in. "Yes, he was my father. I don't like to discuss it, though. It's rather . . . painful," she lied.

Nellie's eyes widened with visible sympathy. "Oh, I'm so sorry."

"Oh, don't worry about it," Clara started. She felt a twinge of guilt at her manipulation, but she reminded herself it was for the greater good. "It's just that I can't help but feel a bit concerned at finding an item like this in my father's things. It doesn't seem to have belonged to him, and I would hate to think that someone had forgotten it there and my father never bothered to return it."

Nellie nodded. "Let me take another look." Clara placed the locket before her. After a moment, Nellie said, "I believe that's Eddie Reynolds. Though I can't say I know how the locket ended up at the inn." She made a face of visible focus. "Unless he'd been there with his fiancé or a past—" Nellie stopped abruptly, her face nearly going white.

"A past . . ." Clara prompted softly.

Nellie stared at her, seeming to consider how much to disclose, before she said, "Well, a past sweetheart, I suppose." Despite the seemingly empty market, Nellie lowered her voice. "You see, he was dating the Mason girl before she ran off."

Clara furrowed her brow. "Who's the Mason girl?"

"I can't quite recall her name now," Nellie said, clearly combing through her memory. "Her parents were quiet folk and mostly kept to themselves. But she and Eddie were sweethearts for a while before she ran off with another man. Left him heartbroken from what I heard. Mind you, all of this was a few years back."

Clara thought of the woman in the mirror, alarm coursing through her. "And where is she now?"

Nellie shrugged. "No one knows. Surely, someone in her family must have gotten in contact with her. She never came back though."

Clara frowned. "Did the police look into him? Eddie, I mean."

"Oh yes. Her parents said she'd never up and leave without telling them, and they had the police take him in for questioning. Constable Davis was mad as a hornet when he found out. That's Eddie's uncle, you see."

Unease coiled tightly in Clara's gut. "Then what happened?"

"Well, Eddie was home with his family all night, so they let him go. After that, people figured he must've been telling the truth. That she'd run off with another man."

"Yet she never returned to—"

A bell chimed and both women jumped, Nellie's voice increasing several octaves as she spoke. "Mrs. Flynn, lovely to see you this morning."

Clara looked over her shoulder to find a small, rather ancient-looking woman wrapped up in a coat, hat, and gloves as if it were the middle of winter. "Good morning, Nellie. I'll need a few things," the woman said as she made her way over to them. She walked with a cane in her right hand yet held an air of dignity that demanded respect. "You know my granddaughter usually helps with the grocery shop, but I guess she's too busy for me this week."

Clara paused a moment, hoping the woman might move along down one of the aisles, but then Mrs. Flynn spoke again. "It's a shame, really. This generation does not respect their elders, not one bit." She looked at Clara accusingly before returning her gaze to Nellie. "When I was young, I always helped my mother and grandmother, no questions asked. 'Run to the shop and fetch some cigarettes,' they'd say. And off I went. No complaints."

Clara got the feeling that her conversation with Nellie was now over.

"Of course, Mrs. Flynn," Nellie said, cutting in naturally. She walked around the counter and offered the woman an arm. "Let me help you right away." She shot Clara an apologetic glance.

"Do you know where I could look into . . . the topic we were discussing?"

Nellie blinked. "I suppose the newspapers would have covered it, but I'm not entirely sure how you can find those now."

"Is there a library nearby?" Clara asked.

"Oh, yes. Just down past the post office."

"Thank you."

With a twist in her gut, Clara turned and walked toward the door.

"Miss Dawson," Nellie said. Clara glanced back at her, hands on the door. "Be careful."

# Chapter 20

The library sat across from the post office, set aside from the other businesses on Main Street. Ivy wound up the sides of the small, red-bricked building, and Clara found that once she stepped inside, it seemed even smaller than it had looked on the outside. Books lined the walls from floor to ceiling, broken apart by a window on either side of the room, letting the only source of natural light into the darkened space.

A large desk sat at the front of the room, and behind it, a petite woman was clacking away at a typewriter, seeming not to notice Clara's arrival. The room appeared empty of anyone but the two of them.

"Hello," Clara said pleasantly.

The woman looked up over the glasses that rested on her nose, a pinched expression on her face. "Can I help you?"

Clara considered how she should go about explaining what she was looking for. She couldn't very well say she wanted to look into a woman she believed her father might've killed.

"Yes. How would I go about finding out . . . local information? Disappearances, perhaps?"

The woman appeared unaffected by her question, asking, "How far back was this disappearance?"

She considered the timeline of when Al had purchased Hollowfield House. "Within the last ten years."

The woman eyed her warily before she stood and turned away from Clara. "This way," she said without a look back. Clara followed the woman into an even smaller room with barely enough space for the round table that sat in the middle. Each of the four walls held rows of drawers—not the kind she'd seen at her job as a typist. These drawers were narrow, no taller than an index card.

"This is the newspaper archive. If it's not referenced here, we don't have it." She looked at Clara as if she expected some rebuttal.

"That's great, thank you." Clara scanned her surroundings. "So, how does it work? I assume the newspapers themselves are not in these drawers."

The woman cleared her throat. "You'll need to look through the indexes here and write down the call numbers for the ones you'd like me to pull. There are paper and pencils on the table there"—she pointed to the round table at the center of the room—"no more than ten at a time. All documents must stay inside this room, and no food or drink is allowed." She looked over Clara as if suspecting she'd smuggled a carafe of coffee beneath her skirt.

"Understood."

As the woman walked out of the room, Clara was filled with a sense of overwhelm. How did one even begin an investigation when they didn't know the names or dates of the women who'd disappeared?

She opened the set of drawers nearest to her and read the handwritten labels on the tabs separating the long line of index cards. They were organized into categories and then into alphabetical order, the first labeled LOCAL EVENTS A TO C.

Time passed slowly as Clara went through the indexes, writing down call numbers for articles that might contain some semblance of information on crimes or missing persons in the area. She mostly found herself reading about petty theft, such as a bicycle stolen from outside the hardware store, until she found an article about a disappearance from 1929. As she skimmed through the article, she froze as she read the name Charlotte Mason. *The Mason girl* as Nellie had called her.

But that wasn't the only thing that concerned Clara. She pulled the locket out of her purse and ran her fingertip over the gold engraved with a swirly C. As in Charlotte.

The article gave some details as to her last known whereabouts—she'd told her parents she was off to meet a friend at the library, only to never return home—along with details to contact the sheriff with any information. Clara's stomach dropped when she saw the number seventeen. Charlotte had been only seventeen when she'd disappeared, starting her final year of high school. Clara's stomach swirled unpleasantly as she considered whether Al was truly diabolical enough to take the life of a young girl. She supposed it might depend on why, on whether he felt he had no choice. Could Charlotte have been witness to something at the inn? Something she shouldn't have seen?

Clara looked over the locket for anything she might've missed—a date, a year, a name. She opened it up and found that same picture staring back at her, the one of a young man she now knew was Charlotte's boyfriend. She pulled out a sheet of paper and began to make a timeline of events: 1925, *Al buys Hollowfield House*; 1928, *date on the photo in the locket*; 1929, *Charlotte Mason disappears.*

Clara returned to the newspaper splayed across the table before her, cross-referencing dates and trying to gather more information. She hoped for some sort of update on the disappearance or any further case developments. Instead, she found another local disappearance dated three years earlier than Charlotte's—a young woman named Hazel Montgomery, age nineteen. She was reported not by a family member, but by her employer after she failed to show up to work one day in 1926.

Clara's heart quickened at the discovery. Two disappearances in the few years after Al arrived in town. It could very well be a coincidence, but what if it wasn't? She thought of the unsigned letter in his belongings, the locket stuffed into his desk. What if he hadn't found those things, left behind from guests at the inn, but what if he had taken them off his victims? She carried on reading through the articles, hoping she'd find some update on the disappearances, some news that they had reappeared unharmed. But she kept coming back to the same question: who had been the woman in the mirror?

Morning turned to early afternoon as Clara continued to go through the indexes, writing down the reference for any article that piqued her interest, then waiting for the librarian to return with the next batch of articles. Fatigue was starting to settle into Clara as she read through each article, finding nothing further. It wasn't until the clock nailed into the wall in front of her reached twelve that she saw a photo that stopped her in her tracks.

The photo was of a young man with dark hair, dark eyes, and a soft smile on his face, accompanied by a caption that read: *Edward Reynolds*. Clara recognized him instantly as the young man from Charlotte's locket. But there was something about him, something in his eyes that tugged at her memory. There was something to his expression in the photo, the new angle, that made her feel like she'd seen him somewhere. It was a strange feeling of recognition, but after a moment, she moved on to read the article below the photo.

The article was dated February 1930 and went on to state that Eddie was brought in for questioning after law enforcement received a tip that he had been the last person to see Miss Charlotte Mason before she disappeared in October of 1929, the same night the young couple of two years broke up. After further investigation, Eddie was officially cleared as a suspicious person in the case.

Clara began to wonder how Charlotte had ended up at the inn if Eddie had been the last person to see her. Had she and Eddie gone to the inn together? Is that where the breakup occurred? That would explain why she might've left the locket behind, especially if he was the one who'd gifted it to her. Yet the article didn't specify her last known location.

Clara sighed, her eyes blurry and her mind weary. Was Charlotte the woman she'd seen in the mirror behind her? She tried to envision the woman. She'd looked young but not seventeen. Perhaps the woman at Hollowfield House was not Charlotte, but Hazel. But then, how had Charlotte's locket managed to get into Al's drawer?

She was out of her depths with no idea where to look next. She briefly considered going back to Nellie and asking her for more information. Maybe she'd even know where Eddie Reynolds lived currently. She did say he was related to the constable. Clara sat back in the chair, thinking back to the article that said he'd been cleared as a suspect. She couldn't help but wonder if the nephew of a constable in a small town would be found guilty of anything. What if none of this was Al—what if it was Eddie? But if Eddie was only seventeen in 1929, he couldn't have been involved in Hazel's disappearance in 1926. Could he?

"We close at two on Fridays." Clara jumped at the librarian's sudden presence in the doorway. She glanced at the ticking clock—it was nearly 1:30 p.m.

"Oh," Clara said, looking back to the librarian, who still had that pinched expression on her face. "Okay, thank you. I'll be done shortly." The librarian seemed unconvinced but turned and walked back to her desk.

Clara pulled the next article in the pile, desperate for something to become clear. Maybe she shouldn't be looking through missing persons and news articles—maybe she should be looking at obituaries. If either girl had been found, at least locally, it'd have to be included there. She went through each of the newspapers in front of her and flipped to the obituaries section, scanning for some update on either Hazel or Charlotte.

By the time she reached the last paper, she was filled with disappointment at finding neither name. It wasn't that Clara wanted either woman to be dead, but the idea that she had just spent the day searching through articles about these women, only to never have answers, filled her with dread. As she flipped to the front of the paper, a headline caught her eye. It wasn't on the first or even second page of the paper but nearly halfway through.

*YOUNG WOMAN DEMANDS JUSTICE FOR MISSING FRIEND*. It was an interview with a young woman named Sadie Collins, dated July 1932. The article shared an interview with Sadie Collins, a young woman whose best friend, Charlotte Mason, had disappeared years earlier, the case being incorrectly labeled—according to Sadie—as a runaway. Clara skimmed through the article, her heart pounding quickly in her chest as Sadie stated that she believed her friend had not run off but had been the victim of foul play.

This was what Clara had been waiting for. Hoping to find some sort of proof that Charlotte's case had been more than just a runaway, and Sadie Collins had seemed to believe it too. She'd believed it so much that, as of last summer, she'd been willing to appear in this article that cast the police in a bad light. If Clara could just talk to the woman, find out what she knew, then maybe she could fill in the gaps and figure out. As she flipped the page, she wondered if Sadie was still local, if Nellie might know how to contact her.

Clara's eyes reached the top of the next page—the continuation of the article—to the small square black-and-white photo printed there. The caption beneath read *left, Charlotte Mason, right Sadie Collins*. On the left was a young woman with long blonde hair and a bright smile. And next to her, her arm looped through Charlotte's, was a girl with hair that appeared light brown, perhaps even red, and an equally wide grin. The expression on the girl's face was warm and joyful, in stark contrast to what Clara had seen last night, but she recognized those features.

Her stomach churned. This was the woman whose reflection Clara had seen in the mirror. That meant Sadie Collins was dead, and she was the one haunting Hollowfield House.

# Chapter 21

Clara tried to inhale the cold air outside of the library, but her lungs refused to expand, and her vision started to blur. She stumbled down the walkway to the set of three steps that led to the main sidewalk, then took a seat on the cold concrete with a thump. Her arms felt numb, her mind spinning as she pictured Sadie there in the photo, her smiling face, unaware that she and her best friend would be killed not far in the future.

That she might be killed by . . .

Clara's chest seized painfully, and for a moment she wondered if she was having a heart attack. Her hands went to her cheeks and came away wet with tears she hadn't realized she'd been crying. Suddenly there was warmth at her back and a soothing voice in her ear.

"Breathe," the voice said softly. "It's alright. Just take a breath."

She looked up and found the bright blue gaze of Mr. Baker, concern behind his eyes.

"Look at me. One deep breath. Take a deep breath in."

In that moment, she didn't care that they were sitting on the main street of Briar Hollow; all she felt was gratitude. She hadn't realized how desperate she'd been for someone to guide her, to tell her what to do, to tell her how to deal with all of this. And in that moment, she allowed Mr. Baker to lead her. She took a deep breath in, slowly as he directed, and out.

They sat there for several moments as he directed her through each breath until finally, the world came clear into focus, her breath steady.

"Are you alright, Miss Dawson?" His voice was soft and his hand was in her hair, brushing it back from her face.

Clara nodded, wiping the dampness from her cheeks and feeling the slow emergence of embarrassment at her outburst.

"I'm s-sorry," she stuttered, her throat thick with emotion.

"Shhh." He rubbed a steady hand on her back in a slow circular motion. "It's okay. Everything's alright."

It took another few minutes before she could properly speak, before she could collect herself. Icy wind washed through her, cooling the warmth of her cheeks. She sat there on the step, looking out at the street, and felt grateful that in all that time, she hadn't noticed a single motorcar drive past to witness her display.

"Want to tell me what happened?" Mr. Baker asked.

The truth fought within her to be free, but how could she even begin to go about explaining all she'd found, all she'd experienced, over these last few days? How could she explain that not only did she suspect her father of killing someone—something only proven by the fact that she had seen the woman's ghost—but that this also confirmed that her entire life, every apparition she'd seen in the darkened corners of her room had not been a product of her imagination but had likely been a real person who had died? People with families and loved ones. People who had, for some reason, been stuck here, lingering, unable to move forward in the afterlife.

Mr. Baker seemed to read the hesitation in her face. "I promise I won't judge," he said, his voice soft, coaxing. "You can tell me." Clara looked at him, at his handsome face, at the sincerity in his eyes.

"I don't think I can," she admitted.

Her mother's words came back to her: *They'll lock you away*. She could only imagine what someone—anyone, really—would think if she tried to explain all she'd seen. But someone of his profession, a man of the law, of logic and reason? He would never believe her.

"Oh, come on," he said lightly, a semblance of gest in his voice. "It can't be all that bad. I'm a lawyer. I assure you, I've likely heard worse."

Clara felt a smile on her face despite herself. She couldn't tell him about seeing Sadie's apparition in Hollowfield House, but perhaps she could tell him about the rest of it. About the tangible things she'd found—the letter, the locket, the scarf.

Clara sighed, unsure of where to begin. "Do you think you could come by the house?" The words escaped her lips before she could second-guess them. "It's just, I have some things I'd like you to look at. I've found some things in the house that are . . . concerning. I would appreciate your professional opinion."

His eyes wandered over her before he responded. "I can do that. I can come by tomorrow morning, if you like."

She nodded, feeling the smallest bit of relief deep in her chest. "Thank you."

Tomorrow. He would stop by tomorrow and she would share all the pieces of evidence she'd gathered, and he could tell her once and for all if there was truly something here, something to all of this.

She looked back at the library behind her, thinking of that picture of Charlotte and Sadie, then of the picture of Eddie. She couldn't speak to Charlotte or Sadie, or even Hazel, but she could probably speak to Eddie, and that would be a place to start.

"Do you happen to know where Eddie Reynolds lives?"

Following Mr. Baker's directions, she found the small house a minute's drive from Main Street, just past the old church that sat at the end of the road. Her mind swirled with thoughts of the articles she'd read. Sadie had seemed to believe Charlotte had disappeared as a result of foul play the same night she and Eddie had broken up. What if Clara's suspicion about Al was wrong? What if Eddie had been the one to attack Charlotte that night, then attacked Sadie years later when she brought the case forward to the media again?

Or what if Eddie hadn't done it alone? What if Al and Eddie had worked together, Eddie bringing Charlotte to the inn on purpose? Clara tried to picture her father, a man in his fifties, deciding to work with a seventeen-year-old boy. It didn't seem likely, but maybe Al had recognized the boy as someone who could be easily manipulated. Maybe he had gotten something out of the deal.

Clara's heart pounded as she stared at Eddie's house. She stepped out of the vehicle, the slam of the car door cutting through the quiet around her. A dog began to bark from inside the house, growing louder with every step she took up the driveway. With a deep breath, she walked up the porch steps, knocked three times on the wood door, and stepped back down the steps while she waited.

From inside the house, a man's voice rang out, shouting at the dog to be quiet. The Eddie Reynolds in her mind was the young man she'd seen in the photos in the locket and in the newspaper, but the Eddie that opened the door was a grown man with something intimidating in his demeanor. He wasn't tall, but the way he held himself made him feel like an imposing figure. In the photos, he had been clean-shaven, but the man before her had a full, neatly trimmed beard and contempt in his dark eyes as he looked at her.

It was then that she realized where she knew him from. It wasn't just the locket. He was the man she'd seen in the diner the morning after she'd arrived. He was the one who'd turned in his seat, stared at her unapologetically. The one who'd made her hair stand on end. She took a step back before noticing she'd done it, and the smug expression that appeared on his face indicated that he'd noticed and been pleased by the reaction.

"I know you." His voice was deep and low, taunting. "You're the Dawson girl."

Clara's heart raced, and she willed herself to calm down. Whether Eddie had been involved in the disappearances or not, he surely wouldn't do something to her right here in the middle of the day . . . or so she hoped.

"I'm Clara," she said firmly, her best attempt at confidence. "And you're Eddie Reyolds."

He shifted, leaning his forearm against the doorframe. "Pretty and smart," he said, his voice dripping with sarcasm. "What can I do for you, Clara?" He drew her name out as he spoke it, and something like fear coiled in her chest. She imagined this was what a rabbit might feel when it found itself in sight of a fox.

"I have a few questions for you. I've been staying at the inn and—"

"I'm well aware." She tried not to show how his words had achieved their desired effect—they had unsettled her. She could see now the similarities between him and Al, and she knew the best chance of getting anything from him was to cut to the chase and give him less to work with, less to manipulate to his liking.

She reached into her purse, pulling free the locket and letting it hang by its chain. "Do you recognize this?"

For just a moment, something flashed behind his eyes as he stared at the locket. Then his dark gaze fell on her. "And what if I did?"

"Do you know who it belonged to?" she asked, tucking it back into her purse, not wanting to give him an excuse to get any closer.

He shrugged. "Doesn't look familiar."

In that moment, something about his demeanor, his arrogance, brought forth a flame in her chest. "That's interesting because your photo is inside." His face dropped, and she relished in the sight for just a moment before his smirk returned.

"Tell you what, Clara," he drew out her name again, emphasizing it as if it was an insult, a taunt, "why don't you tell me what you're here for and I'll tell you if I care to help." He pulled a cigarette out of his pocket then flicked a match, a small flame hissing to life as he lit the end.

She considered the likelihood of him giving her a real answer, anything of value, and decided to leave Sadie out of it for the time being, to focus on the one person she knew he'd been involved with. "I want to know what happened to Charlotte Mason."

He shook the flame out of the match before tossing it into the leaves that dusted the front yard. "Well, if that's the case, you're talking to the wrong guy. I haven't spoken to that broad in half a decade."

"October 1929, wasn't it? You were the last person to see her." A statement rather than a question.

He laughed as smoke puffed in the air around him, a sound with no joy. "The last person in Briar Hollow, maybe. But she's off somewhere in the city." He took a step forward, the wood beneath his feet creaking as he walked down the front steps. "You really come all this way to ask me that, sweetheart?"

Clara furrowed her brows, confusion running through her. He seemed so confident, so convicted in his words. But she supposed that every good liar knew how to make it seem that way. "Did Charlotte tell you that?"

He stared at her, letting silence fall between them. The wind rustled loudly through the trees, shaking the leaves on their branches, and Clara realized what she couldn't hear—the sounds of other people. She was suddenly aware of how isolated this place felt, the house set off down the end of a long driveway. She had the sudden urge to turn and look up the drive, to see how far she'd need to run, but she fought the feeling, keeping her eyes locked on him.

He tilted his head, his eyes curious as he took a step forward, then another, crossing the distance between them. He stopped only a foot away from her and she met him eye-to-eye, the scent of tobacco overpowering her senses. He might not be a large man, but there was an intensity to his movements, an anger that radiated off him, and she knew that if he chose to hurt her, she would struggle to fight back, to get away.

"You want to know what she told me that night?" His voice was low, intimate. Clara swallowed, and his gaze went down to her throat before meeting her eyes, his smirk reappearing. "She told me she'd been cheating on me for months. That she was leaving me to go be with him." He inhaled his cigarette, never taking his eyes off her. Part of her wanted to move, to walk to her motorcar and never look back, but his words pulled at her, sparking her intrigue.

"Leaving you for who?" she asked.

He turned his head just slightly to the side, blowing smoke past her. "Some college guy." His eyes roamed over her, and she fought the urge to fold her arms across her chest. "Turns out, she wasn't the good girl everyone painted her to be." He paused, his gaze burning into her. "You a good girl, Clara? You smell like a good girl." He lifted his hand toward her face, and she backed away. The look in his eyes told her that was exactly what he'd wanted—that in the end, he'd gotten her to break.

Agitation flowed through her like fire in her gut. "And what did Sadie think?"

Eddie tensed, his smirk turning into a frown. "Sadie?" He took another drag of his cigarette.

"Sadie Collins."

His look was one of disgust. "Sadie Collins was, well—" He stopped, the disgust replaced with smug superiority. "I should watch my mouth in front of a lady. But let's just say, Sadie Collins had other interests. Unnatural interests."

Confusion ran through Clara at his words. Was he trying to say that Sadie had been in love with Charlotte? Had that somehow led to Sadie's death?

He flicked the cigarette across his yard, smoke floating through the air around him. “I’d say she’s in a better place now, but you know what they say about sinners.” He gave her a wink and disgust pooled in Clara’s stomach. He turned toward the house, leaves crunching beneath his feet as he walked casually across the lawn, toward his front door. Without another look back he called, “Thanks for dropping by. Now get off my property.”

# Chapter 22

Clara drove back to Hollowfield House in silence, her mind spinning at everything Eddie had said and everything she'd found in the library. After meeting him, she could see her father working with someone as despicable as him. But had Eddie been that way back then, when he was still in high school, just seventeen years old? Or was this who he'd become over time? He'd seemed to view Sadie with contempt, implying she had cared for Charlotte as more than just friends. But was there any validity to his theory? Or was it nothing more than the projection of a hateful man who wanted someone to blame for the way things ended with Charlotte?

Clara's stomach fluttered nervously as the narrow break in the trees that led to Hollowfield House came into view. As the motorcar came to a stop, she scanned the windows for her, for *Sadie*—a shadowy figure looking down, welcoming her back to this dreadful estate—but all she found was the vacant glance of the house, its empty windows staring back.

She'd expected the house to be unoccupied, but as she opened the door, she found Tuck in the kitchen, cloth in hand as he washed a pile of dishes. He looked over his shoulder, pausing a moment as their eyes met.

"You're back," was all he said.

Silence filled the space between them as Clara sifted through her thoughts, unsure of what to say or how to explain. Instead, she gestured to the cloth in his hand and said, "I suppose I should be thanking you for that. I didn't mean to leave my mess behind."

He dropped the cloth in a bucket of water out of sight, though she heard a faint *plopping* sound at his feet before he leaned back on the counter behind him. "Wouldn't be the first time I cleaned up after someone else's mess."

She wondered distantly what that meant but didn't have the energy to dissect his words right now. She also didn't have the energy for politeness, to tiptoe around what she really wanted to know. "So you're angry with me then?"

Tuck crossed his arms, his eyes clearly assessing her. There always seemed to be so much beneath his gaze, and she wondered if it ever exhausted him, having to always weigh his words before he spoke. "How can I be angry with someone who doesn't exist?"

It took her a moment to catch his meaning, and then she remembered the words that had slipped out before she left last night. *Just forget you ever met me.* She might've felt the cut of his words, the cold rejection within them, if she hadn't recognized the tactic. Hadn't used the same tactic herself, time and time again. Reject them before they can reject you.

Perhaps she should take the more mature path, the one where she apologized, telling him she hadn't meant what she said, that it wasn't personal. That her words were only a product of her defensive nature—the part of her that felt unsafe to be open, to be vulnerable, to be . . . seen by anyone. But as she stood in the hallway, looking over at him, she could sense that there was more than just anger here. That beneath it, there was hurt—hurt that she had caused. And suddenly, it felt like too much to face.

Clara turned away from him and walked into the living room, leaving him to linger in the cold on his own as she warmed herself before the fire in the hearth. She pushed one of the chairs nearer to the flame and sat, placing her feet folded beneath her as she tried to push everything from her mind. The guilt, the fear, the confusion of the last few days.

From the kitchen came the sound of cabinets opening and closing. Her curiosity pulled at her, and she felt herself wanting to turn and watch what Tuck was doing, but she resisted, keeping her focus on the crackling of the fire before her. Several moments later, he appeared with two glasses of amber liquid.

She looked between him and the glass he held out to her, unable to hold back the look of surprise that must have been all over her face. She'd recognized the icy demeanor and the cutting words, but giving in so quickly, with a peace offering at that, was something she'd never done.

Clara accidentally brushed her fingers against his as she took the glass from him, turning toward the fire and breathing in the spicy scent of whiskey. She hadn't seen any alcohol in the house aside from moonshine, which had clearly been batched by someone local, yet this looked like real whiskey.

"Where'd you get this?" Clara asked after taking a sip.

Tuck dragged the second chair closer to the fire, his chair now a foot or so away from hers. He didn't look at her as he said, "You have your connections, I have mine."

She furrowed her brow, unsure of what 'connections' she had, but somehow feeling that it was a jab at Mr. Baker and the help he'd given her over these past few days. Perhaps the frost of his mood hadn't quite melted after all.

Clara let the topic drop, returning her attention to the fire and to the drink in her hand. They sat there in companionable silence for several minutes before Tuck spoke again. "So, why did you come back then?"

She filtered through her thoughts, considering which response seemed the most sane. She could easily say she was back merely to stick through the weekend and make it to her meeting with Mr.

Baker on Monday. She could say she realized that whatever she saw, the woman in the bedroom upstairs, had been a product of her imagination and that she had come to her senses. But whatever it was about Tuck, about the way things had unfolded these past few days with him, she couldn't gather such a lie for him.

Clara took a deep breath and lifted the glass to her lips, taking a long sip. Then she took another, crinkling her nose against the burn of the alcohol as she waited for it to loosen her tongue, to wash a sense of bravery through her, maybe even carelessness.

"I came back," she started, taking a deep breath, "because I think my father might have . . . hurt someone."

She chewed the inside of her cheek, waiting for him to say something. It was one thing to state her suspicion in the safety of her mind, but it was another to voice it aloud to another person. Maybe part of her thought he would say nothing at all, that he would get up and walk out, leaving her to linger in the wake of her honesty. But though he was silent at first, she could feel him there, thinking, watching, processing what she had said.

"Why?" he asked, his voice strained. When she looked at him, she saw genuine concern in his furrowed brow, his eyes alight with some emotion she couldn't name. "Did something happen?"

The whiskey had begun to thaw her composure, softening her edges, lowering her inhibition, the part of herself that thought three steps ahead to what he might think of her. So, she took another sip and then began to talk. She told him of everything that had happened since getting to Hollowfield House—the shape in the trees that first night, the creaking in the hall, the bedroom door left wide open. And she told him about going to the library, about the three missing girls—Hazel, Charlotte, and Sadie.

By the time she reached the end of her speech, she felt emotion prickling behind her eyes. God, what a mess. What a mistake it had been to come here, to Briar Hollow, to this house. But she couldn't take it back now, couldn't do anything but move forward.

Slowly, she gained the courage to look up at Tuck from beneath her lashes, to where he sat on the chair next to her. His face was unreadable.

"That's . . . a lot to take in."

"I don't expect you to believe me." But even as she said the words, she tasted the lie in them. She wanted him to believe her, wanted her experience to be enough for him. But she knew better than to hope for that.

"I never said I don't." He rubbed a hand along his jaw. "I don't quite know what to think."

She nodded before sipping her drink, her eyes flickering back to the fire. The weight of it all—of the disappearances, of everything she'd uncovered—pressed down on her, squeezing something tight in her chest.

"Do you think I should go to the police?" She wasn't keen on the idea herself, her childhood experiences with men of the law more than fulfilling her quota for a lifetime, but she didn't know how else to handle all of this.

He looked at her then, something flickering behind his gaze. "Is that what you think you should do?" There was something in his eyes as he waited for her response, and Clara felt discomfort move through her.

"It seems like the logical thing to do in this scenario."

He looked away, scratching at the back of his head. His gestures seemed unsettled, restless. "I don't know that they could help."

"And why is that?"

He shrugged. "The police around here, they're not equipped to deal with anything beyond petty theft. They don't *want* to deal with anything beyond that. It's not like it is in the city, Clara." There was an agitation strewn through his words that made her feel uneasy.

She stared at his profile, at the straight line of his nose, the soft pout of his lips, the way he clenched and unclenched his jaw. Something was wrong. "You're keeping something from me."

He met her gaze, and for the briefest of moments, there was a look in his eyes that told her she was right. He was holding something back.

Tuck looked away, taking a sip of his drink. "I just think you'd be better off waiting until you know more. They won't take you seriously unless you have disprovable evidence."

She thought of the letter, the locket, the scarf. "Do I not have disprovable evidence? Everything I've just shared with you."

He sighed. "They'll poke holes in your theories—it's what they do. The letter, for example, has no names on it. No identifiable features. The scarf could belong to anyone—"

"But clearly it was left by the person who broke in that night." She thought back to that night, the way she'd imagined someone with a key carefully turning the lock, while Clara was just a few feet away on the couch. But now she saw things differently. She could imagine the door opening, Sadie stifling the groan of the hinges, not a single footstep breaking through the silence unless she allowed it. A chill ran up Clara's spine, and she brushed her hands across her upper arms.

"Just because you found it that night doesn't mean it wasn't there earlier," Tuck argued.

Something twisted in her gut. "I would've seen it. I was in that forest during the daytime just the day before."

"I'm not denying that," he said, leaning toward her, "but the police won't see it that way. They'll want facts. Something that can be proven."

"And how do you know all this?" she asked, agitation coursing through her. He stared at her, a tinge of pink flushing his cheeks before he looked away. She furrowed her brow. "What?"

He shrugged. “I read a lot of detective fiction.”

Despite herself, a smile tugged at Clara’s lips. Suddenly she could see that he wasn’t against her—he was using everything he’d learned from detective fiction to anticipate what the police might say to everything she’d uncovered. Perhaps it was fatigue, perhaps it was the alcohol, perhaps her sanity had finally snapped, but a laugh bubbled up to her lips.

He looked at her, surprise on his face. “I don’t see what’s funny about that.” But the corners of his lips had begun to tilt up into a smirk, and she only continued to laugh, fatigue rolling through her. Here she was, trying to solve the potential murder of the apparition haunting Hollowfield House, and her best source of guidance was a man who read detective fiction in his spare time. It was all so absurd, but she let herself feel lightened by it for just a moment.

“What a mess,” she said. “How am I supposed to figure any of this out when I have no idea what I’m doing?”

“I don’t know,” Tuck said softly. “But I have a feeling that anything you set your mind on becomes a possibility.”

Clara met his gaze and felt a flutter in her stomach. But as his words sunk in, they turned sour, the flutter in her stomach twisting painfully in her gut. The discomfort of her vulnerability suddenly made it difficult to breathe beyond the soft haze of alcohol. She’d shared too much—he’d seen too much. She looked away, setting down her drink, and stood. Clara sauntered over to the gramophone, casual in her movements, but eager for the conversation to end.

She kneeled down to look through the records that were lined up neatly on the shelf below the machine. These were certainly no records of Al’s—in her entire childhood, she didn’t recall him listening to music even once. He liked silence. And for the first time, Clara wondered if the reason he liked silence was because it was easier to unsettle someone without the soft winding of music in the background. Music could alter and shift emotions, and she wondered if he wanted to be the only one with the power to do that in their home.

Clara stood tall, the disc from that night she'd gone into the woods still in place on the machine: *After You've Gone; Marrion Harris*. She hesitated for a moment, wondering if this had been the last disc on the gramophone, or if Sadie had chosen it for some reason. Clara pulled the disc from the player, the memory of it unsettling her even now through the haze of whiskey, and exchanged it with the next one at the top of the pile.

It took a moment for her to focus her eyes, but she recognized the song, *Let Me Call You Sweetheart*. Clara placed the disc on the gramophone, cranking the handle before letting the needle drop. Music flowed through the room and she closed her eyes, imagining that she was back in Rochester with Mabel, making their way to a dance hall. She could feel Tuck there, watching her, but in that moment she didn't care.

She swayed with the music, humming along to the tune.

*I am dreaming, Dear, of you, day by day*

She hadn't danced in months—hadn't had the time, it seemed. But she remembered vividly the last time she had. She and Mabel and a few of their friends had stopped into a dance hall. Clara's mother had still been sick at the time, the dreariness of illness filling every inch of their shared apartment and she had suddenly felt eager for a distraction. Peter didn't join them that night, so Clara had moved from partner to partner, happy to have them as no more than a vessel of amusement.

Until their friend Dominic had stepped in. His dark hair had been slicked back and there had been a fire behind his blue eyes. And as they moved, his strong hands against her, Clara had felt something stir within her. She felt an electricity, a connection, that scared her. And it wasn't him she feared, but the way he moved something in her, the way his presence made her want to lean into his touch. That was the moment she knew she didn't love Peter anymore, and the night had no longer been fun.

She had finished the dance and muttered something about using the bathroom, but she'd slipped out from the warmth of the hall into the cold night and walked home, tears streaming down her cheeks. That was the first moment in their years-long relationship that she knew she would not marry Peter, that the ring on her finger was no more than a gesture of good faith, never to be fulfilled.

Her chest tightened at the memory, her throat thick with emotion. She squeezed her eyes tighter, trying to focus on the music and erase her thoughts.

*Let me call you "Sweetheart," I'm in love with you*

She twirled, only realizing that it was a poor idea when she tripped over her own feet. She reached out blindly, hoping to catch herself on the mantle, but warm hands held her firmly, and she found herself looking up into green eyes. A glimmer of emotion moved through her, and she found herself suddenly eager to replace that memory. Eager to make the last time she danced anything but that night with Dominic.

"Dance with me," she said, the room still swaying softly around her though Tuck's hands held her waist.

He blinked. "You're not serious," he said with a laugh of discomfort, yet he didn't release her.

She lifted her chin, the alcohol making her feel brave, and the shame from that night so long ago making her feel bold. "Unless, of course, you're too intimidated." She lowered her voice into something smooth and sultry. "I tend to have that effect on men." It was a challenge. They both knew it, and he hesitated for only a moment before he pulled her in with one hand and lifted his other hand out for her to grasp.

His palm was warm as she placed her hand in his, the callouses rough against her soft skin.

"I don't think I've danced in ten years," he said, the hesitation still lingering across his features.

"Well, that doesn't inspire much confidence." She nudged against him, trying to encourage him to move, to sway with the song, but he stood as unmoving as a brick wall.

He dropped his head down and looked into her eyes, their faces mere inches apart, as he said, "Aren't I supposed to lead?"

She inhaled the warm scent of him and felt a flutter in her stomach. "By all means."

*Let me hear you whisper that you love me too*

She followed his lead, the rhythm of the music guiding their movements, their feet tracing a path across the rug beneath them. Even as the song picked up, Tuck never missed a beat, his movements smooth, impressively so for someone who claimed not to dance.

"You really haven't danced in ten years?" she asked, feeling the flush in her cheeks, the sway of her skirt beneath her.

"I really haven't."

He moved swiftly then, pulling her along with a hand on her lower back. Clara felt herself grin as he twirled her around the room, a laugh escaping from her lips.

The song slowed as it came to an end, and there was a lightness in her chest that she hadn't felt in a long time. She smiled at him, pulling her hand from his and placing it on his chest to steady herself as she caught her breath. She went to step away, but there was something in his gaze as he looked down at her. His features softened, and his eyes flicked down to her lips, sending a current of electricity through her.

She could feel his breath was ragged, as was hers. Her eyes fell down to his lips, and she found herself thinking that he had beautiful lips and wondered what it would be like to kiss them.

*Bang.*

They jumped apart as the sound of a door slamming echoed through the house, the noise coming from the second floor. They stared at one another, confusion between them, as Clara's pounding heart turned into fear rather than excitement.

*Bang.*

Another door.

She waited to hear footsteps, the sound of someone moving from one room to the next, but there was only silence. A chill ran across her skin.

*Bang.*

That one was closer, and Clara thought of Sadie, going down the hall, slamming each door shut in protest of their behavior. Was Sadie angry? Angry that Clara was allowing herself to get distracted? To forget about what she should be focusing on?

*Bang.*

The final door upstairs. The one to Clara's own bedroom.

She swallowed, waiting, her heart still whirring. Then a moment later, Tuck crossed the room.

"Wait," she said. But as the sound escaped her lips, he disappeared into the darkened hallway, the groan of the staircase filling the silence as he ran upstairs.

# Chapter 23

Clara stood at the bottom of the staircase, staring at the darkness at the top of the stairs. She could hear Tuck's footsteps as he moved through the hall, heard the groan of every hinge as he pushed open each door that had somehow slammed itself shut. Her skin tingled with anticipation, waiting to hear if Sadie would show herself to him the same way she'd done with Clara.

After a few moments, Tuck appeared at the top of the stairs, his expression unreadable through the shadows as he came down the steps.

"No one's here," he said, confusion in his voice. "None of the windows are open. I don't understand how . . ."

She almost felt sorry for him, the way he struggled to make sense of it all, struggled to find some logical explanation for what had just taken place. But Clara knew what happened—Sadie happened. Even with that knowledge, it didn't ease the tension inside of her or slow her frantic heart, everything in her body telling her to run from this house.

She turned, walking back into the living room, drawn to the warmth of the fire in this cold, creaky house. She replayed the memory of the slam from upstairs, then the next, then the next. If Sadie could so easily move something as tangible as a door, if she could move it with such speed and force as to make it slam shut, what else could she do? What could she do to someone living and breathing? Or did the rules of the otherworldly prevent such things? Some principle of matter she didn't know about.

"I think you should stay in the cottage tonight."

She looked over her shoulder and found Tuck watching her, ready for a reaction. "That's not necessary." Perhaps alcohol had muffled her instincts, but she didn't think that Sadie would hurt her. Or at least she hoped she wouldn't.

He stared at her. "Do you know what just happened up there? Because I don't. I can't find a possible explanation as to why—"

"You can," she cut in. "If you reconsider everything I've told you. If you tried believing me." She stared back at him defiantly, a challenge in her eyes. *Believe me.* Deep inside, she felt a spark of hope, felt the softest twinge of desire. If anyone would believe her, *could* believe, it would be Tuck. He looked away and she took that as her response. Her chest twinged in disappointment, and she pulled a blanket that was folded over the back of the couch and wrapped it around her, sitting before the fire.

She heard his footsteps, felt the shift of fabric beneath him as he sat down in the chair next to her, but refused to acknowledge him. When he spoke, his voice was quiet but firm. "Are you not afraid to be here? Does none of this scare you?"

It did scare her. It all scared her, every part of her life lately—the thought of being tied to this house, the thought of going back to the city with nothing to show for her efforts, the thought of putting her trust in a man and ending up like her mother, so softened by the security of a husband that she'd sacrifice anything to make him stay. It scared her to think that she'd spent a lifetime trying to convince herself that she was having delusions when really she was seeing ghosts, beings that could close doors and open locks.

Clara sighed, feeling the weight of fatigue on her limbs. "I'm too tired to be scared anymore." The fire crackled before her, the warmth of the flames pulling her closer and closer to sleep. She hadn't looked up, hadn't moved her gaze toward Tuck, but she could feel him there next to her, watching her as if she might vanish before his eyes.

Sleep took her thereafter, and at some point, she became aware of him close to her, the warmth of his scent as he picked her up and placed her gently onto what must've been the couch. She turned into the comfort of the cushions, her body seeking rest, as some distant part of her hoped he wouldn't leave.

The warmth of sunlight was the first thing Clara became aware of the next morning. As the world around her sharpened, her senses returning to her as she peeled open her dry eyes, she found herself still there on the couch. Her eyes flitted to the hearth, to the chairs before them, and warmth spilled through her as she found Tuck there, eyes shut and still asleep, with his head titled back and his arms crossed. Guilt trickled in at the sight—she couldn't imagine that was a very comfortable sleeping position.

Movement outside drew her attention. She waited, listening, confused at who would be here this early, the sun having just barely risen. Footsteps came up the porch steps, then a heavy knock at the door. She looked at the door, unable to see through the sheer curtains at this angle. She considered whether she wanted to open it when she heard Tuck shift awake, saw him sit up and rub a hand across his eyes.

Suddenly the memory returned to her—Mr. Baker said he would stop by. Embarrassment rushed through her as she considered what he might think, what it might look like, for Tuck to have slept here in the main house with her when his cottage was right there.

She looked at Tuck, alarm overtaking her as she whispered, "Hide."

Barely awake, he gave her a look of disbelief and matched her volume as he said, “No.”

*Yes*, she mouthed, sitting up and pushing the blanket off her. She glanced back at the door before whispering, “He’s going to think you slept here last night.”

Tuck blinked, looking back and forth between her and the door. His voice was still low as he said, “I did sleep here last night.”

She considered rolling her eyes but she didn’t have the time. “You know what I mean.”

The pounding at the door continued, and Clara ran her fingers through her dark hair, hoping it didn’t look like she’d just rolled out of bed.

“Making him wait at the door only to find us alone inside is a much worse look.”

She conceded his point and got up, calling out, “Just a minute.” She fixed her crumpled clothing before opening the door. “Good morning,” she said, pulling the door open and speaking quickly. “Thank you for coming. Tuck has joined us.”

The smile on Mr. Baker’s face froze, and it was at that moment she remembered the tension between them a few days earlier. He peered into the room and looked at where Tuck was sitting in the living room. Tuck gave the man a wave and Clara narrowed her eyes at him.

“Well, that’s . . . great.” Mr. Baker stepped into the room, closing the door behind him.

“He knows everything about what I’ve found, so I thought I’d have him here too,” she lied.

“Of course. So, what do you have to show me? I hope you’re feeling better. You seemed quite upset yesterday.”

She flicked her gaze to Tuck, her cheeks heating as she looked back to Mr. Baker. “No, no. I’m perfectly fine, thanks. Just through here.”

As they moved into the office, Tuck followed behind. "Did you want anything to drink, Mr. Baker?" he asked. Clara turned, giving him a look of utter confusion. Tuck wore a pleasant expression as he went on. "Tea? Coffee, perhaps?"

At his cheery tone, suspicion coursed through her. She had no idea what he was trying to do, but given the tension between the men at their last interaction, it seemed he was trying to get some kind of reaction from Mr. Baker.

"I'm fine, thank you." Mr. Baker carried on into the office.

Clara shot a warning glance at Tuck before drawing Mr. Baker's attention to the items laid across the desk, considering the best way to present the information, her mind going to Tuck's detective fiction. She suddenly wished she had inquired further about that. Mr. Baker may not be a detective, but he was a man of the law. Surely there must be some parallel within their lines of thinking.

"It started with a letter I found in Al's things, one that clearly didn't belong to him." She lifted the letter toward him, allowing him to read it. She had made a conscious decision to leave the woman in the trees, Sadie's ghost, out of this version of events.

"Forgive me, Miss Dawson, but this letter hardly indicates a crime of any sort."

"Agreed. But then I found a journal amongst his things—"

"I'm sure he'd be enthused to know you were reading his personal stationery," he said in jest. She swallowed the agitation in her chest and gave a soft laugh.

"Yes, anyway, I found this journal and the entries are somewhat unsettling. He speaks of a woman. The ghost of a woman, really, haunting him and this house."

Mr. Baker's face was unreadable as he said, "I suppose I can't blame the man. Most of Briar Hollow is superstitious. Hollowfield House is practically a local attraction."

"How do you mean?"

Mr. Baker smiled his dazzling smile. "Oh, you know how townsfolk are. An isolated house on the edge of town, the last owner died prematurely. Doesn't take too much imagination to see why some think of the inn as a haunted house of sorts. Especially after what happened with Al, the poor man."

She blinked, thinking back to the encounters she'd had with people in town, at the diner. Had that been why they were so strange? Had it not been a matter of being an outsider as much as a matter of being superstitious?

"I hadn't thought of that." She looked to where Tuck leaned against the doorframe. He was notably silent during this conversation. Had he known people in town believed these things?

"I wouldn't be surprised if the rumors got to his head," Mr. Baker said. "Especially when you add a bit of drink to the equation." Tuck's eyes flicked to Mr. Baker.

"Yes," Clara said. "I suppose that's true." Knowing that background killed the wind in her sails, making her feel a bit unsure of it all. "Well, I also found this." She brought forth the locket, passing it to him. "The owner, I believe, is Charlotte Mason. A young woman who went missing in 1929."

His eyes flicked up to meet hers. "Yes, I believe I have heard that name before." He opened the locket to where Eddie Reynolds' face stared back at him. "But, as you said, she was a local girl. Perhaps she simply dropped it on the property. Left it behind and didn't realize where."

She flicked a glance to Tuck, whose eyes were fixed on Mr. Baker, his own expression unreadable. "Possibly. But why would a girl of seventeen have need to stay at an inn so close to her own home?"

Mr. Baker passed the locket back to her. "I assume the boy in that photo was her sweetheart. Perhaps they came here together. Wanted a bit of privacy."

Something shifted inside her, unease at the concept. "But would a young man still in high school have the money to stay at an inn overnight?"

Mr. Baker shrugged. "Al could've given him a deal."

"And why would he do that?" Tuck asked, his voice cutting through their bubble.

Mr. Baker looked at him, a moment of tension seeming to pass between them. "Couldn't say why. I wasn't close to either of them. But you were close with Al, weren't you, Tuck? You knew him, what, nearly a decade? Why do you think he would've done that?"

Clara glanced between the two men, aware of some deeper meaning beneath their words, but unsure of what. "Is there something you two want to tell me?"

Tuck glanced at her, something behind his eyes. For a moment, she could see that there was something and that whatever it was, he seemed to want to tell her. But Mr. Baker turned back toward her, pulling her attention with his blue eyes bright and a smile on his face. "Nah, just a couple of old friends giving each other a hard time. I'm sorry, Miss Dawson, we're being rude. What else did you find?"

She paused for a moment, sparing one last fruitless look at Tuck before carrying on.

"I also found a woman's scarf. Mind you, I don't know whose it is, and yes, it very well could belong to a guest, but along with everything else, it just seems strange. It feels like there must be some connection here between these things." She looked up at Mr. Baker and found him unconvinced, a pitying smile on his face. She walked around the desk and pulled her notebook closer. "I also did some research. Al bought Hollowfield House in 1925. Then there are three disappearances of young women, all around the same age, in Briar Hollow not long after Al moved here. Hazel Montgomery in 1926, Charlotte Mason in 1929, and Sadie Collins." She hadn't yet uncovered the date of Sadie's disappearance, but she hoped Mr. Baker wouldn't call her on that.

Something shifted in his expression, something like surprise. For a moment, she had the hope that he would believe her, that he, too, would see the connection between everything. "Did you say Hazel Montgomery?"

"Yes." She nodded.

"Well." He gave a small laugh, and she felt her face drop. "Miss Dawson, I can assure you, Hazel Montgomery isn't missing. In fact, I just saw her a few months ago."

Something fractured within her. "What do you mean?"

"I trust that you two can keep this confidential?" He looked between the both of them, seeming to take their confusion as an adequate agreement. "She was in need of legal help a couple of years ago but needed to be . . . discreet. She asked that I not tell her family about our contact, but she's not far from Briar Hollow. Just a few hours' drive."

Clara stilled. "Oh."

"I would think you'd be happy to hear it."

She swallowed. "Yes, yes of course. It's just . . . I didn't find anything in the articles—"

"You wouldn't," he said. "There were personal issues in her family. In all honesty," he said, taking a step closer, "her mental state is not well. She's a bit paranoid. Nice enough girl but not all there, if you know what I mean." There was pity in his eyes, and for a moment, she felt a flash of nausea wondering if he was starting to view her in the same light he viewed Hazel.

"You seem to know her well," Clara observed.

He shrugged. "She's down on her luck. I sympathize with the poor girl. Every so often, I try to buy her a meal. It seems the least I can do. Most aren't as lucky as we are."

"That's quite the coincidence, isn't it?" Tuck spoke from the side of the room. "The very same woman Miss Dawson just found to be missing, found to have some sort of connection to the inn, just so happens to have come to you for council a few months ago so you're able to disprove the whole thing. What are the odds?" His tone was light, jovial even, but there was an ulterior meaning beneath. She felt it in his gaze when it landed on her.

"It almost sounds as if you're calling me a liar, Tuck," Mr. Baker said.

"You said it, not me."

There was tension between the men, and Clara couldn't help but agree with Tuck. It was a rather convenient set of circumstances. What were the odds he had a connection with one of the three young women who had gone missing? A seed of doubt sprouted within her, and she wondered if there was a reason he had for not wanting her to look further into these disappearances. She thought of Eddie Reynolds, of his connection to the constable, and couldn't help but wonder if Mr. Baker, the town lawyer, might have some connections to local law enforcement as well.

"Since you know how to get in contact with her, perhaps you could set up a meeting between us," Clara offered. Beneath the innocent suggestion was a test—if he really did know Hazel Montgomery, if she was really alive, then this should be doable. She watched for his reaction, watched as he smiled tight-lipped, looking between them as they waited.

He turned back to her. "Of course. I have her number back at the office. I'll give her a call and see if she's free." He pulled a small card and a pen from his jacket then wrote something on the cardstock before passing it to her. It was a name and an address. "Tell you what, I have a reservation for two in Hornell tonight, but my client fell through. What do you say I make it three and have Hazel join us?"

"Where's Hornell?"

"About an hour east from here," Mr. Baker offered.

Her eyes wandered over the card, concern tugging at her brain. She was starting to feel like she didn't know anyone in Briar Hollow, not even Tuck or Mr. Baker. But if she wanted the truth, wanted to know if Al had hurt those girls, then this was the path to find out for herself.

"Alright," Clara said. "That'd be grand."

"Make it four," Tuck said from the doorway. "I'll be coming along as well."

Mr. Baker was silent for a moment before he gave a small smile. "Of course. The more the merrier."

# Chapter 24

Clara stood before the dishes, her hands in the warm soapy water. A strange, unsettling feeling spread through her. She stopped for a moment, listening, and looked behind her. The house was still. Slowly, she turned back, raising her hands to wash the next dish.

*Stop*. Clara whirled back around, feeling an icy cold on the back of her neck, but still she found nothing. It had only been the whisper of a noise, muffled as if behind a wall. She scanned each corner of the room.

"Sadie?" Clara whispered.

Not taking her eyes away from the room before her, she reached for the towel and dried her hands. Slowly, she walked through the kitchen and out into the hallway.

The house looked back at her, unmoving, unflinching.

"Sadie?" Clara whispered again. Some part of her wanted a response, wanted confirmation, but another part of her was fearful. She turned and began to walk toward the living room, but then she heard a thump from the office.

It was loud, like the sound that came from dropping something heavy onto wood flooring, and she rerouted, walking down the hall to peer into the office. She found nothing there, but she stood at the door, watching. After a moment, she took a step inside, the floor creaking beneath her, and jumped when the sound echoed—loud, painfully loud—through the other side of the wall, behind the bookshelf.

For just a moment, pain pierced her skull, her vision blacking out before the room appeared before her again, just the same as it had been. She placed a hesitant hand to the back of her head—the pain had been so brief that she questioned whether she'd imagined it entirely. But she could feel an energy in the air, a strange tension.

Sadie was here.

Something flashed by the window, a shadow moving between the house and the forest, and Clara crossed the room quickly, nearly knocking over the small frame on the wall in her haste. She looked at an angle and saw the shape of someone walking down toward the back of the house. It didn't appear to be a woman though. It was a man, and a tall one at that.

As confusion coursed through her, Clara walked back through the office, out into the hall, and out the front door. Cold air enveloped her as she walked down the steps and sped toward the side of the house. The gravel turned to grass beneath her feet as she walked, her heart pounding, unsure of what she'd find. Was it Sadie? It hadn't felt like it, but she didn't feel sure of anything anymore, the presence of Hollowfield House constantly disorienting her.

She rounded the corner with speed, nearly colliding with a tall man who faced away from her. A yelp escaped her lips, and he jumped as well. As he turned around, very much corporeal, a flush of embarrassment washed through her. What was it with her and scaring men on this property?

"Sorry," she said before realizing the man before her was the same man from the grocery store and the diner—Randy. Quickly her tone changed as she asked, "What are you doing here?"

"Sorry," he echoed. "Didn't mean to scare you. I just wanted to check the, uh—" She blinked, waiting for him to explain. "The foundation. It can shift with the seasons. Wouldn't want water getting in there and putting a crack beneath the house."

"Oh," was her only response. She knew little of foundations, but something about his demeanor made him seem less than credible. Perhaps it was that she was under the impression that Randy had worked as a carpenter. "When you worked for my father, what did you do here?" She put an easy smile on her face. "I'm just realizing I didn't ask earlier."

He turned away from her, seemingly investigating the foundation of the house, his eyes focused on the space at the bottom of the wall. "Mostly carpentry," he said. "But you know how it is in a place like this. Everyone shares the duties. One day you're fixing the fireplace, the next you're sealing the foundation."

She supposed that made sense, especially with someone like Al. He wasn't likely to hire and pay more people than necessary. "So, how does the foundation look?"

"Good," he said, looking between her and the house. "It looks good. Glad I stopped by. It was nagging at me, you know?" He walked around the side of the house, and she followed, her curiosity about another matter piqued.

"You were close with Al, right?"

"Of course. Thick as thieves."

"Did you ever see anything . . . strange while you were here? Anything to do with him? Or his behavior, perhaps?"

At first, Randy was silent, the only sound around them the rustling of leaves in the wind. They carried on towards the front of the house as he said, "You have something particular in mind?"

Clara pushed past the discomfort simmering within her. "Did you ever see any young women on the property?"

Randy stopped and stared down at her. "What do you mean?"

She wondered how much to share with the stranger, but she was running out of time to find out what was really going on here. "There have been some disappearances in Briar Hollow ever since Al bought the place—"

"You're not suggesting that he was the cause of that." It was a statement rather than a question, and Clara saw the flame of anger behind Randy's eyes as he turned toward her fully.

"I'm only trying to figure out if there was a connection between it all. Between those disappearances and the way he . . . ended it all."

Randy looked down at her, his posture stiff, yet she didn't feel fearful. She almost felt like she could see him processing, only now considering the ties that bound the things he might've seen.

"How'd you say you know him again?"

She sighed. "He was my father. We weren't close." The fierceness in his posture seemed to soften at that.

"I didn't see you at the funeral."

His words sent a pang of guilt through her. She hadn't gone to Al's funeral, hadn't wanted to be involved in it in anyway. But that wasn't something she expected most people to understand.

"I'm only here for another few days," Clara said, shifting the conversation away. "Please, I just want to know what happened here. You knew him better than anyone." She wasn't entirely sure there was truth to the statement, but it seemed like something he'd want to hear. "Why do you think Al killed himself?"

Silence fell between them for several moments, but Clara could feel him considering, weighing his options before he spoke.

"If you want the truth of it, I don't think he did kill himself."

The words sent a chill through Clara, her mind trying to piece together what it could possibly mean. If Al hadn't killed himself, then who had killed him?

Just as she opened her mouth to speak, Randy turned and carried on to the front of the house, picking up his pace.

"Why do you think that?" Clara asked, trying to keep up with him.

"I can't tell you anything else." He didn't look at her as he grabbed a bicycle that had been lying next to the tree, hidden by the greenery at the edge of the gravel lot.

"Wait," she protested.

"I've already said too much." Randy swung his leg over the bicycle before glancing back at her. "You have a good evening, Clara."

Throughout the rest of the afternoon, as Clara tried to make herself busy, her mind kept wandering back to that strange conversation with Randy. She couldn't help but think there must be some reason he assumed someone had killed Al, and she realized suddenly that she'd never actually been told the details of her father's suicide. How had he been found? Who had found him? What condition was he in?

When she and Tuck climbed into her vehicle later that evening—she'd begrudgingly let him drive, considering she had no clue how to get to this city where they'd be meeting Mr. Baker and Hazel—she knew he was the one to ask for more details on Al's death.

She waited before she approached the topic. She waited until they'd pulled out of Hollowfield House and drove through Main Street, past the buildings, until they'd reached the other side of town and were surrounded by nothing but fields and crops.

"Randy came by earlier," Clara said finally.

"Did he?" Tuck responded, his voice not giving away any emotion.

"He said he wanted to check the foundation." She looked at him, trying to read his expression. He furrowed his brows, but his eyes remained fixed on the road ahead.

"Why would he do that?" he asked.

Clara shrugged. "He said it was something he used to do when he worked at the inn. And then he said that he doesn't think Al killed himself."

Tuck was silent. The only sound between them was the rattle of the engine and the howl of the wind outside.

Her voice softened as she asked, "When he was found . . . did you see him?" She could see on his face that he knew immediately what she meant.

"I was the one who found him."

She swallowed, guilt panging through her. "And what did you see?"

"Clara," he started, his voice soft with pity.

"You can tell me," she argued, feeling a sudden desperation to know the truth. "We weren't close. It won't upset me."

He was silent, but she waited, feeling like she should give him a minute to process, to think through it all. Then, finally, he asked, "Why does it matter?"

"It matters because I need to know what happened. I need to know if he's the one who hurt those girls. Who . . . killed Sadie. I can't just leave it be. And if he did . . . it would finally make sense."

"He hung himself."

She stared at Tuck, her entire body suddenly cold. "Where?" she found herself asking, her voice little more than a whisper.

Tuck shifted in his seat, visibly unsettled by the memory. "The banister."

Clara thought of the staircase, of the railing between the top of the stairs and the wall that overlooked the entryway below. She swallowed, her mind trying to picture it, trying to recreate what Tuck must have seen. "With . . . with a rope?"

Tuck pushed a hand roughly through his hair, a gesture she'd come to recognize as a sign of unease. "This hardly seems appropriate dinner conversation—"

"We're not at dinner yet," she cut in. He flicked a glance at her before looking back at the road. "If you don't tell me, I'll just imagine the worst."

With a sigh, he said, "It was a scarf."

Her gut twisted, and she was suddenly breathless, her mind going back to the red scarf she'd found that night in the woods. "What?" She stared at him, but he didn't repeat himself. "What color was it?"

Silence filled the vehicle, and she knew what the answer would be.

"Tuck?" she pressed forcefully, urgency in her tone.

"It's exactly what you think it is."

She thought of the red scarf, the silky material, and tried to imagine Al tying one end to a banister and throwing himself over, thinking it would hold his weight. "It would've torn," she said aloud. "It couldn't have held—"

"It did hold," Tuck cut in. He didn't look at her as he spoke. "It held until they cut him down."

Nausea climbed up her throat. "The scarf I found in the forest—"

"There are many red scarves in the world," Tuck snapped. After a moment, he sighed, and she could see the tension in his shoulders, the stiffness in his movements. She suddenly felt guilty for pushing him. What must it have been like to find someone that way?

But that scarf she'd found in the forest, the one Sadie had clearly left for her, it couldn't have been a coincidence.

"There may be many red scarves in the world," Clara said, her voice softer now, "but how many of them could be at Hollowfield House?"

It took him a moment to respond, but when he did, Clara could hear the fatigue in his voice as he said, "I don't know."

# Chapter 25

A wave of nausea washed through Clara as she and Tuck neared the restaurant, her mind spinning with possibilities of what she might find inside. Mr. Baker had warned her of Hazel's mental state, but what did that mean, exactly? What kind of things might she have endured in her childhood to make the decision to slip away one evening and never return?

There were times growing up when Clara had considered doing the same. Packing up only the essentials and disappearing into the night, starting fresh somewhere new, and leaving her mother behind without explanation. Sometimes she could even convince herself that that would be the kinder thing to do. That it would give her mother a chance to start fresh too.

But then she thought of those weeks after her father had left, the way her mother couldn't get out of bed. The way she'd struggled to function. And while Clara suspected that her mother would've preferred her daughter leave in exchange for her husband, it felt like the culmination of their disappearances would've broken her. If Clara couldn't bring her father back, she'd reasoned, then the least she could do was stay with her mother. Help her pretend that she was content to be a mother, even if she wasn't a wife.

Clara wondered what Hazel's home had been like. What it must have been like for Hazel to actually do it, to gather up the courage and disappear.

The air was cool and the sun was setting, the sky filled with vibrant pinks and yellows. The beauty of it felt wrong, like a misrepresentation of what surely awaited her inside. As they walked up the sidewalk, muffled conversation spilling out into the street each time someone came or went, she paused at the feel of Tuck's hand on her arm.

"If you want to leave at any point, just say the word."

Clara met his gaze, the final light of dusk shining onto his green eyes before it slipped behind the horizon. There was a gleam of sincerity there that made her feel like he could see straight through her, like somehow he knew exactly what she was thinking. The thought of being so easily read unsettled her and she gave her best attempt at a half-smile.

"I'll be fine," she said, fixing the hem of her jacket for some excuse to break their eye contact. "It's just a conversation." She flicked a glance toward him and found him still watching her, seemingly not convinced by her words. He didn't say anything, simply giving her a nod and holding open the door.

Warmth enveloped her as she stepped inside the restaurant. It looked much like the ones in the city, like the kind of places she'd met Dominic on the evenings when being alone had felt too heavy, her thoughts too dominant to be ignored without distraction.

Tuck gave the hostess the name of their party and they were taken back through the dining room. As they navigated through tables, Clara heard snippets of conversation from the patrons around them, ignoring the smoke that lingered in the air. And then she spotted them. Mr. Baker was leaning in toward the woman who sat next to him, his gaze fixed solely on her. He was speaking to her in low tones, though the woman did not look at him, instead reading over the menu held within her fingers.

The woman looked to be Clara's age, perhaps twenty-five or so, and there was something classic about her beauty. Her wavy brunette hair rested at her shoulders, and she had wide dark eyes and soft features. Both she and Mr. Baker seemed to notice their arrival at the same time. His face lit into a smile as he stood, while Hazel returned her gaze to the menu.

"Miss Dawson, lovely to see you," Mr. Baker said. He looked to where Tuck came in behind her. "Mr. Tucker." His greeting was dignified with a less enthusiastic nod.

The table was against a wall, one side of it a booth, the other side with two chairs. A white tablecloth lay across the surface and small candles sat within glass holders between the drinking glasses. Clara took the seat across from Hazel, trying to meet her gaze, but the woman seemed to look everywhere but at her.

"Hazel Montgomery, meet Clara Dawson," Mr. Baker said.

"Thank you for agreeing to meet with us on such short notice," Clara said as the men sat down. The woman nodded once in acknowledgement.

Silence washed over the table before Mr. Baker cut in. "Clara here is Al Dawson's daughter. The owner of Hollowfield House."

"Can't say I've been," Hazel responded, sparing a brief glance upward before returning her gaze to the menu. A sense of unease flickered in Clara.

"Really?" Clara asked. "I actually found something amongst my father's things. I was wondering if you recognized it."

Before leaving the house, Clara had wondered if she should take any of the items she'd found with her. She didn't know the woman and didn't want to unsettle her, but she couldn't help but feel she should bring something on the chance that it was Hazel's. The locket seemed to belong to Charlotte, and the scarf, well, Clara didn't know whose that was, but the thought of her pulling a scarf out of her purse at the dinner table seemed a bit much. But the letter could fit easily into her purse, and perhaps Hazel would recognize the writing—perhaps even recognize it as her own writing.

Clara pulled the letter out of her purse and unfolded it, holding it out to Hazel. She stared at it for a moment, her eyes flicking up to Clara before returning to the envelope in her hand. Then Hazel took it, slowly unfolding it.

"Miss Dawson, you don't beat around the bush, do you?" Mr. Baker said with a laugh.

Clara gave him a small smile before returning her gaze to Hazel. The woman had stiffened, her expression unreadable. A moment later she tossed the letter back to Clara's side of the table.

"Tell me, Miss Dawson, are you often in the practice of sharing others' personal letters with complete strangers?" Hazel asked, her voice tight.

Before Clara could respond, the waitress appeared, rattling off the specials and taking their orders. Clara pulled the letter back into her grasp, her heart still pounding quickly from the anger in Hazel's voice, in her eyes. Clara folded the letter and tried to focus on the menu long enough to choose an item. When the waitress left, taking their menus with her, Clara spoke.

"I apologize if I upset you. I simply wished to know if you recognized the writing—"

"And why would I?" Hazel cut in. "I told you I'd never been to the place."

An uncomfortable silence fell over the table as Clara tried to figure out how to respond. If she were in any other situation, she might give Hazel's anger right back to her. But she couldn't help but feel she might've touched a nerve, making her wonder if Hazel did, in fact, recognize the letter. Or perhaps, if she was the writer of the letter in question.

"Now let's not get carried away," Mr. Baker said. "I'm sure Miss Dawson didn't mean any offense." He glanced at Clara and she nodded her agreement. Hazel, however, did not acknowledge the statement, choosing to look away from the group and focus her eyes on something in the distance. It was clear she was done with the interaction.

Mr. Baker recovered first and took over the conversation, asking Clara and Tuck about their drive and telling them about Hornell's history. About some attractions nearby. Somehow the conversation ended up back at Briar Hollow.

"I grew up in Briar Hollow," Mr. Baker said. "Wonderful place to raise a family. Wouldn't you agree, Tuck?"

Clara felt Tuck stiffen next to her and she glanced at him, her curiosity piqued. Mr. Baker knew something, and she couldn't help but wonder what it was.

"Certainly," Tuck replied, holding Mr. Baker's stare. The table waited for something more to be said, the tension building in the silence, but then Mr. Baker looked away first, reaching for his drink.

Clara's attention fell to Hazel. "Did you grow up in Briar Hollow?"

Hazel met her gaze for the first time in several minutes. "No." With that, she reached into her purse and pulled out a cigarette and a light. From where Clara sat, she could see the slight shaking of Hazel's hands as she lit the end of the cigarette. Clara recalled Mr. Baker's statement earlier that morning, that Hazel had some mental health struggles.

"Where did you grow up, Miss Dawson?" Mr. Baker asked. Clara looked at him over the candlelight but found herself pulled back to Hazel, something about her making it difficult to look away. She realized that this entire evening may very well go on this way, with Hazel sharing nothing of value. And perhaps she had every right to do so. After all, she didn't know Clara, didn't owe her anything.

But all of this had begun to shift, to morph into something outside of Clara or Al or the inn. A girl had been killed—that, Clara was certain of. If Hazel knew something that could bring Clara closer to the truth of what happened to Sadie, what must've happened to Charlotte, now was the time to draw it out of her.

"When did you move there, Hazel?" Clara asked. There was a shift at the table as the attention was drawn to the two women.

Hazel lifted her chin and blew the smoke to the side, away from their table. "If you must know, I was thirteen."

Mr. Baker tried to speak but Clara cut him off. "What made you move?" Hazel met her gaze now, something fiery behind those brown eyes. Clara felt the warmth of Tuck's hand on her knee as he gave her a brief squeeze—a warning, she supposed, that she was going too far.

"My mother died."

Guilt pinged through Clara, but Hazel's tone was one without emotion. Simply factual. Perhaps she could have shared her own experience—found some common ground between them—but that didn't feel like what Hazel wanted.

"I'm sorry to hear that."

"Why?" Hazel asked, her tone dry. "Did you kill her?"

A laugh erupted from Mr. Baker, drawing every eye at the table to him. "She's always had a great sense of humor. Isn't that right, Hazel?"

Clara looked between them, noticing Hazel's apathy toward Mr. Baker, though he spoke as if he knew her amicably, if not somewhat intimately. "Have you known each other long?" Clara asked, gesturing between the two.

Mr. Baker paused, a smile still on his face before he responded, "Not all that long, I suppose." He gave Hazel a smile, and Clara turned to Hazel as well, unable to stand another moment of these tense niceties.

"Can I be frank with you?"

Something flashed behind Hazel's eyes, but when she spoke, her voice was steady, almost disinterested. "You can try."

"I don't mean to be rude, but I want to know why you disappeared." Hazel blinked, and Clara continued. "See, I've inherited my father's inn. Upon going through the house, I've found some things. At first, I believed they were merely things left behind by guests. But I've come to find a connection between some of these items and the disappearances of three young women from Briar Hollow. Charlotte Mason, Sadie Collins, and you."

"That's a fascinating story, but as you can see, I'm not missing. I'm right here."

"I'm relieved to see it. Unfortunately, the other girls have not been so lucky. At least one of them has ended up dead."

Hazel stilled. Clara was grateful for the noise of the restaurant, the muffled conversation all around them, to disguise the pounding of her heart in her chest.

Mr. Baker shifted uncomfortably, leaning in. "Miss Dawson—"

"Please, Mr. Baker. This is why you've brought us here, is it not?" Clara snapped. He stared back at her, and she turned to Hazel, who had seemed to go white.

"I'm sorry to be so blunt, but I believe it was my father's doing. Now, you can imagine that upon that discovery, I'm trying to figure out the connection between you and the other girls. I'm not trying to pry into your personal life for my own personal enjoyment. I'm trying to find out if my father was a killer."

Clara realized she was breathing heavily, and she sat back, finding Mr. Baker and Tuck staring at her. Hazel shifted in her seat, putting out her cigarette in the ashtray at the center of the table, and stood.

"If you don't mind, I just need to use the restroom."

They all watched as Hazel walked through the tables and disappeared down a hallway at the opposite end of the restaurant.

Clara's stomach clenched. Hazel knew something, she was sure of it. She placed her own napkin on the table and stood.

"Please," Mr. Baker said, standing as well now. "Just give her a moment, Miss Dawson." He lowered his voice, seeming to realize those at the tables nearby were now watching. "I warned you, she's unsteady. No reason for concern, but please, you mustn't agitate her further."

Clara swallowed, looking between the bright blue of Mr. Baker's eyes and the hall Hazel had disappeared into. "Certainly. I'll make sure she's okay." Without another glance back, she followed Hazel's path to the restroom, nerves coursing through her.

But something was here, she could feel it. Hazel knew something about the inn, about her father. It was just a matter of whether Hazel could trust her enough to share it with Clara.

Clara pushed open the bathroom door and found Hazel leaning against the wall, a fresh cigarette lit. What could she say to this woman to convince her she could be trusted?

"Hazel, I—"

"You're stupid to come here." Hazel shook her head, taking another drag from her cigarette. She looked older in that moment, her expression concerned, like the weight of the world rested upon her shoulders.

"What do you mean? You seemed upset at the table, and I just wanted to make sure—"

"Not *here*," Hazel snapped. "To come to this place. With him." With Mr. Baker, surely. She took Hazel in, trying to piece together what she was upset about. "He's married, you know."

Clara tensed, shame washing through her. She hadn't known—had never noticed a wedding ring. Not that anything had happened between them but . . . She took a deep breath.

"Nothing has happened between me and Mr. Baker."

"It will if you don't leave." Hazel carried on, frustration seeping into her voice. "I see the way he looks at you, and I've been on the receiving end of that look. Don't make the mistake of thinking you're special. Men like that, they're all the same. Forget about the inn, forget about all of it." Hazel took one last drag from her cigarette before putting it out in the ashtray that sat next to the sink.

"I don't care about Mr. Baker," Clara reasoned. "I don't care about the inn, either." She felt the truth within the words as she spoke them, the way this had taken on a life of its own, become something outside of herself. "I want to know why you disappeared, why you left. I want to know what happened with the other girls."

Hazel looked at her, something like pity and resentment in her eyes. "You want my advice? Leave this alone." She took one last look in the mirror and walked past Clara, reaching for the bathroom door. "It won't end well for you, Miss Dawson. I can promise you that."

With those words, Hazel left the bathroom, leaving only the sound of her heels clicking down the hall in her wake.

# Chapter 26

The drive back to Briar Hollow was silent, Clara lost in her thoughts. As the city lights eventually gave way to the darkness of the fields now all around them, confusion worked through her. She had been so sure Al had been the one to hurt those girls, yet Hazel was fine, nothing more than a runaway, just as the police had suspected. Did that mean Charlotte was out there too?

But what about Sadie? What had happened to her that made her linger around Hollowfield House? A seed of doubt sprouted within Clara as she recalled Eddie's words. *Unnatural interests.* Charlotte and Sadie had seemed to be good friends, and Eddie had been dating Charlotte just before she'd gone missing. Did Eddie think Sadie had feelings for Charlotte? That those feelings had caused her death, been the reason someone hurt her? Had it been reason enough for *him* to hurt her? Or had the internal battle of those feelings, of loving someone she would be shamed for, been too much for Sadie to live with?

Clara could imagine how difficult it would be in a town like this to have feelings for one's same sex. Even in the city, there was still a stigma around it. An air of secrecy, as if these relationships shouldn't exist, or if they did, should be kept secret behind closed doors. Had it all been too much for Sadie to live with after Charlotte disappeared?

"Well?" The words broke through her thoughts and Clara turned, looking at Tuck's silhouette through the darkness. She had let him drive to spare them both from a repeat of her first night getting lost.

"Well what?" she asked softly.

"You saw her yourself—she's alive. You must be relieved." His voice held no emotion, and she couldn't help but feel he was treading lightly, trying to get a sense of how she felt before he said anything. She couldn't help but feel annoyed at the condescension of it, as if she might be so easily swayed by his opinion that he needed to protect her from his thoughts.

Clara looked back at the dirt path illuminated before them, the dark night falling outside the scope of the headlights. A sigh escaped her. She didn't feel relieved, didn't know what to feel other than confused. But how could she explain that to him? A girl she'd believed might've been killed by her father was alive. She should be comforted, happy to accept it and move on, having done her part.

"Of course," she agreed, sounding unconvincing even to her own ears. Something deep within her nagged at her, pulled at her attention. Something had felt . . . wrong. Yet she couldn't identify what it was. Couldn't explain why seeing Hazel had unsettled her. And she certainly couldn't put those feelings into words to explain them to Tuck.

"But?" he asked.

"But nothing. I'm relieved. Aren't you?" She glanced at him, curiosity emerging.

"We both know this isn't about me," he said, his eyes still on the road. "Did you find what you were looking for? You certainly didn't hold back with the girl."

She felt the hint of a smile pull at her lips, and she turned her face toward the window. "I don't know," she admitted. "In some ways, I feel like I know less now than I did a few hours ago."

"And why is that?"

Clara thought back to Hazel's behavior, to the anger threaded through every word she spoke. Mr. Baker had warned her of Hazel's instability, but Clara couldn't help but wonder if there was something more to it. If, perhaps, that anger had been directed at Mr. Baker rather than a symptom of some mental condition. As she played through the events of the evening, she couldn't help but feel there had been something unspoken between the two. Some bit of context that Clara hadn't been privy to.

"Hazel said something strange to me in the bathroom. She said that I should leave it alone and that it wouldn't end well for me. That I shouldn't trust Mr. Baker." Clara stared at Tuck, unable to read his features in the shadows of the vehicle.

"Well, do you?"

"Do I what?" she asked, some part of her not wanting to face the question.

"Do you trust Mr. Baker?"

She was quiet, her thoughts churning. "I don't trust anyone." Something about the words, about saying them out loud, feeling the truth of them, made her chest tighten.

Tuck didn't respond at first, and then a moment later he asked, "Not even me?"

She turned her eyes back to the road ahead. "Not even you."

The headlights shone on the windows of the inn as they pulled into the drive some time later, exhaustion settling into Clara's bones. She felt like she hadn't truly slept in days, the tense energy of nerves and stress finally crashing into fatigue. She looked up at the house, the way it seemed to loom over her.

"Do you want me to light the fire for you?" Tuck asked as he turned the motorcar off.

Clara fought the hint of relief at his offer and agreed, grateful to have someone else inside the house with her for even a moment. Once inside, she walked into the living room, finding a match and lighting a candle she'd placed on the mantle. She moved back through the room, candle in hand, and made her way to the hall to light the sconces there.

That was when she felt the breeze, saw the way the flame danced on the candle in her hand. She looked toward the front door but found it had been shut, Tuck already in the living room before the hearth. Then she turned to her left and looked down the hall toward the office, its door ajar, the blackness inside staring back at her. She moved slowly, feeling more of the frigid night air the closer she got, alarm rising within her. Had she forgotten to close the window?

The hinges squealed in protest as she pushed the door open fully. The room was darker than she'd anticipated, the moon outside the window almost entirely blocked out by the trees and the clouds that dusted the night sky. Clara stared at the window, her eyes adjusting to the pitch black, trying to understand how she felt the wash of the cold air even though the window appeared to be fully shut.

There was an energy about the room, remnants of something, a lingering scent of tobacco and alcohol of some sort. Clara stepped forward, her heart quickening as her toe caught on something and she stumbled forward, reaching out her empty hand to catch herself on the desk. She turned and stared down at the pile of books that lay there before seeing that the bookshelf stood empty now.

Clara placed the candle on the empty desk and walked around the desk, eager to get closer to the window, to confirm what she already knew deep down. And then she felt something crunch beneath her shoes. She stepped back, finding that the small, framed photo that typically hung on the wall had been knocked over and lay shattered on the ground. She stared down at it, a chill running up her spine before her eyes slowly moved to the window.

The wind howled as it washed over her, and she stepped forward, looking around the desk at the open space beneath the window ledge, where she found the reflection of the dim moon staring back at her in shards of glass scattered across the floor.

Understanding settled into her, and she swallowed back a sour taste in her mouth as bile rose up her throat.

The window wasn't open. It had been shattered.

# Chapter 27

"Nothing else seems to be missing," Tuck said sometime later, meeting her at the bottom of the staircase. "And no one's in the rooms upstairs."

Clara glanced back at the office, the candle she'd brought into the room still sitting atop the empty desk, the flicker of its flame reflecting patterns on the wall. Her mind went to Randy—to his presence earlier, to the things he'd said the other day when he had clearly been drinking. *I always thought he had cash hidden somewhere in the house.* Had this been Randy looking for the money he thought was owed to him? Is that why the books had been thrown about? Had Randy thought Al would have hidden cash in the books on his shelf?

It certainly didn't explain the other things that had been taken from the desk—the locket, the scarf, Al's journal, her notebook filled with everything she'd found at the library.

"I didn't find anything missing down here," she said, her chest tightening, "except the things in the office. The items I had left on the desk." She paused, knowing exactly what conclusion Tuck would come to.

He stared back at her. "Everything you showed to James Baker earlier today?"

She shifted. "I know you're going to say it was him, but he sat across from us all night—"

"You know as well as I do that he could've had someone else break in on his behalf."

"And why would he do that?" she asked, agitation rising in her chest. "If he was involved in this somehow, why would he have helped us get in touch with Hazel?"

"There wasn't much else he could do," Tuck said, taking a step toward her. "Once he mentioned knowing her, you didn't leave him much of a choice."

"If he were trying to keep their connection a secret, he wouldn't have brought it up to begin with," she argued. "And what makes you so certain this wasn't Randy's doing? You were there when he told us about the money. In fact, you were rather quick to cut him off, if I recall." Tuck stiffened and she knew her words rang true. "You know what I think? I think your judgment is so clouded by this grudge you've clearly been holding onto for years—"

"*My* judgment is clouded?"

"Precisely." With a huff, she said, "It seems we're not going to come to an agreement on this tonight." She pushed past him and stomped her way up the stairs, frustration coursing through her.

"Where are you going?" Tuck called after her. She was halfway up the stairs before she realized she'd forgotten to bring a light with her, but it was too late to turn back now, indignation flowing through her as she went.

"To bed," she exclaimed, not bothering to look back.

"To bed?" His tone was incredulous, a note of disbelief that almost made her turn around and challenge him. But she didn't. She reached the top of the stairs and turned into her room as if he'd never spoken at all.

She felt rather triumphant until she heard the groan of the stairs beneath his feet. With a sigh, Clara walked over to the bed and sat at the edge, crossing her arms and preparing for further chastisement.

Tuck appeared in the doorway a moment later, a candle in hand that lit the room. "Are you out of your mind? Someone broke into the house, and you're going to bed?"

"Well, I'm trying to, but I have a feeling you won't allow that to happen." She stared up at him defiantly.

"You're not sleeping here tonight."

"You're not my father," she retorted. "And even if you were, I wouldn't listen to you. So you may go."

"There's a broken window downstairs. You're a woman alone—"

"And what if I was a man?"

He sighed before rubbing a hand through his hair in frustration. "This isn't me trying to exert my authority over you just because you're a woman. I think you know that by now."

She felt a flicker of satisfaction at his annoyance. "Alright," she conceded. "Then what is it? Clearly, whoever broke in earlier already got what they wanted. I highly doubt they'll return so soon."

"That's not a risk I'm willing to take," he replied. "It's a matter of safety." Clara met his gaze briefly, but there was a flicker of emotion behind his eyes that made her look away.

"What would you have me do in this situation?" she asked, her eyes on the wall behind him. "It's not as if I can call the police—there's no telephone in this house. And I can't imagine Briar Hollow has a police department open at this time of night—"

"They don't."

"Exactly. So, what would you have me do?"

Tuck paused, shifting his stance before he finally responded. "We'll go to the constable tomorrow morning. As for tonight . . . we'll sleep in the cottage."

Clara scanned the room before her, seeing inside Tuck's cottage for the first time. On one end of the room, there was a makeshift kitchen—a small table with four chairs—and on the other end was a bed. Between the two was a small couch, the fabric old and tattered, and a hearth made of white brick.

"Excuse the mess," Tuck said, walking past her to scoop up an item of clothing that lay in a heap on the floor. Considering her experience with men who lived alone, the space wasn't messy, it was more . . . untidy. Mugs sat atop a small counter against the wall, a window that faced the main house inlaid above it. Then there were the stacks of books lined up in the space between the fireplace and the bed, many tattered and missing a front cover.

"Are these all yours?" she asked of the pile that stood ten books tall and five books wide. She titled her head to read the spines of those she could still read, the ones whose prints hadn't been worn off with age and use. *The Murders in the Rue Morgue*, *The Hound of the Baskervilles*, *Strange Case of Dr. Jekyll and Mr. Hyde.*

"Uh, yes," he said from somewhere in the room. "I'm told it's excessive."

Her eyes stopped at *Dracula*. "I don't believe this one is detective fiction?" she asked curiously, picking it up off the pile. She'd heard of it of course but had never read it herself.

"No," Tuck said, coming up behind her. "That one's more horror, I suppose."

"A story about a monster," she said distantly. Her thoughts went to Sadie, to where she was in the moments when she wasn't here, lingering in the shadows of the property. For a moment, Clara wondered if it was lonely.

"Mostly," he said, his posture uncertain, almost bashful as he spoke. "But it's not really about the monster. Dracula is the antagonist, yes, but it's more about the other characters. Their commitment to defeating him. Doing whatever it takes to make things right."

"Hm," she said in acknowledgment, placing the book back on the pile.

"It's interesting that you should pick that one," he said. "I think you'd like it."

She furrowed her brows, wondering if there was an insult in there somewhere, before she asked, “And why is that?”

“In the end, it’s a woman who saves them all.” They locked eyes and she felt her heart skip a beat.

Clara stepped away from him, walking toward the hearth, where a couch was placed in front of it. “And what about the other books? Have you read all of them?” She sat down, the couch lumpy and stiff beneath her.

“Well, yes,” he said, seeming hesitant to make the admission. He turned away from her, kneeling down to light the fire in the hearth. “There’s not much else to do around here.”

“I don’t think it’s a negative,” she said to his back. She watched as he placed the logs, lighting the bark aflame with a match. “I used to read a lot when I was younger. I still do, when I can.” She thought of the novel she’d brought with her, still untouched in her suitcase.

“And what did you read?” he asked, sitting on the cold stone next to the crackling fire.

She thought back to that period of her life. The time during childhood when she’d found solace in the library, a building away from home where she could escape into stories of people outside of herself. Her chest tightened at the memory. “I don’t really remember,” she said with a weak laugh.

Tuck leaned back, his arms wrapped around the tops of his knees as he watched her. “Surely you must remember something you read?”

Clara cleared her throat. “There is one that comes to mind,” she admitted, her heart quickening. “When I was around ten or so, we lived just a street over from a library.” She remembered the feeling of calm between those aisles. “I started going there after school. Just a way to delay going home. And one day I found *Frankenstein*. I don’t know why it drew my attention. Maybe I’d heard the title before and recognized it without even realizing it.”

"Why does it not surprise me that you read Frankenstein at ten years old?"

She shot him a mild glare. "I was mature," she said airily. The truth was, she had been mature for her age, not as some accomplishment on her part, but because she'd needed to be as a means of survival. She wasn't afforded the luxury of carelessness, speaking and acting on a whim, unthinking of potential consequences. She'd learned that early on.

"And did you like it? The book, I mean."

"Yes," she said softly, her mind pulled back to years earlier. "It felt like—" She paused, shifting in her seat, unsure of whether she should go on. But then a moment later, when Tuck didn't intervene, simply leaving space for her to speak, she went on. "I remember thinking how much I was like the monster. Like we were the same." As she said the words, her cheeks heated. "That's foolish, isn't it?"

"I don't think so," Tuck said softly. "Why did you think you were the monster?"

She swallowed. "I suppose it was the way he spoke of his creator. It felt so much like . . . how I felt about my parents. About Al, especially. There was so much anger, so much resentment. And there was one line that I still remember. *I am malicious because I am miserable.* And I thought, is that it? Is that why my father's so angry?"

Tuck didn't speak, yet she couldn't stop herself from continuing.

"You know what's funny about it all? The librarian had seen me coming in and told me I could get a library card. And so, I got a card and took *Frankenstein* home. I had a feeling Al wouldn't be happy with that, so I hid it under my bed. I would read it late at night, after he'd gone to sleep." She paused. "And then one day I came home from school, and he was there on the couch, holding the book in his hands." The memory made her chest tighten even all these years later. "He accused me of stealing it. When I told him it was from the library, he said that no one would lend a book to a little thief like me. He tore it up, right there."

She remembered the look in his eyes, the gleam of satisfaction as she'd cried. The message, even then at ten years old, had been clear: anything you love, I can take from you. Anything you cherish, I can destroy. Perhaps that was when she'd decided it was better not to get too attached to anything.

"I'm sorry," Tuck said quietly.

"Don't be sorry," she said. "He left a couple of years later. And then we were free. Well, I was free, I suppose."

"What do you mean?"

"My mother never really escaped it. Physically, sure. But not in her mind." Clara looked away, sighing. "The funny thing is, him leaving was truly a gift. But my mother didn't see it that way. She loved him until the very end. Even all those years later, she never moved on, never remarried." It was one of the greatest obstacles between them—the way that her mother seemed to mourn the life they'd had, the life where Al had tormented them, had broken them down time and time again.

But she supposed her mother had seen some version of him that Clara had not. She had seen the version of him at the very beginning, when he had wooed her. Perhaps her mother hadn't mourned the version of Al that she'd gotten, but the version she'd been promised. "There was not a day that went by where I couldn't still see him there, clouding her mind, like living with a ghost. And yet, she stopped existing to him the moment he walked out that door."

"What makes you so certain of that?" Tuck's eyes were soft, his expression open.

"When I got here and went into his bedroom, it was full of clutter, as if the man didn't throw anything out, ever. But you know what I didn't find?" She looked at him. "Any hint of my mother or me. Any sign of our existence. Out of all that junk, not a single photograph or letter. Not even her name scribbled down somewhere, like he just needed to get it out. There was nothing. It was as if we'd never existed to him." She stared into the fire, taking a breath before she continued.

"Maybe pretending to forget about her was the only way he could avoid the pain of losing her," Tuck offered.

Clara shook her head. "I think you're giving him too much credit."

"Perhaps." The fire crackled gently before them, and a comfortable silence filled the space between them.

She couldn't help but feel bare, exposed, after all she'd just shared. "So what about your family?" she asked, giving him a small smile. "I assume they're lovely and well-adjusted."

But Tuck didn't look at her, his eyes flickering away.

"I'll tell you about my family another time. It's late." He stood, moving over to the bed to fix the blankets. After he was satisfied, he said, "I'll take the couch."

"No. It's okay. You take the bed. It's your house."

His gaze flattened. "I'm not taking the bed while a lady takes the couch." He walked past her and sat down on the couch next to her, gesturing for her to go ahead.

She stared at him, humor and annoyance coursing through her. "Tuck—"

"Take the bed or I'll be forced to sleep on the floor." He gestured to the stone before the hearth. "And it doesn't look very comfortable."

Hesitantly, Clara walked over to the bed, looking at him there on the couch. She laid down, placing herself beneath the blankets, and somehow sleep took her within a few minutes.

# Chapter 28

The following morning, Clara and Tuck made their way back into the house, looking at the wreckage in the light of day. Books were scattered across the floor, glass was littered beneath the window, and she suddenly noticed something strange in the space where the small frame had been knocked off the wall.

"Tuck?" she called from the doorway before walking over to it to get a better look. "What is this?"

Where the frame had hung, a nail stuck out from the wall. And just beneath it was a small cutout built into the wood, a hook attached to a string disappearing into the wall above.

Tuck came up next to her, his voice uncertain. "I have no idea." He reached for the latch, but she slapped his hand away instinctively.

"Don't pull it if you don't know what it does." Her heart pounded in her chest, a strange feeling moving through her. "What if something bad happens?"

"Like what?"

She blinked at him before looking back to the latch. "I don't know. What if the wall comes down on top of us." She wasn't sure what the purpose of such a lever would be, but for all she knew, the entire house was full of traps she'd simply not uncovered yet.

He gave her a flat look. "Unlikely."

"Fine." Clara walked past him, crossed the room, and stood in the relative safety of the doorframe. "Alright, go ahead," she said from across the room.

"Oh, so I'm the one who gets my hand blown off?" He lifted a brow.

"Precisely."

With a displeased *hmph*, Tuck pulled the latch and the bookcase rattled, a section of the wall coming loose and standing there ajar. After a moment where nothing else happened, they both approached the bookcase, pushing the books off to the side and out of the way.

"I guess I should've been wary of him owning a bookcase," Clara said, peering into the gap of darkness. "He was never one to read."

Tuck stuck his hand in the gap and pulled. A section of the wall opened like a doorway, the few remaining items on the bookcase rattling with its revelation. The morning sun spilled in through the office, but the door stopped, refusing to open any further, the light not reaching the darkened space inside.

"It's a staircase," Clara observed. Her eyes scanned the cramped steps that turned sharply around the wall and disappeared into the darkness above. The steps were tall and wooden, dust collecting on each panel, and a strange, musky scent greeted them.

"I think I read this in a novel once," Tuck said with a hint of intrigue as he looked up into the darkened space.

"One of your infamous detective novels?" He shot her a look, and she fought the smile that tugged at her lips. "You didn't know this was here?" she asked.

"Wasn't something Al advertised, no." He stepped into the space, placing his foot on the first step and testing it. The wood groaned beneath his weight as he took the next step, then the next.

"Be careful," Clara whispered, looking up after him. The last thing she needed was for the whole thing to collapse, the frame eaten away by years of termites or some such creature.

After another few steps, she heard nothing but his breathing.

"Well, where does it lead?" she asked a moment later when the creaking had ceased.

"I don't know," he called back, his voice somewhat muffled. "It's too dark to see anything." She heard the shift of metal sliding against metal. "I'm going to climb through."

"Climb through what?" she asked. The squeal of hinges responded from the top of the passageway, followed by a shuffle and a thump. "Tuck?" she called, leaning in to peer up the steps, still unwilling to take her chances with the stairs.

She squinted through the darkness, confused as to how Tuck had vanished. Had he crawled into a vent? At the top of the stairs was the soft glow of a light, though she couldn't identify where the light was coming from. She heard the creak of the wood panels on the second floor, and she pulled out of the staircase and looked straight above her. She followed the steps she heard, peeking out into the hall.

Tuck appeared at the top of the stairs.

"How did you do that?"

"It leads to the bedroom at the end of the hall," he said, excitement in his eyes.

Confusion ran through her as she walked up the stairs, struggling to understand how that could be possible. Tuck turned and led her down the hall, but she stopped as he disappeared into the bedroom. Her heart began to race as she looked into the room—the place where she'd seen Sadie, had felt the weight of her hand. Clara swallowed.

"There's a false back," he said, bringing her back to the present. As she looked into the room, she saw that the armoire's doors were now wide open. She stepped over the threshold to stand by his side and looked into the dresser. At the back, where a wood panel should be, was now a dark hole revealing the top of the hidden staircase.

"It had a bolt on the other side keeping it closed." He moved around the armoire. "And it's nailed to the floor so it doesn't move."

Her eyes flickered to the same place Mr. Sullivan had brought to her attention days earlier. "Why would someone do that?"

"I'm not entirely sure," Tuck admitted, the excitement starting to fade from his voice. "I assume the stairs were a servant staircase."

"But why close them off just to have them directed to this bedroom?"

"Another exit?" he offered. "Another way to get downstairs if something was blocking the main staircase?"

Al Dawson had never been one for safety. She thought of him keeping access open but hidden. Carving out the back of an armoire, placing a bolt on the other side to secure it shut, installing a latch on the lower level to make sure no one but him knew of its existence.

"If that's the case, then why is the lock on the outside?" Clara asked.

A chill ran through her at the thought of someone staying in this room overnight, unaware of the hidden stairwell that led directly to their room.

After a few more moments of looking around at the space, Clara left, wanting to be away from this room and that staircase. The floors creaked beneath her as she walked down the hall and into her own room, opening the armoire there. She pushed against the back of it, feeling nothing but sturdy wood resisting her.

"It won't lead anywhere." Tuck appeared in the doorway, and she nearly jumped at his voice. "There isn't enough space between this room and the one next to it. And besides," he said, walking over to the side of the armoire, "you can see the gap between the wall and the wood."

Her cheeks heated as she followed him, seeing that the armoire stood away from the wall. "Oh. Well, either way, I've never felt more inclined to go to the police." She walked out of the room and down the front staircase. As much as she found the whole discovery unsettling, it only added to the validity of everything she'd found.

It was further proof that something strange had happened in this house, and that Al had been at the helm.

"Clara?" Tuck called from behind her as she reached the bottom of the stairs.

She stepped into her shoes left by the door. "Don't fret, you'll be coming with me. I haven't a clue of how to find—"

"Clara."

She looked up at him, to where he stood halfway down the stairs, his voice firm. "You can't tell the constable about the staircase."

She blinked. "I beg your pardon?"

He carried on down the steps, something unsettling in his demeanor. "I need you to keep this a secret."

Confusion and agitation flared within her. "And why would I do that?"

He sighed. "I can't tell you why. But take my word that it's in everyone's best interest."

She felt as if she'd been slapped. After everything she had shared, all the ways in which she had bared herself to him emotionally, given him enough to judge her and question her sanity, here he was still keeping secrets.

"I'm not pretending we never found this," she said. "In case you've forgotten, a young woman died—was likely murdered in this house. The police need to know about this." Clara never thought she'd be defending her desire to speak to the police, but here she was, desperate for some kind of help in all of this.

Tuck stared at her, stepping forward, his voice softer, almost pleading. "I need you to trust me on this. Please."

She wanted to push back, to refuse to do as he asked, but something in his demeanor told her this was something serious.

"Fine," she said, her voice weakened. "But just know that if you had something to do with these disappearances, I would stop at nothing to see you held accountable." With that, she stepped out onto the porch, her mind swirling with questions about what Tuck was hiding.

Tuck drove them to the constable's house in silence. They were greeted at the Davis's front door by his wife, who told them he was out at the moment but she would gladly send him over once he returned home. Clara couldn't help but feel uneasy at the whole thing, at the way crime in Briar Hollow was viewed with such a lack of urgency. But she wanted help and knew this might be her only chance to speak to someone from law enforcement, so they thanked the woman and drove back.

It wasn't until an hour later that Constable Davis arrived at the front door.

"If it isn't the youngest Tucker," the man said as she stepped inside, clapping a hand on Tuck's shoulder. "How's your old man?"

"He's doing well, sir."

"Glad to hear it. So, I hear there's been a break-in?"

"Yes," Clara said. "Just through here." She led the constable into the office, her eyes lingering on the bookcase, which was now closed, and the latch now covered with the small frame. "Be careful, there's glass. I didn't want to sweep it away in case—well, I don't know. I suppose evidence?"

"Not a problem," he said. He walked through the room, avoiding the chaos of the books and broken glass. "Was anyone home when this happened?"

"No," Clara said. "We got back around nine or so, and we found the room like this." She flicked a glance at Tuck who stood in the doorway, leaning against the frame.

"Anything stolen?"

Clara nodded. "I had some things on the desk here. It was a locket and a scarf. There was also a journal—"

"Can't imagine why someone would steal a woman's journal," Constable Davis cut in.

She frowned. "Well, it wasn't my journal. It was my father's."

"Why don't we just stick to the items of value? Anything valuable taken?"

Clara shifted on her feet, discomfort coiling tight within her gut. "The locket. And the scarf seemed rather . . . sturdy material. But I don't think they came for something to resell elsewhere. They left everything else in the house. What reason would someone have to break in and then leave behind everything that could be sold?"

Constable Davis took a slow exhale. "Anyone mad at you for anything? Any altercations lately?"

"No. I've only been here a few days."

"Well, my best guess is it was nothing more than a few kids."

She blinked. "Kids? You think . . . kids did this?"

The constable nodded. "Bored on a Saturday night. Decided to go down to the spooky house in the trees, far away from everyone. I don't mean to upset you, Miss Dawson, but as you know, there was a death here. That tends to bring out curious kids, telling ghost stories, that sort of thing."

"What do ghost stories have to do with breaking into someone's house?" She felt her anger rising.

"They were probably playing around. Daring each other to go up the steps and touch the front door. The game escalated, and they wanted to see who was the bravest in the group. You know how boys are."

There was such confidence in his words, in his theory. It was as if, as the very words left his mouth, he'd already believed them. As if he'd been here, watched it all unfold.

Frustration churned in her stomach. She desperately wanted to tell him the truth of everything, to tell him about Sadie, about the disappearances, about the staircase they'd just found, and the way all of this was so clearly connected. But even if she could, even if she had the evidence before her, if Tuck had allowed her to show him the staircase, would that change anything?

"What do you recommend I do then?" she asked.

"Nothing to do," he said. "They didn't steal anything of value—you said it yourself. They didn't damage anything. Well, aside from the window here. But even if you could track down the kids who did it, you wouldn't be likely to get more than a poor excuse for an apology."

"And what if I think it's something more?" she asked. He furrowed his brow. "Ever since getting here, I've had a series of break-ins. There's never been damage though. I assumed whoever was doing it must've had a key."

"And you didn't report this?" Constable Davis asked.

She blinked, suddenly feeling as if she was the one doing something wrong. "Well, as you said, nothing was stolen. Nothing was damaged either," she said, pointedly looking at the broken window. "I can't help but wonder if there's a reason for it."

Constable Davis glanced at Tuck, then back at her. "How do you mean?"

She took a deep breath before going on. "I've found some concerning things in my father's belongings, or rather, that seemed to belong to some missing young women. And it just so happens that those were the items taken last night."

"And what missing young women are you referring to?"

She swallowed, her mind going back to last night, to seeing Hazel. She supposed she was no longer a missing person, even if her behavior unsettled Clara. "Charlotte Mason and Sadie Collins. They each—"

"I don't need to be educated on the cases, Miss Dawson. I was on the force for both of them." Agitation coursed through his voice, and he sighed. "Listen, I understand you've been staying here alone, and

I'm sure that's frightened you. Hell, my wife wouldn't last three days sleeping here alone." He laughed and looked at Tuck to agree, but Tuck's face remained neutral, unreadable. "It's unsettling, I'm sure. But letting your mind wander does nobody any good."

"I'm afraid I don't understand."

"You wouldn't be the first to get carried away, thinking there's some big scheme going on with all these missing girls. But the simplest explanation is often the truest. Kids run away. They leave. Especially young women who've spent their entire life under their daddy's thumb, following the rules. There's never been evidence that any foul play was involved in either case you mentioned. I assure you, we've looked into it."

She glanced at Tuck, whose eyes were firmly on the floor now. She could argue, try to make the constable understand, try to explain everything she'd seen. But what were the odds that she, the one who was new in town, only visiting for a few days, would be the one to change this man's mind on anything? The more likely concern was that she'd be viewed as unstable, having a constable recommend she be put in a mental health institute.

"My suggestion," Constable Davis started, walking toward the front door. "Make the place look lived in, especially when you leave the house. Fix the window, install some lights on the outside of the house." He opened the door, turning to them briefly. "I'll write the report if you really want me to, but I don't see this being a problem again."

She gave him a polite smile. "Thank you, Constable. I'll do that." Clearly if she wanted answers, the police would be of no use to her. She supposed she should've known as much after her encounter with Eddie. After all, Nellie had told her that he and the constable were related.

"We appreciate it, sir," Tuck said, shaking the man's hand before they said their goodbyes.

It wasn't until Tuck closed the door behind the officer that Clara spoke. "Well, that was a waste of time." She walked over to the door and peeked through the curtains, waiting for him to leave.

Tuck sighed. "I told you, it's not like Rochester. The police here aren't equipped to deal with any real crime."

She watched as the man stepped into his vehicle, the engine revving to life.

"Aren't equipped or aren't interested?"

"Both, I suppose."

As the constable disappeared from view, Clara walked through to the living room and grabbed her jacket off the couch. She slipped her arms through the sleeves and wrapped it around herself.

"Thank you for not telling him about the staircase."

"No need to thank me," she said, looking up at him. "I'll find out the truth one way or another." She walked over to the front door and stepped into her shoes.

"Where are you going?" he asked.

"Don't worry," she said, pulling her dark hair free from her jacket, "I'll be back soon enough."

# Chapter 29

The wind rocked against Clara's vehicle as she drove down the country road toward Main Street. The constable had been of no use, she knew Tuck wouldn't share anything more with her, and she couldn't help but feel that Randy was the one who'd broken into the inn last night, which meant that he wasn't someone she wanted to return to with questions. There was, however, one person who had insight into Hollowfield House that she hadn't truly spoken with yet. Evelyn.

After a quick stop at the market to get the address from Nellie, Clara was back in her vehicle and driving toward Evelyn's house. As she reached the end of Main Street and turned left at the old church, Clara noticed the graveyard that lay just behind it. Morning fog still clung to the grounds even though it was nearly 11 a.m., and she found herself wondering if, somewhere within that black iron fence, Al lay inside, deep within the ground beneath.

Evelyn's house was only a minute's drive from the graveyard, one of the many small white homes that sat side-by-side with little more than a few feet of grass separating them. Nerves coursed through Clara as she walked up the pathway, unsure of how the woman would respond to a near-stranger asking her all kinds of questions about what she'd seen while working at the inn, and whether she thought a crime had taken place.

Clara raised her hand and knocked on the front door. She stood there for a minute, hearing the distant yells of children playing outside of one of the other houses, just out of view.

The door opened, though it wasn't Evelyn looking back at her but a small elderly woman. In fact, it was the very same woman she'd seen at the grocery store.

"Oh," the woman said, looking rather disappointed. "You're not Evie."

"Uh, no, I'm not," Clara said with a flustered smile. "I'm here to speak to Evelyn."

"She's not here at the moment. She went to drop by a friend's house. Said she'd be back in time to take me to church." There was an accusation in her tone, and Clara wasn't sure if it was directed at her or Evelyn. "You know, in my day, you weren't late for church. It was a matter of respect. You went every Sunday and you wore your best attire. None of these pants for women and all that racket. A lady dressed respectfully." The old woman eyed her up and down, clearly not impressed by what she saw, and Clara felt her cheeks flush.

"Right. Well, do you happen to know if she'll be back soon?"

The woman blanched. "You don't know what time church starts?" She narrowed her eyes. "Are you the new girl? The Denson girl?"

"Dawson," Clara supplied. "You know what, maybe I should just leave her a note. Do you have paper and a pen I could borrow?" She glanced behind the woman into the entryway of the small house.

The woman hesitated a moment before turning and sifting through something out of sight. Clara heard the woman muttering softly, "Always wanting to read and write, these girls." She passed a scrap of paper and a pen to her. "Make it brief, dear. She won't have time to read a novel when she gets back. We need to get to church. In my day, you simply weren't late for church."

Clara fought the urge to tell her she'd already said as much but instead scribbled a note and handed it back to the woman. "Thank you."

"We'll see you at church, dear."

Clara looked back, but the woman was already shutting the door.

As she rounded the corner, heading back toward Main Street, she noticed the church and the cemetery again. Suddenly, she wanted to see Al's grave. To sense the finality of it. She pulled off the road and into the small white church's dirt lot, passing by a group of four people who stood by the front, donned in their Sunday best. The motorcar crept around the side of the building until the cemetery came into view, and she parked in the empty backlot. Her chest clenched as she looked out over the headstones, debating if she really wanted to do this—if she wanted to see Al's headstone for herself.

She stepped out into the cool, damp mist that clung to the air. From where she stood at the edge of the lot, the cemetery appeared to be empty of anyone but her. Green grass squelched beneath her shoes as she walked over to the entrance, and a squeak cut through the silence as she opened the short wrought-iron gate.

Headstones littered the field, so different from the neat rows of other cemeteries she'd visited throughout her life. This one seemed to have no rhyme or reason, simply fitting in a lot where there was space, each tombstone a different size and shape from the last. Her eyes scanned over names she didn't recognize, people of all ages who had passed, from the young to the old, death making equals of them all.

As she reached the far end of the cemetery, the headstones grew smaller in size—less intricate—some made of wood rather than stone. Crows called from the trees nearby, protesting her presence. This side of the graveyard was lined by trees and blanketed by the leaves that had fallen from their branches. She waded through them, crunching beneath her feet, and realized that many of the plots at this end weren't maintained the way the ones near the church had been. She wondered what factors determined who ended up here at the neglected end. Was it simply those without close family? Those without money to pay for the luxury of having one's final resting place cared for? Those who hadn't committed their Sundays to worship in church, repenting from the wooden pews under the eye of God?

And there, at the end of the line, sitting amongst the dead leaves and blanketed in autumn gloom, was the burial site for Al Dawson. There were no kind words engraved into the wooden plaque, simply his name, his date of birth, and his date of death: September 1933.

It was real. He was well and truly dead.

She had known it—been told as much by many people at this point—but there had been no internal confirmation. There had been no part of her, still connected to Al through some parent-child bond, that had felt any different from one moment to the next, from before his passing to after. She supposed that was the nature of relationships that died while both people were living. Maybe there had been no paternal bond to begin with. Maybe Al had laid eyes on her as an infant, fresh into the world, and saw her as no more than an unwanted burden he was forced to provide for.

She looked down upon the grave and felt . . . nothing. Even here, the confirmation clear before her, she did not mourn for the man who robbed her of the person she could have been. Did not mourn for the man who ensured she did not live a day or night without fear, without feeling as if everything could crumble beneath her at any moment. Perhaps a better person would have felt something—a kinder person with more compassion than she was capable of feeling—but she felt no more for this man, maybe even less for him, than she would an unknown name marking any of these graves.

She thought of each person who had heard a sliver of her story—knowing nothing of Al, of his character, of the way he moved through life—and told her, 'But he's your father. Think of the regret you'll have when he dies one day.' And as she looked down at the grass, the decaying leaves, the wooden plaque, she felt no regret. If anything, she felt thankful that he had died so soon. His death had closed off that lingering worry in the back of her mind—the strange, irrational fear that somehow he may still try to come back, find her, and demand something from her. Now she knew she was free.

On her way back through the graveyard, her shoes damp from the moisture that clung to the grass, Clara noticed someone standing at her vehicle. The fog made it difficult to make out her features, casting a thin veil over the woman until Clara got close enough to see it was someone she didn't know. The woman was tall, her blonde hair was perfectly waved, falling to her chin, and her face was beautiful, but her expression was pinched. She wore a wool knee-length wool jacket that was belted at the waist and held a black handbag tightly in her gloved hands.

As Clara stepped through the gate and took the final steps toward her car, the woman finally looked up at her asking, "Do I know you?"

Confusion and agitation swirled through Clara. "I don't believe so, but you're standing in front of my car." The woman didn't move, staring at Clara, an emotion behind her brown eyes that made Clara feel unsettled.

"How do you know James?"

It took a moment for Clara to realize who the woman was referring to, for she had really only known him as Mr. Baker. "He's my lawyer," she said, recognizing the confusion in her voice.

The woman took a deep breath, her expression remaining unsatisfied. "He's married, you know."

Clara blinked, trying to piece together what on earth this woman was talking about. And then, realization sunk in. She looked to be somewhere in her mid-thirties, and a glance at the diamond on her left hand confirmed Clara's suspicion.

"Are you his wife?"

The beautiful blonde only stared, her mouth pinched, before she said, "I saw you." Each word seemed measured, as though she needed to be careful with what she said next, what she revealed. "In front of the library."

Clara combed through her memory that day at the library—it seemed like it had been so long ago now. The way she'd broken down right there on the sidewalk, unable to hold herself together. She remembered the warmth of Mr. Baker's hand on her back, trying to comfort her.

The woman—likely Mrs. Baker—looked over her shoulder toward the church. From here, Clara could hear the rumble of engines as they began to fill the small parking lot.

"I know he was with you last night," the woman said, turning back to Clara. "That he went to the city to meet you."

"Well, yes, I did meet Mr. Baker last night. But we weren't alone. He was introducing—"

"Don't bother making excuses," the woman said. "I'm only here to warn you. I know what you must think. That he cares for you, that you're special to him, but you're not. You're just the same as every other girl, and soon enough, he will leave you heartbroken. He always does." Her voice was cold, but Clara could see a glimmer of tears pooling in her eyes.

A moment later, the woman turned and walked across the dirt lot toward the church. Clara watched after her, wondering if the woman had followed her here or if she had simply recognized her as she pulled into the church parking lot. She thought about Hazel, about the things she'd said, repeating much the same sentiments.

As Clara watched the woman turn the corner of the church, she couldn't help but wonder if this was the first time Mrs. Baker had felt the need to intervene, to approach someone she thought might be seeing her husband. *I'm only here to warn you*, she'd said. But was the warning that Mr. Baker—if Clara had really been having an affair with him—would break her heart? Or was this simply a warning before Mrs. Baker took action of her own?

# Chapter 30

The soft grey sky had darkened as Clara pulled into the driveway of Hollowfield House. The wind picked up, tossing the slim tree branches back and forth, rattling the leaves that clung to them. A storm was coming—she could feel it—and she hoped it'd sweep through quickly, leaving by tomorrow afternoon when she was set to return to Rochester. The last thing she needed was to navigate these roads during a downpour.

As she rounded the bend of trees, she found a motorcar there before the house and Tuck loading something into the vehicle. Clara parked next to him and stepped out, the wild wind tossing her hair all around her.

"Where'd you get the motorcar from?" she asked, meeting Tuck's eyes as he shut the trunk.

He stepped around the vehicle. "A friend in town loaned it to me for a few days." She furrowed her brow, fear creeping in. "I received a telegram. My father—he's . . . I need to go see him."

"Oh." She tensed, unsure of what to say or how to comfort him. She didn't know much about Tuck's relationship with his father, but she assumed it wasn't like the one she'd had with Al. "I hope he's alright."

His face was grim as he spoke. "He lives in a care facility a couple of hours away." Clara felt a spasm of guilt in her stomach. She thought back to all the times she'd spoken poorly of her father in front of Tuck, and yet his own father had been unwell this entire time, in a care facility, and he'd never brought it up. She couldn't help but wonder if he'd resented her in those moments. "I'm not sure when I'll be back," he said, meeting her gaze. "It could be tomorrow, or it could be a few days."

And she was leaving tomorrow. So this was to be their goodbye. With the chaos of Al's office and bedroom cleared out, she had no reason to stay regardless of what choice she made tomorrow. She couldn't even if she wanted to—she needed to go back to work, to make up financially for the last several days. The realization sent a pang of anxiety through her at the thought of that decision tomorrow. She'd been so consumed by Sadie, by trying to figure out what had happened with Charlotte, and even Hazel, she hadn't realized that time had nearly run out.

Thunder grumbled nearby, the sudden violence of the sound making her flinch. She looked up at the darkening sky, the smell of rain heavy in the air. She fought the disappointment simmering within her—it was foolish, really. She knew she'd never live in Briar Hollow. She knew it would do her no good to let herself grow attached to someone here. And yet she felt it, embedded deep into her chest, like an invisible string connecting them. She didn't want to say goodbye, and she couldn't help but resent herself for the feeling.

Clara swallowed, pushing aside the unwelcome emotion that spread through her as she said, "I hope everything goes well for you." She looked at Tuck, trying to read the glint of emotion behind his gaze.

"I don't feel right about leaving," Tuck said, looking past her at the house. "With everything going on—"

"I'll be fine," Clara cut in, "if that's what you're worried about." She gave him a small smile, a sign of encouragement that felt artificial. "I'm used to being on my own." She'd meant it as a positive, yet his eyes snapped to hers at the statement and he didn't seem comforted.

"You could come with me."

Clara stilled at the words, looking for some sign of humor. She found nothing but sincerity looking back. A lump formed in her throat at the offer, but she knew she couldn't go with him. She didn't belong in Briar Hollow, and going with him, letting this attachment continue, would only muddy things further.

The sky opened up and rain fell down around them, bringing her back to reality. She took a step back, then another. "Go," she shouted through the sound of rain, forcing a smile to her face. "Make sure everything's okay with your father." He stared at her, unmoving, as if he didn't feel the water dampening his clothing, his hair. She swallowed before forcing out the words. "Hollowfield House will still be here when you get back." Then she turned and ran up the front steps and under the covered porch.

"Clara."

She looked back at where he still stood next to the car, his shirt clinging to his skin. "Sleep in the cottage tonight."

For a moment, she felt the familiar pattern take shape within her, the desire to be stubborn and petulant, to make some remark. But as she met his gaze through the rain, she found herself only nodding, saying nothing at all as her gut twisted.

With that, Clara opened the front door and disappeared into the house.

There was no sunset that evening. The clouds and rain blocked out the light of the sun as it moved through the sky. A feeling of unease began to sink into Clara, and she fluttered through the house, sweeping the dust into the garbage, finding ways to stay busy. But as she cleaned, her mind wandered back to the staircase they'd uncovered—to the secrecy of it.

She couldn't help but think back to her conversation with Randy, the way he'd been convinced that Al had hidden a stash of money somewhere in this house . . . If that money existed, a hidden staircase seemed like the likeliest place for it. She moved through the first floor, lighting the sconces on the walls on her way to the office. She slowed as she reached the doorway, feeling the cold night air as it blew in through the broken window. Tuck had haphazardly nailed a thin wooden board across it, but the breeze still spilled in through the cracks at the edges.

Outside, the sky had darkened to deep charcoal, and she crossed the room quickly, taking advantage of the faded natural light, a candle in her hand the only other thing lighting her path. Tuck had pushed the bookshelf back in place before the constable arrived, and she walked over to the latch, pulling it hesitantly, and nearly jumping at the sound of the wall coming loose.

She set her candle on the desk and slipped her fingers into the opening, pulling it open. It was heavier than she'd expected, and the flame of her candle flickered from the breeze as it opened, revealing nothing more than shadow inside. Her heart began to pound, that same instinct from childhood kicking in—the fear of the dark, of what might be watching from the shadows. She fetched her candle and brought it closer, inspecting each step for some latch or lever that might reveal another hidden compartment.

She walked up the steps, her heart stopping for a moment as her toe caught on the edge of a step in the dim lighting. She took a deep breath and carried on, reaching the second floor and holding the candle out to make sense of the backside of the enclosure—the last bedroom at the end of the hall just on the other side. She slid her hand across the wood plank, across the walls around her, as her eyes squinted through the dim light of the candle.

Frustration built in her chest as she took a step down, trying to understand what she was missing. There was something here—there had to be something here—she was almost certain of it. Randy had seemed so sure, yet it was Tuck's reaction that made her suspicious. He had refused to talk about it, not wanting the constable to know about the staircase. There was something here, whether cash or something more nefarious.

Clara took a step down—one hand on the candle, one flat on the wall next to her—and she felt her candle tumble from its holder. Her heart stopped as she waited for the flame to catch on the fabric of her dress, to burn as it touched her skin, but the fall extinguished the flame, casting her in darkness. She was left holding the stone stem as the hardened wax end tumbled down the steps. She swore under her breath, a chill of fear tingling between her shoulder blades.

The small space was silent save for the sound of her breathing as she grabbed onto the stair in front of her, then blindly stretched her foot out to reach a step below. The wood groaned softly beneath her foot and she slowly climbed down the staircase, feeling her way in the dark. It wasn't until she'd reached the bottom step, hand outstretched and holding onto the lip of the stair above, that she noticed why she'd tripped on that step. The wood on that stair stuck out further than any of the others.

Clara froze, excitement and terror coursing through her. She slowly slid her hands further along that same step: above it, then below. She felt along the wood, felt the grooves beneath her fingertips and then . . . something else. It was small—smaller than the latch at the top of the stairs, the one that had led into the bedroom—and was tucked right under the lip of the step. It stuck as she tried to slide it, and the iron dug into her skin as she used all of the force of her thumb and index finger, determined to get it open.

She ignored the pain at her fingertips, readjusting her grip on the small latch until, finally, it squeaked open with a loud protest. She pushed up against the step and felt it move, lifting open like a toy chest. Her heart pounded furiously in her chest, afraid of what she might find in this hidden space. What if Sadie's body was here all along? What if that's why she was trapped in this house, tethered to this property?

But it wasn't the stench of decay that washed over her as she opened the top of the stair, it was the burn of alcohol. She looked down into the pitch black, trying to make her eyes adjust, to see some shape within the darkness, but she saw nothing.

Clara pushed herself away from the staircase and fumbled through the dark office toward the hallway. She went into the kitchen and grabbed the lamp sitting on the table there, taking it with her back through the hidden passageway. The wood dug into her skin uncomfortably as she kneeled on the step, shining her light down into the compartment, illuminating rows and rows of jars filled with a clear liquid. She reached down into the space, the damp air burning her nostrils, and lifted one of the jars to eye level.

Everything made sense now—why Al had decided to settle down and run an inn, isolated, away from the city. He hadn't been living a simple life, running an honest business—he had been running hooch. She'd heard of people like this—storing moonshine, hiding it from Prohibition officers, helping transport the stuff across the country to take a cut of the profit. The inn had been a front for bootlegging.

It made so much sense she nearly started laughing. As she looked down at the space that appeared nearly two feet deep, she wondered if Randy was one of those smugglers as well. If he had been looking for the recent stash Al had been holding. As she placed the jar back in its spot, she wondered about the cash. She understood now why Randy was so certain Al had stored his money at the house—he certainly wouldn't bring smuggling money to a bank.

Clara placed the candle on a lower step and leaned down into the space, but she couldn't see anything but shadow. She pulled herself out, looking at the candle but feeling too nervous to risk sticking a flame into a tight space filled with alcohol. She wondered if this was the opening of a crawlspace beneath the house—if she'd be able to see it easier in the daylight.

She sat back on her heels, staring at the shadowy compartment. If Randy had been the one to break in last night, he hadn't seemed to find the staircase. Yet, he must've known about the bootlegging, had to have been involved if he thought some large amount of cash was owed to him but hidden in the house. Unless Al was the only one who knew about this compartment. Clara thought back to Tuck's reaction to the space, the curiosity that came off him as he climbed the steps. Had he truly been that good of an actor? Or had he been left in the dark as well?

But Tuck hadn't wanted her to tell the constable about the staircase, which had to mean he'd known what it was used for. That he'd known what the constable would find inside. Betrayal twisted like a knife in her gut. What else did Tuck know about Al's actions? What else had he kept from her? What else had he been involved in?

A series of knocks came in quick succession from the front of the house and Clara jumped, looking through the office and toward the hallway. She closed the hidden compartment, sliding the latch in place, and quickly moved from the stairs, taking her candle with her. She considered closing the bookcase, but it had been so heavy and the knocks came again, an urgency in their cadence.

Her thoughts went to Tuck. Maybe he'd returned. Maybe everything was fine with his father and he was back. But the thought of his return now made her feel nauseous. What if he somehow knew she'd found the very thing he was trying to keep secret? What if he would be angry with her? But it couldn't be Tuck. He couldn't have gone to his father's and back that quickly.

Her heart beat furiously in her chest as she stepped out of the darkness of the office and walked out into the hall.

# Chapter 31

As Clara approached the front door, she saw the silhouette of a woman turned away from the house, looking toward the trees. Clara opened the door and a gust of wind swept in, carrying the scent of rain as it tapped overhead on the porch's roof.

"Evelyn, come in—"

"I can't stay," Evelyn cut in, her arms folded tightly across her chest. She looked over her shoulder, out into the night behind her. Clara's eyes followed, scanning the shadowed treeline for some sign of movement but saw nothing but the gentle sway of leaves still holding tight to their branches.

"Is someone with you?" Clara asked, that gloom of paranoia clinging onto her now, too.

"No. No one can know I came here," Evelyn said, turning back toward Clara. Her voice dropped, a hushed tone but firm. "I got your note. I need to tell you something, but you can't let anyone know it was me who told you where to look. I can't be involved in any of this."

"Any of what?" Clara asked, lowering her voice as well.

Evelyn looked past Clara into the house. "No one's with you, right?"

"No, it's just me. Are you sure you don't—"

"I'm sure." Evelyn took a deep breath, tucking a strand of hair behind her ear and avoiding eye contact. She lowered her voice. "A little over a year ago, sometime in the summer, I pulled into my driveway and this girl came in behind me. She asked me if I worked at the inn, and I told her that was none of her business. I had no idea who the girl was until she gave me her name. Said she was looking into the disappearance of her friend Charlotte and that her name was Sadie Collins."

Clara felt a chill up her spine.

"I told her I didn't know a Charlotte and started walking into my house, but she said she disappeared from Hollowfield House in the fall of 1929. Told me that she knew I was working there at the time, and she just wanted to know if I'd seen anything."

"Had you?" Clara couldn't help but ask.

"No. I'd never seen a young girl here. Never seen anyone but men most of the time. But I only came to the inn once every two weeks and always during the day, so I have no clue who visited here outside of that."

Clara thought of the moonshine beneath the hidden stairs and wondered if Evelyn knew about that. If, during her time working here, she'd managed to come across things she shouldn't have, perhaps even getting involved for a cut of the money. But it didn't seem the time to ask, not when she had more information about Sadie.

Evelyn pulled her arms in tighter, bracing herself against the cold, damp air. "She told me more about the girl, Charlotte, but I told her I couldn't help her and that was that. After that, I started hearing talk around town that this Sadie girl was looking into the disappearance of a local girl. She was causing all kinds of scandal. Going around town, asking questions, interviewing people. There was even an article in the newspaper about it."

Clara recalled the article she'd found at the library—the one with that picture of Charlotte and Sadie side by side, looking so young. She imagined the whole town whispering about the matter, about this girl who couldn't let go of her friend's disappearance, even after it was determined she had run away. Eddie's words came back to her. *Unnatural interests.* If Eddie's view of Sadie was any indication of what the constable thought, then that article couldn't have gone over well with law enforcement.

A snap sounded from off in the distance and they both looked toward the noise. Clara imagined someone watching them from those woods, straining to hear their hushed tones through the rain.

Evelyn looked nauseous with fear as she turned back around. She spoke more quickly now, and Clara had to pay close attention to make out each word. "Sadie came back a few months later. She appeared one day and told me that she knew I didn't want to be involved, but she had nowhere else to go. Said her parents didn't believe her and that the police were no help. Told me that someone had broken into her house, but she had no proof other than some of her things were moved around and missing."

A chill ran up Clara's spine at the thought of the break-in last night. She'd kept going back to Randy as the likely culprit, but the one thing that didn't make sense was the fact that nothing had been taken aside from those items on the desk.

"She just seemed so . . . afraid. She was young, still. Couldn't be more than a year or two out of high school. She said she just needed me to hold on to something for a few days—to keep it safe while she figured a few things out."

"What did she need you to hold onto?"

"It was a box, like a shoebox. She said I could open it if I wanted to, but I told her I wouldn't. I didn't want to be involved, but she begged me. She said that girl, Charlotte, was like a sister to her. Asked me if I had a sister, and what I would be willing to do if my sister had been hurt by somebody and everyone looked the other way." Evelyn sighed, seeming to be pulled back into the memory, reliving it in her mind. "So I took it. I glanced in the box to make sure there wasn't a bomb or something inside, but it was only a bunch of notes and letters."

"What did they say?" Clara asked.

"I don't know. I never read them. I told her, I didn't want to be involved in this. But then she never came back."

Clara's blood ran cold. "When was this?"

"Last September. A few days passed, and I was a bit annoyed at the whole thing, wondering when she'd come back and take the damn box back. But then people started talking in town, some saying the girl had run away, some saying she had killed herself."

"Did—did they find her body?"

Evelyn shook her head. "I don't think so. At least, I never saw evidence that they did. It was just rumors. But she never came back. I never saw her again. I asked around a bit, but no one knew where she'd gone. Nothing concrete, anyway. And then I couldn't help but feel like maybe she wasn't so crazy after all, thinking that someone was after her." Evelyn took a deep breath. "I think they got her in the end."

"Did you tell the police?"

"Of course not. She said herself the police didn't believe her. For all I know, the police were the ones who did it."

Clara thought of Constable Davis, of Eddie. For the first time, she wondered if it hadn't been Randy who'd broken in, but Eddie. She thought back to their interaction, the way he so clearly wanted her intimidated. What if Constable Davis had been closer to target than she'd thought? What if it hadn't been a local teenager but Eddie trying to frighten her?

"Did you ever go through the box?" Clara asked.

Evelyn's eyes went wide. "No. I couldn't. My grandmother needs me. I can't be wrapped up in some murder case with girls going missing."

"So where is it now, then?"

"Upstairs."

"It's here? In the house?"

Evelyn nodded. “If someone was willing to kill for it, I didn’t want to keep it at my house. So, one of the days I came to clean, I hid it under the floorboards in one of the bedrooms upstairs.”

“Which one?”

“The last one at the end of the hall.”

“Can you show it to me?”

Evelyn took a step back. “I’ve taken a risk just by coming here. I can’t get pulled into this. That’s everything you need to know—that’s everything I know.” Evelyn looked over her shoulder again, glancing behind her into the darkness of the trees. “Please, just, don’t tell anyone I was here.”

Before Clara could say anything else, Evelyn turned and ran down the porch steps, running through the rain and getting into her car, a shadow against the dark night. It took her seconds to start the engine and peel out of the lot, disappearing into the night.

# Chapter 32

The wood creaked beneath Clara's feet as she made her way up the staircase, the candle in her hand the only light shining upon the second floor as she reached the top step. Rain tapped against the shingles on the roof above, competing with the sound of Clara's heartbeat loud in her ears. She looked down the shadowed hallway, the light from the candle only touching the few feet before her.

As she lifted her foot to take a hesitant step, it was as if a veil had been pulled back and she was seeing another night, another moment in time. The wall sconces were lit down the hallway, and a familiar woodsy scent overwhelmed her. Clara blinked and the vision was gone, replaced by the dark hallway where she stood, alone. Like the dream she'd had that night in her car, it was as if she were seeing a memory that didn't entirely belong to her. As if she were following in the footsteps of someone else, in some moment from the past.

Clara froze, afraid to take another step. Her stomach churned.

"Sadie?" Clara's voice was barely a whisper.

She waited, but there was no response.

With a deep breath and a heart that felt as if it might break free from her chest, she took another step, and then another. The wood that groaned beneath her sounded too loud in the quiet. Her skin prickled, the hairs on the back of her neck standing up.

She could feel something here. Someone.

She reached the doorway, the light of her oil lamp casting a glow upon the room. She saw herself reflected in the window, but beyond, the night outside was black. As she crossed over the threshold, she heard the faint murmur of words, muffled, as if they were being spoken through a wall.

*Just to give us some privacy.*

Clara jumped, looking over her shoulder for the owner of the voice, but as she turned in a circle with her light held out, she saw that no one was there. The voice had been deep, a man's voice, but as she tried to replay it in her head, she couldn't place it. Her hands shook, the flame of the candle wobbling, and she put it down on the side table next to the bed.

It was Sadie.

Clara could feel it in her bones. Sadie was showing her something. Trying to help her see. Everything in Clara's body told her to run, to get out of this house. To get to the safety of the cottage where she could flip the lock and pretend she hadn't experienced any of this. But she had come too far. She needed to know. Somebody needed to know.

How many people had looked the other way? Had decided that what had happened to those girls wasn't their problem? It had become more than just validating her own sanity. About more than whether or not her father had been a murderer—another piece of evidence to prove that he was the villain, that *he* was the monster, not she. About more than just confirming she wasn't the one to blame for the way he'd treated her.

If it weren't for those experiences that made her question her own sanity, would she have even bothered? If it hadn't become personal, would she have cared enough to keep looking? She knew the answer to that. Could feel its claws digging into her. The sharp sting of a truth she'd spent her life trying to avoid. Could see her own fears and instincts mirrored in Evelyn's inaction.

A monster could only exist in the shadows, and she'd spent her life avoiding shadows at all costs, unwilling to shine a light on them, unwilling to even look. She had spent too long pretending not to see what was right in front of her. She'd spent too long resenting her mother for doing the same, for making excuses for her father's behavior, unwilling to accept that she'd let him in and let him stay, day after day.

Clara knelt down on her hands and knees and looked between the slim gaps in the floorboards, lifting her candle from where it sat on the nightstand, using it to illuminate the floor beneath her. It took only a few minutes for her to find it, a small gap just a bit wider than the others. She placed the candle on the floor next to her and dug her nails into the small gap, prying the board up.

It lifted slightly before falling back into place. Her heart pounded in her chest, drawn on by the fact that the board existed, that just beneath this board could lay the answers she'd been looking for. Her fingers hurt as she dug her nails into the crack of the board again, lifting upward and getting some leverage. She grunted in frustration as it finally lifted just enough so she could slide her fingers beneath it and pull it out of place.

She lifted the board and looked down into the narrow gap beneath the floor. A shoebox was turned on its side, just as Evelyn had said. Clara stared down at it, breathing hard either from the exertion of trying to pry up the board or the knowledge that what lay inside that box, the information that Sadie had gathered, had been worth killing for.

She reached down with both hands and carefully lifted it out of its spot, placing it on the floor between her and the candle so she could see inside. She ignored the pain of the wood digging into her knees, shifting to sit cross-legged before she opened the lid.

Through the quiet came a sound from downstairs—music. The gramophone began to play, its melody spreading through the house, loud enough for Clara to hear it clearly from up here. It was the same disc she and Tuck had danced to a few nights earlier, and she felt a pinch in her chest. Clara glanced up, looking toward the open doorway, the darkened hallway. Was Sadie encouraging her? Telling her to carry on?

She looked back at the box and lifted its lid, placing it to the side. Inside, there was an assortment of folded notes and letters stuffed on either side of a small black journal. Clara reached in and pulled out the first piece of paper, unfolding it and reading the soft loopy handwriting.

*Friday September 27. Before the pep rally Charlotte admits Jay has another sweetheart that he's been with a long time. Said that's why he couldn't come/why they couldn't be seen in public together.*

*Thursday October 3. C told me she was going to see Jay that weekend. Said he's going to break up with his other girl for her.*

*Friday October 4. Eddie claims to drive her home after school. Says she broke up with him because of Jay. Rumor that C was seen driving toward Hollowfield House on Friday evening.*

*Sunday October 6. C reported missing.*

Sadie. This had to be Sadie putting together a timeline of events. Trying to piece together what happened that led to Charlotte's disappearance. But who was Jay? This was the first she had heard that name used. She tried to think back, scrounging her memory for some semblance of familiarity, but nothing came to her.

A noise came from behind Clara, and she gasped, turning around to find the windowsill thrown open. The curtains swayed in the breeze and the rain splattered onto the floor beneath the window. It took her a moment to realize no one was about to climb through the second-story window, that Sadie had been the cause. Clara stood up to close the window, sliding the latch back into place. That was when she heard the music still playing downstairs, but louder, if that were possible.

Did Sadie not want her to find this? Did she want Clara to hurry up? Clara's hands shook as she returned to her spot on the floor, pushing the note aside and digging into the shoebox. She pulled out another piece of paper that had a note written in a different hand. It was unlabelled, listing simply a time and place.

*HH. 10/04. 8 p.m.*

Something about the handwriting tugged at Clara's memory—a familiarity in the loop of the numbers. But she couldn't place where she'd seen it before.

Clara put the note aside and pulled out the journal, written by another hand. This writing looked soft and feminine, and she couldn't help but think of Charlotte. She skimmed the first page, which confirmed it was definitely the diary of a young woman. The first entry was from January 1929, the year Charlotte disappeared. It spoke of school, of Eddie, and Clara found herself unable to shake the unease that clouded her mind as she read the words of a young woman who had likely been murdered just months after these entries were written.

She flipped to the last entry; it was near the end of the book and dated October 4.

*I broke things off with Eddie. He certainly didn't take it very well, but what could I do? He acts as if he's my father. As if he's the one who can tell me what to do with my life. Maybe that worked at one point but no more. I know what real love feels like thanks to J, and I have never felt even a fraction for Eddie as what I feel for J. So he can carry on feeling angry about it, but it really isn't his business anymore. I am none of his concern from this day forward.*

Clara paused, realizing suddenly that it wasn't Jay who Charlotte had been dating, but J. As in, the first letter of a name. A way to talk about him with Sadie without using his full name, without identifying him. Clara swallowed, a heavy feeling weighing on her chest. Why would a seventeen-year-old girl need to hide the identity of the guy she was dating from her friend? Unless it was someone she shouldn't be dating.

*Now all that's left is to tell J the news. About Eddie and about . . . well . . . our little surprise. I know he'll be ecstatic but I can't help but feel butterflies. I suppose I'm nervous about how that woman will react when she finds out. But he's not happy with her – if she truly wanted what's best for him, she would see that he's moved on. But none of that matters tonight. Tonight is about celebration. Who knows, by the end of the evening I may even be engaged!*

Nausea roiled through Clara as she read the last few words. This was the night Charlotte disappeared. She was pregnant. She was pregnant and she was going to tell J. Clara's stomach churned.

J could be many people. It was a letter that stood for many names.

But it was that handwritten note that gave it away—the handwriting she'd recognized. It'd taken some time for it to sink in. For her to remember where she'd seen that writing. And then that last line, Charlotte's certainty that her secret boyfriend might propose. A boyfriend who was not seventeen then. A boyfriend that was taken and older, maybe much older.

Yet even with the thought in her mind, the possibility of it being him, the sight of him now, here, appearing in the shadowed doorway, chilled the blood in her veins. Panic flooded through her, and all at once, she realized the gramophone, the window, had not been encouragement but a warning that he was here.

# Chapter 33

"Well, isn't this cozy?"

Mr. Baker stood in the doorway—James, as Charlotte would've called him—his body relaxed as he leaned against the frame. Even in the dim light of the single candle, his blue eyes sparkled. From downstairs, the record continued to play, filling the house with music.

"What are you doing here?" Clara tried to sound calm, casual even, but her voice wavered. She'd locked the front door, she was sure of it.

He shrugged, nonchalant. "I heard you were here alone for the night, and I wanted to check in on you." Then he met her gaze as he said, "I hope Tuck's father is okay."

She leaned back slowly, trying to put space between them, her stomach sour. "And how did you hear about that?"

He gave her a playful smile. "Oh, Clara. My darling girl. I'm cognizant of a great many things." He gestured to the papers spread out in front of her. "But you knew that already."

She swallowed. "I was just—"

"Don't let me stop you," he cut in, crossing his arms over his chest. "Go ahead, keep reading. This is what you've been waiting for, isn't it?"

The sound of her heartbeat filled her ears. Every fiber of her being was on high alert. She needed to get out. To get around him, down the stairs, out to her car.

"I don't know what you mean."

James Baker stared down at her. "Is that so?" His voice was still playful, as if he hadn't just broken into her house. As if he weren't here to hurt her. "Why don't you read it to me then?"

It was clear he didn't believe her. He knew what she had found. He'd likely been the one out there in the woods, the sounds Clara and Evelyn had heard from the shadows. If she were going to get out of this, get past him, she'd need to be strategic.

"Why don't you tell me about it instead?" She reached behind her to the edge of the bed and pulled herself up slowly, keeping her gaze on him the entire time. "I'm sure you had a good reason for what you did." She tried for a weak smile. "Tell me your side."

He stared at her for a moment, seeming to assess the situation before he sighed.

"It looks bad, I admit." He lifted his hands in mock defense as he continued. "But you had to know Charlotte. She wasn't right in the head."

The same thing he'd said about Hazel.

"Try me." She forced levity into her tone, but her voice sounded weak even to her own ears. She sat on the edge of the mattress, folding her hands on her lap to hide the way they were shaking.

"She wasn't like you," he started. "She was so desperate for attention, for love. And it was never enough. An endless pit of need." There was disgust in his voice, and then he paused, seeming to catch himself. His voice lifted into something more casual. "And that was with a boyfriend on the side. Eddie. You remember him. You met him the other day."

She tensed, thinking back to that day, to the sympathy in James Baker's eyes as they sat there on those steps just outside the library.

Clara took a deep breath, reminding herself that she needed to gain his trust. Needed to make him believe she wouldn't say anything. "That sounds difficult," she said.

"Oh, that wasn't the half of it," James said with a sigh. "She lied all the time. Twisted things. She was impressively manipulative for her age." Clara's stomach folded over on itself at that. The reminder of her age. Only seventeen when she'd been killed. "I thought she was just a girl with a crush. But there was something about her—something not right. She was obsessive. Spun these stories about us being together."

Then it settled in, the realization that he wasn't owning up to what he'd done, but trying to convince her that everything she'd just read was lies. Disgust filled her just as hope sparked within her chest. If he could believe that she would take his word for it, then maybe he would let her go.

"So this"—Clara gestured to the box, to the assortment of different papers written by different hands—"is all made up?" She kept her voice steady.

But before he could respond, a memory flashed behind her eyes. Not her own but someone else's. She felt it, heard it, all at once. The loud *thump* as her head hit the wood floor, the feeling of hands grasping her ankles tightly, the scent of dust and damp mixed with the scent of alcohol. Clara flinched at the pain in her skull, but then she was back in the room, sitting on the edge of the bed, James Baker watching her carefully.

It was the staircase behind the bookshelf. That's where the memory had been—Sadie was trying to show her what happened. Or maybe trying to help her escape? Clara couldn't tell which, but she now had to fight the instinct to look to her right, to let her eyes glance over at the armoire.

"Are you okay?" James moved toward her, and she flinched before scrambling backward on the bed.

They both froze, staring at one another. Something shifted in his handsome face, a look in his bright blue eyes.

"Sorry," she said, exhaling shakily. "Just tired and . . . cold."

It took a moment for the tension in his features to melt away. "Well, I would offer you my jacket, but it's soaked from the rain." As if to prove it, he slid out of the jacket, revealing his buttoned shirt beneath it. He held it out for a moment before letting it drop on the ground with a heavy clunk.

Clara stared at where it lay, a puddle on the floor.

It was so small, so innocuous a thing. Yet with that one gesture, a show of carelessness, she somehow knew he would not let her leave this room.

He had already decided, likely had decided before he climbed through that window, that she wasn't leaving this room. That she would be silenced tonight, just like he'd decided for the others.

She stared at the jacket, a flame igniting within her chest. Anger. Anger at the way he felt he could make such decisions. At the way he had taken their lives—Charlotte and Sadie. She knew it now, was confident in it.

He had viewed Charlotte as no more than an object to do whatever he wished with. She doubted anything romantic had ever happened between him and Sadie—doubted Sadie could ever stand to even pretend to view him that way once she knew what he'd done. But that didn't keep her safe from him.

Sadie had known too much—this box was evidence of that, and that's why she'd asked Evelyn to hide it for her. But it wasn't enough. He needed to tie off each loose end. That's what Sadie was to him—a loose end to be dealt with. Clara thought of that strange moment in the hall, the flash of something, a memory that was not her own, the heavy scent of cologne, woodsy and warm. It had been James with Sadie that night. He had brought her here, knowing what he needed to do. Knowing he would kill her.

Clara looked up at him, meeting his gaze through the dim of the room, the single candle flickering on the floor where she'd left it. And suddenly the fear was not separate from the anger but was part of it. The two emotions mixed together so seamlessly she couldn't tell where one began and the other finished—she just knew she hated the man before her, and if he would be her end, it wouldn't be like this.

He would know what she thought of him. Would know that, at the end, she'd seen through the mask and found him to be lacking. And so her voice didn't waver when she spoke next.

"Tell me about Sadie."

# Chapter 34

James Baker stared at Clara, his expression unreadable as the moments passed. And then he released a deep breath and gave her a smile that chilled her to the bone.

"She was stubborn, that one. Fiery. Maybe it was the red hair." He gave a short laugh as if they were having a casual conversation at the dinner table.

"Is that why you killed her?"

James stilled. Adrenaline pumped through Clara's veins and she tried to act as if she wasn't terrified.

"She gave me no choice." He spoke slowly, holding her gaze. "She was like a damn dog with a bone. Just couldn't let it go."

"Couldn't let go of . . . Charlotte's murder?"

"Murder?" he echoed, his voice filled with amusement. "That wasn't murder. That was mercy."

Clara thought back to the letter, to the excitement palpable within every written word. She swallowed the thickness in her throat. "She was pregnant."

"She was seventeen," he snapped.

"That didn't stop you from taking up with her." The words rushed out before she could think better of them.

He took a step toward her. She pushed backward, slowly trying to put space between them but not wanting to trigger the predator within. Suddenly he reached out and grasped her ankle, pulling her toward him.

A scream left her throat, and he held her face in his hands, staring down into her eyes like one would a lover. But behind his bright blue eyes was nothing but cold rage.

When he spoke, his voice was low, steady. "You think you're so high and mighty. So superior." Clara tried to pull away, but James gripped her tighter, his fingers digging into her jaw, her throat. "But you're no better than me. I've seen how you operate. You skipped your own father's funeral but showed up once you found out about the inheritance." Her gut twisted at his words, at his proximity. "When it all comes down to it, you do what it takes to survive, don't you? You're no more than a cockroach." He lifted his hand slowly and brushed a strand of hair out of her face. Her skin tingled with disgust. "What, nothing to say?"

She stared up at him for a moment before she said, "Maybe you're right." She felt his grip slacken, and then, as hard as she could, she slammed her closed fist into his crotch.

He buckled forward in pain, and with all her might she shoved him off her, pushing past him toward the door, fear coursing through her.

Clara felt a harsh tug at her scalp as he grabbed her by the hair, pulling her backward. She landed on the floor with a loud thud, air whooshing out of her lungs, and felt the heat of fire briefly against her skin as she knocked the candle out of its base.

Suddenly James was atop her, pinning her wrists above her head. Panic bubbled up her throat as one of his hands reached for her throat. She tried to twist out of his grasp, turn her head away, and then her eyes landed on the armoire.

If she couldn't make it through the door, she could go down the stairs—

He wrapped his hands around her throat and panic crashed into her as she struggled for breath. She reached for his face, but he leaned back slightly out of reach, his hands still gripped around her throat. Hot tears wet her cheeks, and warmth trickled down the side of her face.

Out of the corner of her eye, she saw a glow, as if a lamp had been turned on, lighting up the corner of the room. And then she smelled the smoke. Heard the crackle of flames climbing up the wooden night table.

Something flashed across her vision and suddenly she was on the bed—no, not her, Sadie. She was seeing through Sadie's eyes as James Baker pinned her down and wrapped something tightly around her throat. Hands reached up, trying to scratch at his face.

Clara blinked and she was back in her own body, lying beneath James on the floor, digging her own nails into where his hands were wrapped around her throat. She tried to kick, tried to move, to get out from under him, but he was so heavy, his full body weight on her as he cut off her airway. She looked up at him, trying desperately to breathe, to inhale, and saw the rage in his sparkling blue eyes, the determination. That's when the realization settled into her—she was going to die. She was going to die just as Charlotte and Sadie had, and he was going to leave her body to burn in this fire.

Blackness filtered around her vision and she felt herself losing consciousness, felt the fight fading from her limbs.

And then she felt it. A shift in the energy. Her skin tingled like a thousand insects crawling over her body. The air was cold, icy, biting at her cheeks. It was a familiar feeling, but stronger—so much stronger—than anything she'd ever experienced. There, just behind James, standing in the middle of the flames, stood Sadie.

Suddenly, the pressure released from around her neck, and the weight lifted off her stomach. She gasped, flipping over onto her stomach, coughing and sputtering as she struggled to catch her breath. Clara glanced behind her and saw the flames licking across the threshold and up the doorframe, the nearness of the flame hot against her skin. She dragged herself away from the fire, toward the armoire, ignoring the sounds that filled the air.

Her limbs were weak, fatigue weighing her down like an anchor. She tried to push herself up toward the knobs, fear coursing through her as she heard the rattle of James's cough from somewhere in the room. Just as her fingertips reached the knob, her arms buckled beneath her, and she collapsed onto the wooden floor. The sound of the rain had been replaced by the sound of flame eating through the wooden floor, the furniture, the walls. She began to cough, the scent of smoke overpowering, dry against her throat.

She glanced over her shoulder, fear and confusion coursing through her at why James had let her escape, where he had gone. And then she saw him. James Baker was hanging in the middle of the room, his feet lifted from the ground as he kicked frantically, that red scarf tight around his throat. And before him, standing in the flames, was Sadie, looking up at him with no sign of emotion on her face.

The horror of it, of someone being hung before her very eyes, made bile fill her throat.

As she looked up at the armoire, her only option of escape, a sob escaped her lips between gasps of air. She pushed onto her knees, then pulled herself up the side of the armoire, pulling the door open and dragging her body inside. She could still hear James's desperate attempts at breath as she pushed through the fake backing of the dresser and dragged herself head-first down the dark staircase, not daring to look back.

Clara's head throbbed as she reached the bottom of the stairs, pushing through the gap in the hidden doorway and crawling out into the office. She felt the cold of the room instantly, heard the splash of rain coming through the broken window, the board once nailed there now gone, letting in the howling wind.

She fought the fatigue that pulled heavily on her as she pushed herself onto her hands and knees, crawling toward the office door. When she reached it, she stopped, leaning against it and gasping for breath. The front door seemed so far, every cell in her body begging for rest. Sleep called to her seductively, promising freedom from the pain coursing through her.

Clara struggled to keep her eyes open, her eyelids heavy as she forced herself to keep going. The fire had lit up the second floor so brightly it could've been day, the crackling so loud that it filled her ears even from the first floor. The scent of smoke was inescapable, clawing at her, making it difficult to breathe even now.

She dragged herself across the wood floor, pulling from energy she no longer had in order to reach up and grasp the doorknob. She just needed to get outside. Get away from the house, from the fire. She couldn't think about James Baker, about what was happening upstairs, about the possibility that Sadie might do the same to her. All she could do was get herself outside.

A gust of wind pushed her hair across her face as she got the door open and pulled herself onto the porch, then down the stairs. As she reached the gravel, she felt it digging into her palms, but she kept going, the distant pain a welcome confirmation that she was still alive.

Rain soaked her skin and hair, dampened her clothing, but every muscle in her body begged for sleep. Somewhere deep inside her mind, there was a whisper to keep going, to get up, get help, but the voice felt so far away, and her eyelids were too heavy for her to fight the feeling any longer. Her eyes fluttered shut, her head resting on the wet gravel beneath her, as comfortable in that moment as any bedding she could've hoped for. She was tired. So tired.

Using the last of her energy, she forced herself to open her eyes, looking at the house that stood before her, the bright light of the fire clear through the upstairs windows. And on the first floor, standing on the porch mere feet away, was Sadie. Her expression was soft as she looked over Clara. Part of her felt she should move, should run, but she couldn't gather the fear she'd need for fuel. She only felt numb, the pain in her body momentarily subsided.

Sadie stepped down the porch and walked over to Clara, kneeling above her. Sleep was pulling Clara under, tugging at her limbs like cement bricks, and her eyes drifted close as she heard a gentle voice whisper to her.

"You're safe now. Sleep."

That was the last thing she heard before the world went quiet.

# Chapter 35

The burning in Clara's throat was the first thing to greet her when she awoke at the hospital. She peeled her dry eyes open to find that she was lying atop a small bed with a white curtain to her right that blocked out the other side of the room. The edges of her vision swam as she slowly scanned the space, her mind fuzzy as she tried to make sense of what she was seeing. To her left was a window that revealed the beginnings of a sunrise, the charcoal and navy sky tinged with gold at the horizon. In front of the glass pane stood a familiar figure.

"You're awake," Tuck said once he noticed her eyes were on him.

Clara tried to speak, but her throat protested, resulting in a coughing fit that felt like her brain was rattling around in her skull. When she opened her eyes again, she found Tuck there with a small cup of water held before her, instructing her to drink.

The cool water both soothed and burned as it slid down her raw throat. Memories flitted back to her—flashes of fire, hands gripped around her throat, James Baker's legs as he kicked and bucked in the air.

"What happened?" she asked, her voice little more than a whisper.

"I found you outside the inn," he said. "The place was up in flames and you were just . . . there." He swallowed, emotion in his eyes as he looked at her. Clara had the distant thought that she didn't want him to be upset, that he might be upset with her, but her mind felt cloudy, the thoughts fading as quickly as they'd come.

He took her hand and she let him, relishing in the warmth of his touch. But then, there was one question that emerged, feeling more urgent than the rest.

"And what about . . . James?" There was another flash of his feet kicking, of the sound of him choking. She squeezed her eyes tight, hoping to wipe the vision from her mind.

"Clara." Tuck's voice was a whisper as he reached out to her, his thumb brushing across her skin. Without meaning to, she flinched from the contact, and he pulled his hand away, a frown on his handsome face. "It's okay," he said, his voice soothing. "You're safe now."

The words brought forth a memory. Rain pelting her skin. *You're safe now. Sleep.* Tears pricked her eyes as her throat thickened with emotion, though she couldn't articulate why.

"What's wrong?" Tuck asked, sitting on the edge of the hospital bed.

"Sadie." Her voice broke on the word. The flash of her face. The red of her hair. She was dead. Gone. And so was Charlotte. The edges of the room softened and blurred, her eyelids growing heavy with emotion and fatigue. They must have given her some medication to ease the pain. She could feel it pulling her under, drawing her into sleep. "Don't leave," Clara whispered, her eyelids fluttering shut.

Just before she slipped away, sleep taking her once again, she heard him whisper, "I won't."

When Clara woke hours later, the constable arrived to talk to her about what had occurred. She sat there, leaning back in the hospital bed, with Tuck on one side of the bed and Constable Davis on the other. The fog in her brain had lifted slightly, discomfort sitting heavy in her stomach as she told them of what had happened, without the mention of Evelyn's appearance at her doorstep. She also didn't tell them about the fear and relief that ran through her as she saw Sadie there. She didn't tell them of the sounds James Baker had made as Sadie held him there, that red scarf tied around his throat while he kicked, desperate for air, desperate to live.

She knew now that he had been a man far worse than even Al had been—that his deception was one of great practice, great skill—and she hated him for what he'd done, the way he'd felt entitled to take the lives of Charlotte and Sadie. But as she remembered it, looking up at him as he struggled, she couldn't help the tears that spilled from her eyes.

"Did he . . . survive?" Clara asked, drying her tears. It wasn't that he deserved to live, but the thought that she had witnessed someone's murder filled her with dread.

Silence filled the room, both men watching her until the constable spoke. "James Baker is deceased. He was found hanging from the banister." Clara felt numb, like ice easing through her chest, dulling her senses. A moment later, Constable Davis added, "It seems you might've been right with your suspicions. Can't think of another reason he would've ended it that way."

Clara thought back to Sadie, to the neutral expression on her face as she looked up at him and watched him struggle. A chill crawled up her spine.

"The fire consumed a large majority of the house," Constable Davis continued. "The entire back half, really."

She tried to picture it in her mind, to see the inn that had stood there a day earlier, now burnt to rubble. Her head throbbed and she took a deep breath, ready for the conversation to be over.

After the interview, she was granted permission to leave the hospital. Briar Hollow didn't have a hospital, so Tuck had taken her to the next town over. As they pulled out of the parking lot, heading toward the inn, she remembered the telegram Tuck had received.

"Your father," she said, turning to him. "Is he alright?"

Tuck's hands tightened around the wheel and his eyes flitted toward her before returning to the road. "He's fine. When I got there, they couldn't figure out who had sent the telegram. Turned out, it wasn't any of them."

Confusion swirled through her. "But you don't think—"

"Yes," Tuck said, a bite to his tone, "I do."

James Baker. He had sent the telegram. He had planned what he would do that night—had planned to get her alone in the house. She wondered now how he would have done it. Would he have made her disappear as he had the others? Would he have staged a suicide, easily dismissed as a symptom of her madness? A family curse, the same as—Al. Something clicked into place and Clara's stomach churned.

It hadn't been Al who'd chosen suicide. It had been chosen for him . . . by Sadie.

Which had to mean that he had been involved.

She thought back to the news articles, to the scarf, the locket, trying to piece it together. And then she remembered, that flash of a memory, the crack of a skull against the hard floor, the hands on Sadie's ankles, which meant . . . there had been another person there to help James Baker dispose of the body.

Deep inside, she knew it wasn't Tuck, knew it couldn't be. But then she thought back to the hidden staircase, to the way he'd asked her not to tell the constable about what they'd found. She turned to him, looking at the profile of his handsome face, and took a deep breath.

"It's time you tell me everything," Clara said, her voice still scratchy from smoke inhalation. He didn't look at her, his eyes fixed on the road, but she watched him swallow, watched him consider her request.

"What do you want to know?"

"Did you know about Sadie? Charlotte?"

"No," he said immediately. "I told you from the beginning, if I knew about any of that I would've told you."

She felt a weight lift from her chest at his response, her mind shifting to another question she'd been holding onto. "Did you know about the moonshine?"

He was silent for a moment. Clara wondered if he would avoid her question, if he would go down that same pattern of withholding things from her, but then he said, "Yes."

And to her surprise, in that car ride back to Briar Hollow, he told her everything. He told her about Al's moonshine operation, something he hadn't initially known about but had become clear after living on the property for a few weeks. That it had been an endeavor between Al and Randy, and that Tuck had agreed not to tell anyone as long as they didn't involve him, going into his cottage each evening at 5 p.m. and refusing to come outside and be entangled in their schemes even as he heard vehicles come and go at all hours of the night.

It made sense to Clara now how James Baker might have brought young women to the inn without Tuck ever being aware of it. Tuck was committed to not seeing or hearing anything that might incriminate him when it came to Prohibition, and that had created an environment where Al and James could do as they pleased without being held accountable.

The part that had, somehow, been most surprising to Clara was finding out about James' involvement in the scheme. That just a few years earlier, Randy had let it slip to Tuck that Al wasn't the one at the head of the operation, he'd been recruited by James Baker, looking for men to run the liquor on his behalf and with his connections. And then she thought back to the strange behavior of those in town—the hostility from Eddie Reynolds, the nephew of the constable. She wondered how many other locals had had their own suspicions about what was really going on at the inn, and how many of them had assumed she must somehow be involved.

By the time they pulled into the driveway of Hollowfield House, Clara couldn't help but look at the property through new eyes. There had been so much deception woven into the walls of this inn, and now the outside of the house matched with the felony that took place inside. From the front of the house, things almost looked normal, a mask of credibility, but as you peered around the side of the house, you could see the back half collapsed, blackened with soot.

Clara got out of the vehicle and stood there on the gravel lot, staring up at the place, and wondering if, somewhere on this land, lay the bones of Sadie and Charlotte. If they had been buried here, tied to this dreadful land for eternity.

She felt Tuck's presence as she came up beside her. "Come on," he said, sliding his warm hand into hers. "Let's get you inside."

Clara let him pull her gently toward the cottage and lead her inside the front door. But once they crossed the threshold, he stopped suddenly. Clara followed his gaze to the kitchen table, to where an envelope sat with the name *Tuck* written across it.

"This wasn't you're doing it, was it?" Tuck asked, looking at her.

She glowered at him. "I was in the hospital this whole time. You were with me."

He looked back at the envelope. "Just checking." He walked over to it, ripping the envelope open and pulling out the letter inside. Clara watched as his eyes scanned down the page, his expression unreadable. Without another word, he passed the letter to her before crossing the room.

"What is it?" she asked before reading the words.

*This is your half.*

*It's the least of what we deserve.*

*Check the cupboard.*

There was no name signed beneath it, and her heart pounded as she looked up to find Tuck across the room, pulling out yet another envelope from behind a cabinet door, but this one was bloated. She watched as Tuck glanced inside and his face went white.

"What is it?" she asked, her voice sounding weak even to her own ears.

Tuck swallowed, taking a moment before he looked up at her and said, "It's . . . money."

Clara furrowed her brows, confusion roiling through her. Tuck came over and pulled a stack of bills free from their envelope. She felt herself gasp. She couldn't remember a time when she was this close to a stack of money like this.

"He finally found it," Tuck said, his voice tinged with wonder and disbelief.

"Who?"

"Randy."

She thought back to Randy, to the way he'd seemed so sure that Al had money hidden somewhere in the house. Likely, the product of their bootlegging. Something he couldn't very well take to the bank. And based on this envelope stuffed with cash, it appeared that Randy was right. She thought back to the hidden compartment in this staircase and wondered if the money had been there, stuff far back in the crawlspace. She wondered if Randy had already cleared the space out of moonshine.

There was tension in the air as she watched Tuck count the bills, the total going higher and higher until he reached the last of the pile. It was roughly the equivalent of half a year's pay for Clara and all she could do was stare at the money in disbelief.

"Looks like you didn't need to sell the place after all," Tuck said.

"Me?" she asked. "The envelope had your name on it."

Tuck stared at her for a moment, and when he spoke, his voice was soft. "It was Al's money. He left the inn to you. It's yours."

She frowned, a mix of emotions crashing through her.

"He didn't leave the inn to me," she clarified. "He died without a will—there's a difference." She stood up, pacing back and forth, suddenly antsy.

"What's the difference between taking this and selling the inn?"

"One was acquired through a federal crime," she said, her throat tightening with anxiety.

Tuck's gaze softened as he stood, walking over to her. He hesitated for just a moment before he placed both hands softly along the sides of her face, turning her eyes up to his. She felt herself soften under his touch. "Clara," he said, his voice little more than a whisper, "take the money."

She saw the sincerity in his eyes and found herself suddenly light-headed.

"I need to sit down." She took a step back and walked over to the bed, fighting the nausea that climbed up her throat as she sat on the edge of the mattress.

Surely she couldn't just take the money. Selling an inn was one thing, but accepting a wad of cash snatched from somewhere in the house seemed entirely different.

"If you don't take the money, I'll have to take it to the constable," Tuck said. "And once they find out this much cash was hidden in the house without an explanation . . ."

She met his gaze, understanding sinking in. The bootlegging. If the police started poking around the property and asking questions, Tuck would be one of the people caught in the crossfire.

Clara exhaled deeply and fixed her gaze on the wall in front of her, her mind spinning as she tried to process everything. She heard Tuck approach, felt the weight of him as he sat on the mattress next to her, felt the warmth from his nearness.

"Have you told me everything?" she asked, turning suddenly and looking into his eyes. She scanned the depths of the green, searching for any sign of deception.

"Yes," he said, meeting her gaze.

She found herself nodding. "Okay. But I'll only take the money if you take half."

He stilled, silent for several moments before he finally spoke. "It's not my money. I couldn't—"

"That's my one condition," she cut in. "If you don't want me to tell the constable about all of this, then you'll take half."

Unsurprisingly, Tuck didn't agree right away. In fact, after going back and forth for nearly twenty minutes, they eventually agreed to pause the conversation for now, Tuck insisting on Clara resting her voice and having something to eat.

That night, as fatigue weighed down her limbs and a heaviness sat on her chest, she didn't argue with him about not taking the bed. Instead, in a moment of weakness, she asked if he could lay with her, an attempt to counter the dark shadows that crept into her mind as the night fell outside.

As he lay behind her on the bed, his fingers making slow circles on her back, they whispered to each other in the dark. After some time, he finally relented, agreeing to her condition, and she fell asleep, wrapped in his scent.

# Chapter 36

The next two days were spent mostly asleep. There was a tiredness deep in Clara's bones that she couldn't shake. Tuck would wake her long enough to drink water and eat something, but once she'd eaten, she'd be pulled under by sleep again.

She didn't dream most of that time, experiencing the mercy of darkness. But one night she did. She dreamed of Charlotte, a look of panic in her eyes as James Baker leaned over her, his hands wrapped around her throat, with a fire growing nearby.

Clara woke crying that night, too distressed to feel shame as Tuck appeared at her side, wrapping her up in his embrace and stroking her hair as her tears fell. After she'd cried herself dry, she fell back into sleep, and neither of them ever spoke of the incident again.

On the third day, reality arrived as a knock at the door.

Clara had been in a state between sleep and wakefulness when Tuck had answered the door. She'd heard the concern in his hushed tones, heard the way the muffled conversation went back and forth, and couldn't help the curiosity that piqued within her. Clara hadn't known who she expected to see behind that door, but it certainly hadn't been Mrs. Baker.

The woman was as beautiful as she'd remembered—far more put together than Clara could have imagined, given what must've unfolded for her in these past few days. Tuck had been hesitant to step away, to leave them alone, so Clara stepped out onto the path and shut the door behind her. At least it gave the illusion of privacy, though she knew Tuck would likely stand on the other side of the door, listening, waiting for some opportunity to step in.

"I'm glad to see you're well," the woman said, her tone as icy as the wind that washed over them.

Clara crossed her arms over her chest and considered the words. Was she well? It didn't feel like it. But perhaps well was a relative term—relative to those who had survived in the same incident where others had died.

"Thank you," was all Clara could respond. She looked past the woman and out through the trees, to the place where the house once stood. Leaves tumbled across the gravel lot, and from this viewpoint, Clara could almost pretend the latter half of the house wasn't entirely demolished. Could almost pretend it wasn't her fault.

Perhaps if this had been another time, Clara would have been filled with questions—eager to know what Mrs. Baker had known, what she had missed. Eager to understand the monster she'd mistaken for a man. But now, after all that had happened, she couldn't draw up enough emotion to care about anything. She'd reached the end of her fear, pain, and anger, and now she had nothing left to draw from.

"Was there something going on between you?"

Clara looked up at the woman, into the depths of her brown eyes, and noticed for the first time the fear that lingered there. Even now, after all the woman must have learned from the constable, she still feared that her husband's greatest deception might have been his love for her.

"No."

"Then why—" Mrs. Baker paused, seeming to collect herself. "Then why was he here?"

Clara's brow furrowed, something twisting in her gut. "Because he wanted to hurt me." Perhaps the words were unkind, but they were true, and that was all Clara could offer.

Mrs. Baker stared at her, uncertainty in her beautiful face. "That's not James. James is—" Her voice broke, tears filling her eyes. "James was a good man. He would never have done the things you're implying."

These were not the words of a woman who was left in the dark—these were the words of a woman who'd had a light shone upon her life and been left unwilling to accept what she saw before her. Perhaps it was a fair response to this kind of news. Perhaps it would take weeks, months, even years for her to accept the true nature of who her husband had been, to untangle the depth of deception before her.

Perhaps another woman would have more compassion for Mrs. Baker—more understanding as she tried to reconcile the man she knew with the actions of a monster. But as Clara looked up at her, she couldn't help but see her own mother. A woman who'd seen the truth time and time again but chose to make excuses to keep her husband, to stay a married woman—even if that marriage wasn't a good one.

For women like her mother, perhaps like Mrs. Baker, admitting that they'd loved a bad man would reflect poorly on them as well, and that wouldn't stand. Instead of accepting the pain of the truth, they were left to rearrange their perception. To twist and distort in the name of justifying the love they'd still felt for him, even after the reality was laid before them.

"Perhaps, I'm a liar," Clara said.

Mrs. Baker froze, drying her tears. "What?"

"That's what you want to hear, right? That I lied. That I made it all up. That your husband was a wonderful man and you made a wonderful choice when you married him." Silence washed between them. Somewhere in the distance, a bird crowed in the trees.

"Of course not," Mrs. Baker said, clearly flustered. "I just want to hear the truth."

As Clara looked into the woman's eyes, saw the hesitation there, the way she refused to hold her gaze, she knew it wasn't what she really wanted, what she was really here for. Mrs. Baker wanted someone to blame, and it wouldn't be her husband.

"You want the truth?" Clara asked. "Look back at every moment when you questioned something he did or said, when you felt like it didn't quite add up. Look back at everything you've ever feared might be true about him, every time you felt it in your gut, that little voice telling you he was lying, that knowing deep inside. That is where you'll find your truth."

Clara stepped into the house and shut the door behind her without another look back.

# Chapter 37

Tuck had insisted on driving Clara to the diner. She'd tried to reason with him, reminding him that tomorrow she'd be making the several-hour journey back to Rochester alone. Somehow, that did nothing to convince him.

As they pulled into the diner's parking lot, she thought of the last time she'd been here. How different everything had felt. She'd known nothing then—had nothing but a desire to get the house sorted and be gone. Now everything was simple, really. The house was uninhabitable. James Baker was gone. Nothing was left for her here. No reason to stay, to worry about Briar Hollow.

Yet there was one very clear reason to want to stay. No matter how deeply she knew she couldn't have a life here—that she would never be happy in a place like this, in a town tainted by so much tragedy, a place so deeply tied to Al—she couldn't deny the small spark of hope in her chest. The little voice that whispered *but what if* to her when she thought about leaving.

Tuck cut the engine and a hush fell upon them.

"If you insist on being here, you'll need to sit at the bar top," Clara said as they climbed out of the vehicle. "She won't feel comfortable with you here glowering at her."

Clara almost expected a protest, but he gave her a nod and said, "As you wish."

They walked through the door, and Clara glanced at the small number of tables inside, her gaze landing upon Hazel Montgomery.

"I'll be over here." Tuck left her, taking a seat at the bar—the same place she'd seen him that first night.

Clara turned back to Hazel, who hadn't noticed her yet. She sat at a booth, a cup of coffee before her. As Clara approached, their eyes met, and they were both silent as she took her seat across from Hazel. There was a second cup of coffee before Clara, steam still coming off the top.

"Thank you," she said, gesturing to the cup. Hazel gave a weak smile. Clara could feel how much was going on behind Hazel's eyes, feel the way she was hesitant to speak.

"Is it true?" Hazel asked eventually. "Is he . . . gone?"

Clara saw the wariness in her eyes. "Yes."

Hazel nodded, staring down at the mug before her. "You know this is the first time I've been in Briar Hollow in . . . I don't even know when."

"What happened?" Clara asked.

Hazel looked away, shifting her gaze out the window, looking at something off in the distance. "I wanted to tell you, you know. That night at the restaurant."

"Why didn't you?" Clara asked.

"I was afraid," Hazel said, her voice steady, factual. "Afraid of what he could do. How he might try to ruin my life if I said too much."

"Is that why you disappeared years ago?" Clara thought back to the article she'd read about Hazel's disappearance, about her employer who'd reported her missing rather than a family member. "Were you running from him?"

Hazel shook her head. "No." She swallowed, shifting in her seat. Then she lowered her voice and said, "I found out I was pregnant."

Clara's stomach dropped, her mind going back to Charlotte. To her excitement about her own baby, to share the news with James Baker. But Hazel must've been first, her disappearance from 1926. "How old were you?"

Hazel exhaled a shaky breath. "It was just before my eighteenth birthday."

It appeared James Baker, a man who would've been in his late twenties at the time, had a very particular type—high school girls. Clara wondered what might've happened if Hazel hadn't gotten pregnant. Would he have lost interest shortly after?

"Did you tell him?" Clara asked.

Hazel averted her gaze, then cleared her throat. "I was scared to tell him. It felt like . . . something he wouldn't want. I don't know why I felt that way, it was just an instinct, I suppose. I knew he was married." She said that last word like it was a cuss. "I figured he might not take it well. But I brought the topic up one night. We were sitting in the backseat of his motorcar. I just asked him if he wanted children. He didn't have any at that point, though I think he does now. Or rather, did." She paused, stirring the spoon slowly in her drink. She brought the cup to her lips and took a sip.

"What did he say?"

"He said no," she said with a short laugh that lacked any joy. "He said children only tied people down and made women cranky and fat."

Clara cringed.

"I didn't know if I was for sure pregnant at the time, but I'd missed two of my monthlies. I didn't have many signs but I just . . . felt it. I could feel it in my body that something was different. And when he told me he didn't want to be a father, I knew I was alone. I knew he wouldn't change his mind. James never did. He was stubborn that way. If it was a no now, it would always be a no."

Clara thought of his wife at home, those years when they were married without children. What must it have been like then? Was he denying her children? Trying to put off his wife's pregnancy? Or had they been trying all that time, Mrs. Baker unaware of him sneaking off with a teenage girl?

"And James hadn't noticed?"

Hazel smiled. "We didn't undress when we . . ." She tucked a strand of hair behind her ear. "And it was usually dark, in the back of his motorcar."

A bell chimed from behind Clara and she turned instinctively, looking over her shoulder. It wasn't until her eyes landed on a small, elderly man slowly making his way through the front door that she realized her heart was racing. For a moment, she'd expected to see James Baker walk through the door. She turned back to Hazel, flashing her a look of apology.

Clara took a slow sip from her coffee, allowing the warmth to steady her before she spoke again. "Did he ever find out?"

Hazel took a deep breath. "I was going to tell him one night. It was my birthday, and he was supposed to come to see me." There was something in her gaze, a flicker of sadness, almost. As if she was back there, in that moment so long ago, feeling the pang of emotion. "He never did show. And I suppose . . . that's when I knew the truth. That he didn't love me the way he'd said he did."

Clara shifted, placing her hand on her coffee mug for the first time, considering taking a sip, but stopping, a question on her mind. "I don't mean to be insensitive, but didn't it bother you that he was married?"

A short laugh escaped Hazel's mouth, her eyes landing on the table before her, a bitter smile on her face. "He told me they didn't love each other." Their eyes met, and Clara could see the shame there. "Said they hadn't loved each other in years. That they slept in separate bedrooms, no more than housemates, really." Hazel took a slow breath in, then exhaled. "He said they both wanted a divorce, but they didn't want to ruin her reputation. That he cared for her as a person, as a friend." Hazel swallowed. "I thought it was sweet of him."

Clara could imagine it—Hazel as a young woman, never married, unaware of the cliches, the things men would say to try to get a woman into bed, to overlook their infidelity. She must've seen this man, this beautiful, successful man, and felt truly . . . special. That of all the women out there, he'd chosen her.

"What happened with the baby?" Clara asked, her voice soft.

Hazel stiffened and Clara couldn't help but feel guilt course through her. She almost didn't expect Hazel to tell her, but after several moments of silence, Hazel said, "My grandmother found me one day—walked in when I was changing. And so she brought me to a home, a few hours away. A home for other girls in my situation."

Clara's chest tightened. She'd heard of pregnancy homes for fallen women. A place to stay, away from everyone, to have one's baby in peace, give it up for adoption, then return as if nothing had happened at all.

"I was there for a few months. I hadn't told anyone, of course. And then, one day, we all went out on a field trip of sorts. They took us to a local market for the afternoon, a break from the house. And I looked up, and there he was."

"What did he want?" Clara asked.

"It was quite obvious that I was . . . with child. And so he asked me who the father was. And you know, he had been my first. We'd met when I was sixteen. He was my only at that time. And he knew that." Hazel swallowed. "Looking back on it now, I think it was a test. He wanted to be sure I wouldn't say his name."

"And did you?"

"No," she said. "I just stared at him. I couldn't believe he had found me." Hazel took a sip of her coffee, silence passing between them as Clara considered her words. "I told him I wouldn't be keeping it. That it would be going to a real family. To one that could care for it." Hazel smiled tightly. "You know, I was so scared when I first went to the home. And then, they told me, I'd have the baby, the child would go to a good home, and then I'd move on, as if nothing ever happened. They told us that every day. 'Your baby deserves a mother *and* a father. Your baby deserves a house, a yard, good clothes, food. You can't provide that. You're not fit to be a mother.' And I believed them."

Clara's chest tightened. She couldn't imagine being in such a situation, being so young and having to make a choice like that. Being made to feel like she couldn't be enough for her own child. "Do you still believe them?" Clara asked.

Hazel met her gaze, and there were tears there. "No," she whispered. "No, I don't." She used her tablecloth to pat the corners of her eyes, stopping the tears from spilling. With a sniff, she said, "Anyways, it's in the past now."

For a few moments, neither of them spoke. Clara didn't know what to say, how to comfort the woman. This didn't seem the type of pain that words could ease.

And then Hazel said, "You may think poorly of me for saying this, but I'm glad he's gone. For me, but also for them. Knowing that he's not out there, with the knowledge of that baby. With the connections he has to the police, to who knows who else." She met Clara's gaze. "This was the only way it could've ended."

# Chapter 38

A rush of wind swirled around Clara and Tuck, pulling loosened leaves from their branches as they walked down the footpath that led to the gravel lot of Hollowfield House. Clara gazed at what was left of the remnants of the fire.

"Do you think there's really money buried somewhere?" Clara asked as Tuck came up beside her, carrying her case.

"I think he probably said that to make Randy think he could pay him back for whatever he stole." He walked toward the car, lifting the trunk. "And whatever he did have was likely lost in the fire."

Clara looked at the blackened rubble around the side of the house, now dusted with leaves from the nearby trees. The place where the remnants of James Baker had been pulled by police. She couldn't help but wonder about Charlotte and Sadie—about where they had ended up. She hadn't seen or felt Sadie's presence since that night. She hoped that wherever the dead went to rest after life, she was there now, finally freed from this God-forsaken town.

The slam of the car door jolted her attention. "You're all packed up," Tuck said, turning to her.

"Thank you." She pulled her cardigan more tightly around her, fighting the chill of the air.

"It wasn't much trouble."

"No, I meant for everything." Silence fell between them as he searched her eyes. Before he could speak, Clara said, "And I'm sorry for burning down your place of employment."

Amusement lit Tuck's gaze. "I don't think that was your doing."

"Considering I'm the only surviving witness, I think that's really up to me to decide." She gave a small smile despite the heavy feeling that settled in her stomach.

"Are you going to be okay? Truly?"

She felt herself stiffen at the question. At the thought of someone—of him—caring about her answer. And it felt like he did care. That it wasn't a question for the sake of politeness but out of sincere concern.

"Of course," she said with a smile she didn't feel. "I'm too stubborn not to be." Clara turned then, opening her motorcar door and stepping inside. Her chest tightened as she shut the door between them, a strange sensation spreading through her.

Her hands shook slightly as she placed the key in the ignition and the motorcar sprang to life. She should roll down her window, should say goodbye to him. It would be the polite thing to do. Yet she didn't reach for her window pump. Didn't look anywhere other than at her steering wheel.

The wind whistled as she pulled away slowly, turning onto the short drive toward the road. Gravel crunched beneath her tires and branches brushed the top of her vehicle as she drove down the path, her fingers gripped tightly around the wheel.

A sound cut through the wind and she glanced in her mirror to see that Tuck was running toward her motorcar. Concern flooded through her as she stopped and let him catch up to her. He met her at her window and gestured for her to roll it down, his expression unreadable.

She pumped the window and asked, "Is everything okay?"

And then she was surrounded by his scent, feeling the warmth of his lips on hers, his thumb resting gently on her jaw as he pulled her in. Something sparked within her, a desire to stay here in this moment, with nothing on her mind but him. Her hand found his face then the back of his neck, and she pulled him in, warmth flooding through her.

It felt like a mere moment and an eternity all at once, and then he was gone, taking his warmth with him, leaving nothing more than a hand on her jaw, his thumb brushing her cheek. Clara leaned into his touch instinctively, too caught up to feel embarrassed by her action.

"Promise you'll write to me." He stared down at her, such hope in those green eyes. She nodded, unable to stop herself from readily agreeing.

"I promise." It came out as a whisper, carrying the surety of an oath.

He stayed there another moment, staring at her—at her eyes, her lips, her hair—seeming to take her in. To memorize every inch of her while he could.

"I'll be waiting with bated breath."

And then he was gone, and Clara was alone in her car, the cool air touching her blushed cheeks. She looked in her mirror and saw him walk away without another glance toward her. She rolled up her window and pulled to the end of the drive, turning onto the road and knowing she'd never be back to Hollowfield House.

# Epilogue

Clara pulled open the front door of her apartment building and stepped inside, relief flooding through her as she escaped from the crowd and the noise—two things she still hadn't quite adapted to in the nearly two weeks she'd been back in Rochester. The push of the crowds on the sidewalk, the streetcar ringing its bell as it drove past. It was enough to make her almost miss the solitude of Briar Hollow. *Almost.*

"Who's there?" Mrs. Gibbs called from inside her unit, her door ajar, as always.

"It's Clara," she responded, peeling off her gloves as she walked toward the staircase.

"Oh, you've got a package just on the table there."

Clara turned, her eyes landing on a small bundle that sat atop the table. At first, she thought it might be a birthday gift from Mabel, but it seemed strange that her friend would feel the need to mail something when they'd be seeing each other tomorrow for the Halloween party. As Clara neared the item, rectangular in shape and wrapped in brown paper, she saw the return address listed Hollowfield House, and her breath caught in her throat. For a moment, she was back in that room on the second floor, the shoebox before her with Sadie's notes inside, the gramophone playing, and *he* had found her—

Clara stepped back, willing her heart to settle. An unpleasant tingle ran through her hands and up her arms. This was nonsense.

She wasn't in Hollowfield House. She was in Rochester, and James Baker was gone.

She exhaled sharply and forced herself to reach out and take the box before she could think better of it. She noticed the weight of it, the size and shape flatter than a shoebox—nothing like Sadie's box of evidence. As Clara looked again at the return address, afraid of the name she might find there, she saw Tuck's name instead, something she'd missed at first glance.

"Did you find it?" Mrs. Gibbs called, seemingly unwilling to come out of her apartment and look for herself.

"Yes," Clara replied. "Thank you."

She tucked the small rectangle beneath her arm and walked up the staircase to the second floor, nerves coursing through her as she let herself into her small apartment. Clara placed the package on the kitchen table and peeled off her jacket, hanging it over the back of a chair before disappearing into her bedroom to change into something more comfortable. All the while, her mind churned with curiosity. Had she forgotten something in Tuck's cottage? It seemed unlikely, given that most of her belongings had been lost in the fire.

Clara walked back into the small living area, flicking on a lamp and returning to the package. With hesitant fingers, she tore into the paper, peeling it back slowly until she caught the sight of engraved lettering.

She stilled, tears pricking her eyes before she could chastise herself for the foolish response. With a shaky breath, she tore away the rest of the paper, revealing the bound novel beneath—an all-black cover with a pattern embossed into the cloth, the title *Frankenstein* written across the center in gold.

Clara thought back to that night before everything had happened—before the death of James Baker and the fire that could have killed her too—back to that night in Tuck's cottage when he let her see his books, their edges torn, their covers ripped and mangled. To the night when she'd told him—the only person she'd ever told—about the book she'd brought back from the library all those years earlier. The one Al had torn to pieces in front of her. And now, in her hands, was one of the most beautiful books she'd ever seen.

Instead of replacing one of his own tattered editions with something brand new, Tuck had gifted her the one book that had meant something to her so long ago. Tears pricked Clara's eyes, and she tried to swallow back her emotion as she reached for the book and ran her fingertip across the material. She flipped open the front cover to a scrap of notebook paper that had been slipped inside, a note scrawled in what must be Tuck's handwriting. *I didn't want to ruin your book by writing in it.* Clara laughed, wiping away the traitorous tear that escaped down her cheek. *Happy birthday. I hope to be with you for the next one.*

She thought of the warmth of his hand in hers, the feel of his lips as he'd kissed her. And suddenly she was eager to speak with him, to sit next to him by the fire, to just be near him, as foolish as the desire may be. But she knew she could never go back to Briar Hollow, and she knew Briar Hollow was all Tuck had ever truly known. It could never work, the two of them together.

But even that doubt didn't touch the flame of hope within her chest, the part of her that didn't know how it could ever work but dared to wish that it would. Maybe one day they would find themselves together in the same place at the same time, and she would finally be unburdened from the pain that still sat heavy in her chest after everything she'd experienced.

And even though she knew it was foolish to hope—especially now when she felt more broken than ever before—she let that longing lead her to pull out a pen and paper and begin on another letter to Tuck.

# Acknowledgments

First and foremost, thank you to my family who provided me with the support, space, and encouragement to write this novel.

To my editors—Freia, Mallori, and Maria—thank you for your invaluable contributions that helped shape this story into what it is today.

To Jada M., my unofficial project manager, alpha reader, beta reader, and social media manager—thank you for being my sounding board through every late-night vent and ramble.

To my beta readers, who generously took time out of their busy lives to engage with this story in its earliest stages, thank you for your thoughtful and invaluable feedback. A heartfelt thank you to Alin N., Allison R., Brittany Y., Cait B., Chastity K., Christine J., Claudia R., Echo M., Ela G., Eve M., Heather W., Lauren B., Maggie F., Priscilla M., Tana B., and Yanitza V. Your insights made all the difference.

To everyone who shared about the book before its release and offered encouragement along the way, thank you for your kindness and support.

And to my dogs, Braxton and Paisley, who may not be able to read, but who have been by my side during every step of this process.

# Content Warning

The following subject matter and themes are included **on-page** and experienced by or witnessed through the eyes of the protagonist: Consumption of alcohol (some scenes); Mild abuse of alcohol (minimal scenes); Homophobic attitudes (minimal scenes) (no slurs used; hateful rhetoric by a secondary character); Violence (minimal scenes) (no gore); Witnessing a violent act that leads to death (one scene) (no gore)

The following subject matter and themes occur **off-page** but may be referenced or described throughout the novel: Childhood neglect and abuse (referenced throughout); Parental abandonment (referenced throughout); Domestic abuse (referenced throughout); Death of a parent (referenced throughout); Suicide of a parent (referenced throughout); Terminal illness of a family member (referenced throughout); Mental health struggles & mental distress (referenced throughout; includes negative & potentially offensive references to mental health asylums); Murder and death (referenced throughout); Alcoholism of a parent (referenced in some scenes); Grooming of a teenage girl (referenced in some scenes); Accidental pregnancy (referenced in some scenes); Pressured/forced adoption (referenced in minimal scenes); War and conscription (referenced in some scenes); Death of a loved one in war (referenced in minimal scenes); Infidelity (referenced in minimal scenes)

# About the Author

Amelie West is an author and fiction editor from Toronto, Canada, who crafts dark, atmospheric gothic mysteries featuring strong, complex heroines. She draws inspiration from authors like Simone St. James, Deanna Raybourn, and Ava Reid. When she isn't lost in her latest manuscript, Amelie can be found wandering old bookstores or enjoying the company of her two loyal companions—a French bulldog and a pug mix.

For details on her upcoming releases, you can follow her on Instagram @ameliewestbooks.

Made in United States
North Haven, CT
13 February 2025